WITHDRAWN

D1284909

3 4028 09215 0992
HARRIS COUNTY PUBLIC LIBRARY

Fiore
Fiore, L. C.
The last great American
magic
$17.99
ocn967966240
First edition.

THE LAST GREAT AMERICAN MAGIC

Also by L.C. Fiore

Green Gospel: A Novel
The Trench Garden

THE LAST GREAT AMERICAN MAGIC

by
L.C. Fiore

THE LAST GREAT AMERICAN MAGIC
By L.C. Fiore

Cover and text design and typesetting by Patricia A. Lynch
Cover art © Doug Hall – Somerset Fine Art

© 2016 by L.C. Fiore

All Rights Reserved. No part of this publication may be re-produced or transmitted in any form or by any means, electronic, digital, or mechanical, including photocopying and recording, or by any information or storage or retrieval system, including the Internet, without permission from the publisher. Permission is hereby given to use short excerpts with proper citation in reviews and marketing copy, newsletters, bulletins, class handouts, and scholarly papers.

ISBN: 978-0692717073

Published in the United States of America by Can of Corn Media, Durham, NC.

First edition.

For Amelia,
who had the courage
to go on Quests of her own.

1813

Upper Canada

After you die, your ears still work. Someone had told him that, once. He couldn't remember who. That hearing was the last to go. That even in death was sound.

He closed his eyes and listened. Musket fire faded. The shouts of soldiers receded and beneath these, the rustling of dried leaves overhead, the hues of red and orange that now, like him, clung to life, rattling against the wind.

Tecumseh was shot, and he was going to die.

He lay on the forest floor. He felt the wet ground against his skin, on his neck. The smell of churned mud. Each time he breathed, his chest blossomed with pain.

There had been times in his life when he'd been lucky. There'd been valiant escapes. More than once he'd lurched toward death, only to be yanked away again, to life. Some considered them two sides of the same plum stone, living or dying. Black or white. But he knew now that wasn't true. There were men who never seemed to die; men who died and were reborn; men who only knew how to kill and one day, were finally killed themselves. He didn't wonder anymore what kind of man he was. Life and death were fluid. His part in it was washed in gray.

He'd dressed as if he'd known. For the entirety of the campaign, this endless, borderless war, he'd acquiesced and worn the uniform of a British officer, which by all rights he was—serving under Major-General Procter, commanding a unit of some 500 native warriors. Wyandot and Pottawatomie and yes, plenty of his own tribe, the Shawnee. He'd donned the sash, the black polished boots. The red jacket with epaulettes. But not today. Instead, he'd worn his deerskin hunting shirt, his breechcloth. He painted his face black. He wove a long, white feather through his hair. And his quartzite necklace—he was glad to have it. He wouldn't have wanted to die without it. Now, sprawled in the underbrush along the banks of the Thames, he felt the cool stone against his throat.

He listened: he could hear the leaves. He could hear boots moving across the ground, toward him.

Suddenly there were hands on him—sitting him upright, pawing at his chest, yanking the feather from his head. He felt his leggings being loosed and pulled free. He could not resist. He could not even open his eyes.

He hadn't seen the man who shot him. He regretted that. He'd been charging a cluster of soldiers hidden in the trees. He thought he accounted for each, but then someone had gotten off a shot, and the bullet had burned beneath his arm and all his breath had been taken from him.

He would have liked to have looked his murderer in the eye. He wondered how many would stake a claim. Scores, he thought. Probably every soldier in the American army would say they were the ones to kill Tecumseh.

Even the great William Henry Harrison.

The thought of Harrison persisting when he himself would not made Tecumseh bolt upright. He gasped; he opened his eyes. He was being dressed again, by a white man—an American. The soldier's chest was wider than a barrel. Sprouts of black hair stuck up through his shirt collar and covered the backs of his hands.

"I know you," Tecumseh said.

"Lie still," the man said. "We've changed your clothes so no one else will find you."

Tecumseh studied the length of himself. It was true: he wore trousers now and black polished boots. A red jacket, but no shirt. Dressed as any nameless British soldier, without adornment or rank.

Hadn't he told his lieutenant, Roundhead, to stay close to him during the fight? He'd given him his flintlock rifle.

"Should I fall tomorrow," he'd said the night before, when they'd gathered around the fire, "strike my body four times with the ramrod. Then I will lift myself from death and find victory."

He had given away all his weapons. Had gone into battle with only his war club, which his brother Chiksika gave him long ago. The vanity of that—a war club against guns. He'd gotten what he deserved.

But now he turned his head. The American was dressing a dead brave in the clothes he himself had worn into battle. Tecumseh's feather, his hunting shirt. The dead warrior was Roundhead. So much for the flintlock rifle, the promise of the ramrod. He hadn't seen Roundhead fall.

"Poor lad." The white man returned, shaking his head. Tecumseh searched his memory for the name but couldn't find it. He'd had so much hair even then. The hair he remembered. "You've not much longer. I'm sure I don't need to tell you."

Tecumseh let his head fall back. He stared into the trees. When a breeze blew, shards of sunlight blinded him through the swaying and the edges of the leaves touching one another, gently at first, then clattering as the wind picked up. He shut his eyes again.

Soon his own men would come to collect his body. They would give him a proper burial. The Americans wouldn't have the satisfaction of robbing his teeth and hair for souvenirs.

"Easy," said the American. "Know how much we respect you that we do this thing in your honor."

This was something—respect from an American. He wondered what his father would think, or Chiksika. He knew this white man from somewhere, from many years ago. All his life he'd—no, better to try and think of something else. Something good. To savor these last few moments. To count each minute, every second. He noted the trembling of leaves and knew as long as he could hear their sound, he wasn't dead.

The leaves passed their impatience to one another like whispers through the branches, the way rumors spread, or fire. It had been a short life in many ways. He had not done all that he'd set out to do. The certainty of youth had faded into something else. He doubted that in fifty years, or even ten, anyone would remember his name.

The only thing he was certain of was that today, Tecumseh, the Great Panther Crossing the Sky, would die.

1774

Ohio Country

WHATEVER IT WAS THEY WERE GOING TO FIND—whatever it was they would one day be—waited for them below the ice. Tecumseh and his two brothers stood naked, shivering on the riverbank. They huddled together for warmth. Up before dawn, their father had marched them to where Massie's Creek fed the Little Miami River, reminding them the entire way how much had changed since he was a boy.

"Maybe my sons wear trousers and linsey shirts like white children," he said, "but some things remain the same. Now you are six years old, you need to find your pawawka tokens, as I did long ago. Certain things make us Shawnee, and these will never change."

Tecumseh hopped back and forth. Frosted grass crunched beneath his feet. His breath came in short, anxious bursts, visible in the breaking light. His father, draped in heavy bearskin, stood with arms crossed, a switch in hand. Ice lined the bank, and the river current slogged against the freeze.

He was the oldest by minutes, and he was first to feel his father's switch against his back. The pain was brief but amplified by the cold: it stung worse than it should have.

But he did not wait. He bolted for the water. When his feet hit, he sunk past his ankles through the slush. He plunged on and soon was waist-deep, breaking up the ice with his knees. The frigid slash of the water against his chest emptied his mind and strangled his breath in his throat.

The hope was that the pawawka token would find him, as a kind of sign. The token would be a clue for what his life would be after this. Though he knew that at the bottom of the river lived the Great Horned Snake, he was not afraid. Half the stories about drownings and deathly tides were just tales the older boys made up to frighten children—or so he told himself. He set his teeth and folded his hands above his head and dove.

Underwater was silence. He could see nothing in the darkness. He stretched out his hands to the river bottom, warm and slick. He grabbed two fistfuls of muck and then kicked hard toward the surface. Breeching, he saw the current had carried him downstream. He struggled against it, fists clenched, kicking, and swam back to shore, the jumpy silhouettes of his brothers guiding him in.

On the riverbank again he collapsed and coughed up water. His father draped a blanket over him, but still he could not keep his teeth from chattering. His father knelt and brushed ice slivers from his eyebrows and ran fingers through his straight, dark hair, shaking out the water so it would not harden.

"Show me what you brought up from the river bottom," his father said.

Tecumseh felt his breath draw even. He felt the ground

beneath him and the flat, white sky above, the cold in his limbs and eyes. All were one: he didn't know where his body ended and the sky began. He didn't think he could unpeel his frozen arms from where he kept them clutched at his side for warmth. But he produced two trembling fists. His father uncurled the fingers, one by one, and Tecumseh watched closely because the fingers did not feel like his own.

His right hand held only river crud. But opening his left revealed a marbled stone. Small and square, it radiated heat. He felt its warmth spread from his fingertips past his wrist and up his arm.

"Quartz," his father said.

The mineral's warmth spread as far as his shoulder. His arm tingled and throbbed as feeling returned. He held the quartz to his eye. The stone revealed many colors: blurs of deep red swirled with a color of yellow deeper than the corn at harvest. White flecks sparkled in the sunlight now pouring through the empty trees. The longer he examined the stone, the more colors he saw. And they seemed to shift or trade places with one another, first more red than yellow, then so much yellow he thought it would run from the edges of the stone and soak the earth.

"This is your pawawka token," his father said. "Keep it close. It will protect you."

But the second brother, Rattle, believed in the Great Horned Snake that lived at the bottom of the river. He refused to jump. Even when his father hit him with the switch, and then again, he whimpered and shook his head and rubbed his eyes with his fists. He said the snake was waiting for him. He said the snake would pull him under and he would drown.

"Where is your pride? Your self-respect?" Their father was furious. "How will you ever take my place as war chief?"

The switch fell, again and again. Its sound was crisp as a shot on the frozen river. Tecumseh flinched each time, wishing his brother would get on with it.

Finally Rattle stumbled knock-kneed toward the water, hands outstretched as if groping against the dark. His eyes were shut and his fleshy mass quivered, mottled by the cold. His back was inflamed by lashes. The fat rolls above his knees smacked together with a kind of wet, mucking sound. He hit the water; he hurled himself into it. But he hadn't forged deep enough. Instead he tumbled in the shallow current, breaking up the slush. On his knees now he tried to plunge his head below water. Then he rolled onto his back to cover himself as bits of river-bottom, the green, oily tendrils of fungus and mire, clung to his arms and back and buttocks. He splashed and thrashed like a netted fish.

"Go deeper," Tecumseh called, feeling shame for and because of him. "You haven't gone deep enough."

But Rattle was no kind of swimmer. Their father took two steps into the water and hauled him onto shore. The boy wept and shivered. He coughed and sputtered on his knees, cupping his private parts, the sad mass of him shaking.

"Show me your hands," their father said.

Rattle opened his hands but there was nothing inside them, not even mud. His father put his foot against the boy's flank and kicked him. He groaned and flipped onto his back but he did not rise. He only lay there weeping as their father snapped his fingers and motioned for the third brother to enter the water.

Open Door did not need the switch. Before their father could strike, he walked calmly into the river. Once he was waist-deep, he paused to look back at them. He turned toward his reflection in the broken pieces of ice and then looked back at them again.

"Is this me?" His arms hung at his sides. "Is this really me?"

Tecumseh knew his brother imagined he was like all the other boys. But their mother, Methotaske, had said that in her womb she knew there was a difference among them: that two had moved together while isolating the third. How Tecumseh had come first, then Rattle, bawling, and finally Open Door, small and squirming and silent, his skin so blue they could almost see through him. They had to pinch his toes to make him cry. Even then the sound was pitiful, weaker than a mewing kitten.

"Put your hands in the water," their father told him.

But Open Door was weeping now, chin quivering. Round tears rolled down his face.

"Is this me?" he asked again. "Can this really be me?"

He had never seen himself before. And now he faced his reflection in the ice. Tecumseh knew what the ice revealed: a long, narrow head, his forehead too broad, his left eye hanging below his right. A clot of spittle clung to the corner of his lip.

The river revealed everyone for who they were. Tecumseh knew this—it was the power of the Great Horned Snake. Some considered it evil, but it had also given the blackest, most potent medicines to the shamans. The river reminded the boy that there was evil in the world, and there always would be. He could either learn to live with it and try to control it, or placate it with offerings. Many things in life were not strictly good or bad, and the river was one.

The brothers could recite the story of their birth. Methotaske had told it to them many times. How on the night a comet appeared, a white flash bridged the southern tree line to the silhouette of the hills. The Shawnee capitol was consumed by light as the first child emerged, barking and gasping, pushing his way out of his mother's womb. And his father, in great excitement, swept the shriveled infant in his arms and swore it was a sign. "We will name him Tecumseh," he said. "The Great Panther Moving across the Sky."

But Tecumseh's birth brought no relief to Methotaske. The labor pains went on. She grimaced and clenched her teeth while the midwife plunged her hands again between the mother's knees. Moments later she resurfaced, clutching a second child, this one rounder and meatier than the first and louder, too—he had lungs like the whistle of a steam engine. Everyone in Chillicothe heard his cries. Packs of dogs stopped to cower and to howl. The child's face was swallowed by his scream. He held his fists by his ears and shook them. They named him *Tenskwatawa*—the Rattle.

Even as Methotaske's thoughts were absorbed by the wailing infants in her arms, she felt a new stirring below as her muscles clenched, weakly, against a third delivery. The sweat cooled on her arms and legs and she made a small noise and the third child was born—a third boy who emerged silent and nearly still, giving only the smallest, involuntary shiver against the sudden fresh air, shaking out his cramped legs.

The midwife slapped this child's behind and finally it let out a pitiful mew, a helpless sound of surrender. He was half the weight of his brothers and so pale that Methotaske could see his veins and below those his organs and bones as if through a thin sheet of ice. She named him *Sauwaseeku*, the Open Door.

The rhythm of Chillicothe then, the many pots and kettles set boiling outside the wigwams. The impromptu games among the men; a space in the afternoon set aside for tobacco. The brothers swaddled and strapped flat to their boards and carried everywhere Methotaske went—gardening, cooking, washing clothes in the creek. At night, while the town sang and danced, the children were set upright on their boards in a spot away from the fire, where the shadows cast by the dancing men fell across them, where the thrum of the water drum shook their still-soft bones, while the fire burned and the flames leapt.

Returning from the river, the brothers warmed themselves beneath bearskins. Their father sat shaving the bark from a short, plump stick and working the point of his knife into the wood flesh to hollow out its middle. The boys had sticks of their own, young saplings, and they peeled back the bark and scraped at the green underskin with their fingernails. It was rare for their father to spend so much time with them, but then he was leaving soon.

"Why do you go?" Tecumseh asked.

"There is a war," he said. "The Shawnee must again choose sides."

He explained how white settlers from Virginia were pushing far down the Ohio River, further and further each year. That together with the Mingos, the Shawnee would try to stop them. That if the settlers came too far downriver, the Shawnee way of life would be no more.

"And our way of life is sacred," Rattle said. It was something they'd heard from their father many times. "The best way of life."

"It's the only way of life," he said. "Or the only way of life I'm interested in, anyway."

He told them how before they were born, there had been a different war. The Shawnee had been on the losing side, not by any fault of their own, but because the French had not helped as they had promised. The British, as victors, demanded the tribes return all their white prisoners, including the women and children.

"This was very difficult." He put the stick to his mouth and blew. Wood shavings blasted from the other end. "Many of the white women had been with us for years. They had children with Shawnee men. And most of all, they had come to love our way of life. How our women are seen as equals."

The tribes had brought hundreds of white prisoners to the appointed place, where the Tuscarawas met the Muskingum River. So many that the British were overwhelmed. There was much weeping and sadness on the banks that morning as the women said goodbye to their children. As white children, who had been taken by the Shawnee as infants, screamed and fought and had to be carried onto the waiting boats and hauled away.

"I learned our way of life was unique among men." Their father put his lips to the hollow stick. When he covered the bottom hole and then uncovered it, quickly, his hands moving like the slow flapping of wings, there was a low and wavering whistle. "It is worth fighting for."

Springtime. The sense of having put winter behind them. The quality of daylight in the afternoon: the hills ran with it. Something buttery in the air that Tecumseh could sift through his teeth. Everything trembled with life. A feeling in his heart, swollen and wobbly, like a cup that had been filled to the brim. A slightly sick feeling in his belly. The possibilities of life opening up.

On a nearby hill hung a thick vine that was knotted somewhere far up in the branches, too high to see. But there was slack to the vine, and the brothers could walk it up the hill a ways and then run with it, downhill, and leap, clutching the vine, kicking their legs soaring through the air. Open Door shrieking as he held on, Rattle forgetting to let go and falling back to earth with it and dragging himself through the leaves—all of them laughing and hooting and feeling like this day, this life, would never end.

It was still Shawnee land, all of it, and the brothers believed it belonged to them. Many of the men in their village, including their father and their oldest brother, Chiksika, were away for long stretches at a time, following the Shawnee chief Cornstalk. Leaving the boys unsupervised. Leaving the trees, the river, the sky: leaving all of it to the three brothers who had been born at the same time, under such a fortunate sign.

Tecumseh and Rattle sometimes walked together with Open Door out in front by fifteen paces or more, flushing rabbits from burrows and putting birds to wing as his brothers hurled sticks after them—the boys not yet old enough for real weapons. Open Door scampered through the undergrowth on all fours, barking.

"He thinks he's a dog," Rattle laughed.

Tecumseh snapped a branch and hurled both halves high into the trees. "At least he's being useful."

Since finding his pawawka token, he'd taken to wearing it around his neck on a string. Each night before he fell asleep he squeezed the stone and tried to feel its magic. He did not talk about it with his brothers. The river had not been as generous with them. But there were many ways to discover your purpose. It did not happen the same for everyone.

They came upon a settlement a hard, two-hour walk from their village. This was the furthest they had ever pushed from home. They waited for a time in the underbrush, watching. But there were no voices or animal sounds. Only herb gardens strangled by weeds, and stalks of corn that were far past ripe, bending from their own weight. Having come upon the settlement on the southeast side, they followed the outer wall and found the front gate open. They came racing around, pushing one another and jockeying to be first inside.

"Get out of my way." Tecumseh planted his feet and grabbed hold of Rattle, trying to spin him to the ground.

But his brother fought back. "Why do you get to go first?"

"I'm older."

They could see inside. There were two cabins. They knew the settlement was abandoned because it was cold, the way you could tell something was dead just by touching it.

Rattle freed himself from his brother's grip. "You're only older by a minute."

But, Tecumseh thought, it was a minute that mattered. If Rattle had been first, he would have been named

The Great Panther Crossing the Sky. The thought was so absurd, he punched his brother in the arm.

Rattle plopped down, pulling at the fabric of his shirt to keep it away from his fat. "What happened here, do you think?"

"It could have been our men, or the Delaware," Tecumseh said. "Or they could have decided to move to a larger settlement further east. Closer to people of their own kind."

Settlements frequently emptied. Most of the time, you never learned why. Men came, built walls, put homes inside the walls, lived for a while. They planted crops. They hunted the woods. And then one day—well, it was different for each.

He put two fingers to his lips and whistled. The tone was piercing and clean. In a moment, their youngest brother came scampering around the east wall. Nettles were in his hair. Faded dandelions clung to his elbows and knees. He wagged his tongue and pretended to rub against Tecumseh, growling a little.

Rattle reached into his pocket and produced a green apple, something their father had brought back from Virginia. He said they were valuable and rare. That Americans had only just started growing them near the great sea. Their father had given them the apples for their eighth birthday and the taste, when Tecumseh bit into one, was fleshy and sour. The fruit made him thirsty.

"Here, boy." Rattle hurled the apple through the open gate. "Fetch."

Open Door took off after it, disappearing inside the compound, still staggering forward like a dog.

"Perfect." Tecumseh stood, brushing grass from his knees. "I guess one of us better go get him."

The settlers had lived there a long time. There was a wagon with a harness for the horses. There were hoes and axes. Someone had planted flowers, yellow and blue and white. Blooming without their gardener—whoever it had been. Tecumseh was only a few yards inside before Rattle came up behind him, breathing heavy.

Open Door stopped at the first cabin. He knelt before the shut door, pawing at the seam. He stroked the door with stiff fingers and whimpered like a pup. Rattle went to him.

But there was something vibrating at the base of Tecumseh's throat, insistent. He clasped the quartzite that hung from his neck. The stone was hot. It felt alive in his hand.

Their father had said the token would protect him—it warned when there was magic nearby. Tecumseh couldn't get the words out fast enough.

"Wait—"

But Rattle put his shoulder to the door. The door swung open. The stench unleashed itself upon them, having been cooped up long enough for the air inside to take on a physical quality. The smell had a taste—Tecumseh swallowed against it. He covered his nose and mouth and with his brothers tried to see into the blackness of the cabin.

Sunlight revealed debris in bits and pieces. The room

was trashed as if a great, spiraling wind had swept through. Wax candles, tin sconces, straps of woven baskets—all strewn across the floor. A spinning wheel was upside down against the far window. There were smashed kettles and an overturned table with chairs, their legs snapped. There were books and loose pages. Curtains were torn, not rendered in half, but as if someone had taken a knife and drawn it down their lengths. And the smell: it hit Tecumseh high in his nose, a sour and suffocating odor that forced itself onto the back of his tongue and down his throat. Sour, but sweet. It reminded him of something.

Rattle spit. "Smells like piss."

Tecumseh crossed the threshold. Whatever had befallen this settlement, whatever had caused the people here to flee, had not been peaceful. Open Door pushed past them both into the dim room, having set aside his game of playing dog. He stepped very carefully now, one foot in front of the other, as if balancing on a log above a deep gully.

"Here kitty kitty," he said. "Here kitty kitty."

That was it—that was what Tecumseh smelled. The distinct odor of cats. Sometimes his father would bring back a wildcat from a hunt, long and powerful and graceful. Sometimes he was given the task of taking the great cat's skin. This room, as he walked through it, carried the feline smell of wilderness and night prowls and also, of death.

He paused at the window. He ran his fingers along shreds of curtain, feeling them shift. He traced the upturned tabletop, along gouges where something had made deep cuts in the surface. It didn't seem possible for a wildcat to have caused all this. But he had never heard of them traveling in packs.

His foot kicked something. His eyes were still adjusting. He reached for what his foot had brushed against and touching it with his fingers knew by its heavy wetness what he held was a heart—and that it was human.

He leapt back, dropping the piece of flesh, stumbling against the cockeyed spinning wheel. He wiped his hands on tendrils of curtain and saw them all then, the many human remains, those glistening and soggy internal masses. What he had mistaken for shadows along the floor became blood stains. He recognized the room then for what it was.

Rattle called to him from the doorway. "What did you find?"

But he couldn't speak. Whatever had done this, whatever was able to murder these settlers was something much more terrible than a wildcat. They were standing in the aftermath of a massacre.

"We need to—"

He had heard Shawnee war cries. He had heard buffaloes moan as wolves dragged them to the ground. He had heard dogs howl, and women wail out of deep mourning, and he had heard feral cats make their low, quavering incantations facing off against one another in the night. But the sound he heard then outside the cabin was something beyond even these. It yanked the air apart and jolted his bones. Open Door dropped, covering his ears. Rattle dove inside and slammed the door behind him, throwing the latch.

His eyes were full of tears. "What is it?"

Tecumseh reached for his brothers and they came to him and waited, listening. The scream sounded again, higher in pitch now, and below the scream was a throaty, inhuman rumble that he could only describe as that of a cat in rut—a very large, very terrifying kind of cat.

The door shook as something slammed against it. The cabin too. The brothers shouted out, clinging to one another. This something threw itself against the door again. The latch held. And then the beast began to circle. They could tell where it was by the way it hurled itself against the wall and by the sound of its claws rattling against the wood. Tecumseh thought that whatever had eaten the people who used to live here was now just outside—it had come for them.

The creature caterwauled. The floor seemed to shudder. The quartzite around his neck was standing straight out now as if upheld by a strong wind. As the creature clawed and shrieked, the quartzite spun, lassoed only by the string that held it. Responding to whatever terrible magic was trying to get in.

He could see its shadow slip past the slits in the logs. He could smell it: the deep, dark scent of animal blood.

"Here, kitty kitty. Here, kitty kitty."

Open Door was crawling for the entrance, his face radiant. The beast outside dragged its claws along the length of the north wall. Their youngest brother reached the door and threw back the latch.

"Get him," Rattle begged.

"No." Tecumseh couldn't feel his hands. "You."

Both of them were too afraid to move. And then Open Door was outside, the cabin door thrown wide. A rush of air; the live and horrible smell of the creature; Open Door then standing in the front yard, arms outstretched.

"Here, kitty kitty."

Tecumseh scrambled to the threshold but no further, stayed by a shadow falling across the yard, originating someplace he couldn't see, casting Open Door in darkness off the blind corner of the cabin.

"No," Rattle said from behind him.

A change came over Rattle then. He sucked in his belly. His hands were fists at his side. His chin did not quiver. Only his nostrils, a slight flaring, the breath moving in and out. On the floor was a black book. The words *Holy Bible* were written across the front in gold font—Tecumseh had seen this book before in the hands of surveyors and other whites. Now Rattle picked up the volume and held it to his chest. He went to the door, took a deep breath, and stepped into the yard.

Tecumseh lunged after him, to pull him back. He wanted to save his brothers, but he was also afraid to die. He wanted the beast outside to quiet and wished they'd never come into this settlement—but he also wanted to sacrifice himself for them. He felt all of these things as he groped for the door, determining finally to shut it and save himself. But he could only watch as Rattle strode into the yard, stopped, and held up the book.

The creature came around the side of the cabin faster than he had seen anything move—faster than any wildcat, faster than a horse at full gallop. It was upon Rattle then or almost: his brother did not flinch but held the book up to it. The creature reared back. The two stood facing one another, Rattle extending the book toward it, his shirt riding up to show the flabby swell of his belly, and the creature pulling itself to full height and unleashing a roar. Open Door was on his knees, mouth caught in a stupid half-smile, paralyzed by fear.

The beast was taller than any man—taller than the cabin. Its lower half, its back legs and feet, were feline. Its fur was long and black and crusted, its claws curving blades. But its upper half was female. Smooth, brown skin along her back, her breasts caked with mud and the ravages of her slaughter. She circled Rattle, sometimes bending low to snap at him, showing her fangs. Her face was part cat, the mouth and nose, but her eyes were human, and her black hair was matted to her head like fur, with coils ensnaring her face as she circled, unwilling to come closer so long as Rattle held the book.

"Be gone with you." Rattle's voice did not waver, his hands did not shake. *"Yea, though I walk through the valley of the shadow of death, I will fear no evil: for thou art with me; thy rod and thy staff they comfort me."*

The creature shrieked, and cowered, and covered her cat ears with hands that were also claws, her nails long and sharp. Rattle spoke again, louder now—he seemed to be quoting something in a language Tecumseh did not know. His brother gestured with the book and the creature seemed to fear it, recoiling, hissing at the black book and shuddering at the words until, finally, she screamed, swiped once at the boys, and sped away through the settlement gate into the night.

Tecumseh went to them. "It's okay. It's gone."

Rattle lowered the book and, taking one last glance at it, tossed it to the ground. "It was the Wampus Cat."

"I know."

"It actually exists."

He rubbed his brother's arms: his skin was cold. "What were you quoting there?"

Rattle shook his head. "I once saw a man reading from a black book like that. Just something I memorized somehow. I guess I liked the way it sounded."

"How did you know it would work?"

"The white man brought the Wampus Cat here. It fears their god."

The brothers made their way to the gate. They held Open Door's hands between them. They were still hours from home.

"The white men have a saying about that beast." Rattle whispered so that Open Door would not hear. "They say that when the Wampus Cat screams, in three days, someone will die."

They told their mother about the Wampus Cat. She was laughing before they finished. She threw her head back and roared and fell off the stump she was sitting on.

"You were never in any danger," she said, breathless.

"But the Wampus Cat killed those settlers," Rattle said. "She would have killed us."

"You acted bravely." She petted Rattle and pulled him close. "But you are Shawnee. We are not afraid of these monsters."

They were eager to make her love them. Fair but demanding, she kept careful watch over them and pushed, sometimes mercilessly, if they were lazy, or if she felt they were somehow not living up to their birthright. They wanted only her approval, to fulfill whatever vision she had for them. They weren't the only ones: many in their village felt the same.

She had flawless skin—that was the first thing anyone said about her. Smooth and unblemished, despite how hard she worked. Her hands, small and quick, flashed as she peeled and chopped, mashed and wove. She was, as a young woman, or so their father told them, the most beautiful girl in Chillicothe.

Of all the brothers, Tecumseh looked most like her. How her eyes and nose seemed to have been coaxed from the soft clay of her face, little by little, so as not to overpower the rest. How her lips, set tight, tugged a little at their corners as if, at any moment, she might smile. And yet the way her eyes were set a bit too close together, the pronounced V of her brow, made it also seem as if her smile, given quickly and freely, almost perfunctorily, to set her audience at ease, might be a precursor to some intelligent, insightful, and sometimes cutting remark. Hers was a face that deserved to be gazed on and was, but not as one admired the moon or a budding flower, in appreciation of their symmetrical beauty. Her charm lay in the animation of these features. Her good looks—and by extension Tecumseh's—could disarm her listener, and secure another's trust instantly. The heavy-lidded eyes that were also a bit sleepy—again, just another way to set her listener at ease, unassuming, unthreatening—would suddenly focus as if expecting something more from her sons than they were even sure they had the ability to offer. A question, or two, that cut to the heart of whatever issue was being discussed and then, a solution. Or at least, action. The girls of the village, and many young women too, would sit and hold her hands and braid her hair, which had remained full and black and hung to her waist. They would gossip, and seek advice, and share secrets. She was still beautiful, even after bearing so many children.

She led her boys to the outskirts of the village, not far from where the horses were kept. There, in a faded cabin, lived a medicine man named Knotted Pine. Tecumseh knew of this man and had watched him cross their village with his hesitant, shuffling steps. It seemed he covered no distance at all until he suddenly arrived. Everyone saw he had great power.

Methotaske dragged her sons inside without knocking. Tecumseh could not settle his eyes: there was a small cooking fire in the center of the room and on the walls were pelts and the blanched skeletons of woodland creatures, jackrabbits and groundhogs and buffalo horns like daggered scythes. There were baskets stacked high against the wall. There were painted turtle shells. There were small dishes of herbs and powders and vials of bright liquid set in rows along the floor. Knotted Pine sat among these things—he was part of them. His hair was white, his face creased and folded. He wore only a bearskin. His skinny legs and arms jutted out from beneath the fur. He worked his jaw and looked at them. Tecumseh swore his eyes changed colors, green to yellow to black as he looked at them all in turn. "I've been expecting you."

"My sons have had a run-in with the Wampus Cat," Methotaske said.

Knotted Pine worked his lips as if to spit, then swallowed instead.

"I thought we might show them why they should not be afraid."

"One should always be afraid." The old man rocked himself to standing. He shuffled to the doorway and parted the curtain. "Not to fear, to assume these new monsters are like the old, is foolish."

They followed him into a space the size of a corn crib. They crowded into the small room, two adults and the triplets. They stood so their elbows touched. Their mother put her arms around her sons to make sure they were listening.

"What do you see?" she asked.

An object hung from the ceiling, suspended by a string. The boys had to stand on tiptoes to peer at it from above. A hollow stone, about the size of a bread loaf, hung wrapped in deerskin and buffalo hide. In the bowl of the stone was a steady flame.

"There's no kindling," Rattle said.

Tecumseh saw his mother and Knotted Pine exchange an impressed look. He felt a flash of jealousy and studied the fire more closely. It was true—the blue flame danced and flickered but there was nothing beneath it, and no smoke.

"Very good." Knotted Pine examined the light. "This is the sacred fire. Chalaakaatha carried it across the sea, on his back. This flame is eternal. It prays to Our Grandmother on our behalf. It keeps us safe so that the lesser gods—and these monsters, such as your Wampus Cat—cannot harm us."

Rattle stepped forward and touched the base of the stone. "But how does it burn without fuel?"

"This fire does not require wood, but is everlasting."

Methotaske explained how the skin surrounding the stone had been renewed three times since it was brought to the Shawnee. The flame itself was very, very old. There were always two men to keep the flame, one—Knotted Pine—who lived with the flame and another who lived close by. These keepers of the flame did not travel with the war party but kept the sacred fire burning. One day the flame would save the Shawnee from their enemies and renew the world with its heat.

"You are not, then, the strongest or the fastest?" Rattle said.

The shaman seemed surprised by the question. "No. I am an old man."

"Knotted Pine has always been an old man, even when he was young," their mother laughed.

"It is true." He snorted, clearing some kind of blockage behind his nose. "But I've kept this flame burning for over a generation."

"Perhaps one day I will keep the flame," Rattle said. "Perhaps one day Open Door and I will be the two who keep the flame and save our people from our enemies."

But Open Door was often sick. Many mornings he stayed in bed while his brothers went off to do their chores. He spent afternoons in the shade, watching his mother shuck corn and dig in the dirt with her fingers. It seemed he was not born with enough strength to last each day.

Other times, he was left to lie with his eyes closed. Tecumseh would stand over him then, waiting for him to breathe, holding his finger beneath his brother's nose until he felt the slightest breath on his skin. To make sure Open Door was still alive. Sometimes it was hard to tell otherwise. His skin could be so much lighter: sometimes he looked like a smudge mark, as if he weren't there at all. His chest did not rise and fall like most boys sleeping. He took sips of breath and then a wisp of air drifted out, disturbing nothing.

"Let me read your fortune."

Rattle wouldn't sleep. He wouldn't let Open Door sleep either. He explored his brother's wide forehead with his fingertips. "Come on, dummy. Let me read your mind."

The nights were growing cool. The brothers slept wrapped in deerskins, Tecumseh and Rattle with Open Door between them.

Rattle, fingers outstretched, probed his younger brother's cheeks and ears. He threatened to slide one thick finger up his nose and then laughed and slapped him lightly on the head. Open Door whimpered, twisting side to side, craving but also resenting the attention. Rattle waved his fingers and hummed.

"It's very faint, your mind." Rattle closed his eyes. "I sense almost nothing."

"Go to sleep," Tecumseh urged them both.

"Wait." Rattle rolled himself into a sitting position and clamped the palms of his hands over Open Door's face. "I see an ugly wife. Fat, covered with warts. She will bear you six ugly children, each one uglier than the last. And one day, your fat wife will be so tired of looking at all your ugly faces, she'll leave you."

Tecumseh laughed and pulled his blanket up over his head. He could picture them all, twenty years in the future—a plump wife who bossed his brother around and six runt kids with heads like gnarly carrots.

Rattle's eyes glistened in the dark. "But somehow, you

won't mind. The seven of you then, you and your six ugly kids, will travel west. Somewhere far away—Dumb Canyon. Perfect for dummies like you."

When he took his hands away from Open Door's face, they saw their youngest brother was crying. A snot-bubble balanced in his left nostril.

"Don't cry, dummy." Rattle stroked his hair.

"I don't want to move away from you," he said. "I won't."

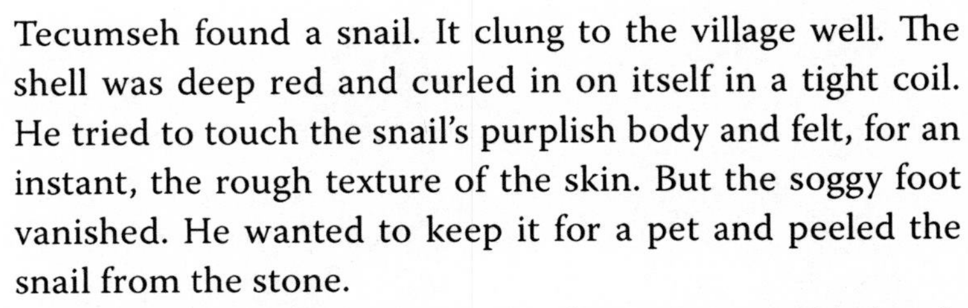

Tecumseh found a snail. It clung to the village well. The shell was deep red and curled in on itself in a tight coil. He tried to touch the snail's purplish body and felt, for an instant, the rough texture of the skin. But the soggy foot vanished. He wanted to keep it for a pet and peeled the snail from the stone.

He sprinted home, cupping the creature in his hand. He would show his mother. He would raise the snail. He would feed it grass and dandelions, moss and twigs. Once, as he ran, the snail stuck out its head and looked at him with tentacle-eyes. Tecumseh felt the cool slime of its body on his fingers. Surprised, he dropped the snail, and when he picked it up again he saw that luckily the shell had not cracked. But the snail did not stick out its head again.

Methotaske was not in their wigwam, but the cooking fire still smoldered. Tecumseh saw the rabbit she had skinned and butchered. But his brothers were not in bed where he left them.

Outside again he saw a woman he knew hurrying toward the Great Council House. He followed. The House was long and tall and built with straight planks of board. There was one large door and no windows. He and his brothers were never allowed inside—not until they were older. How much older, no one ever said.

He found his mother there, and his brothers, and most of the village. They stood outside. He tugged at his mother's leggings, at the fringe there, which he sometimes ran his fingers through and which he liked to feel brush against his face. He held the snail up for her. She would think the snail was funny, as he did.

But his mother did not laugh. She did not take the snail; he did not think she saw it. Instead, she grabbed his hands and pulled him close.

There were horses approaching. He felt the ground tremble and heard the thunder of hooves: Shawnee braves returning. They had been gone a long time, fighting a war. His oldest brother Chiksika. His father.

He couldn't help grinning. Whenever warriors came home there was much dancing and food and laughter. But he looked around and saw that no one was smiling. He glanced up at his mother and saw an empty expression that was the opposite of joy. His brothers were rubbing sleep from their eyes and also clinging to her.

The warriors came out of the woods, one by one. The air was heavy with the night's rain. A low fog clung to the ground. Emerging from the trees, the men seemed to float and hover on the haze. Their faces were painted with smears of red and black. They were bare but for their loin cloths, and they cradled their rifles in their arms.

Tecumseh saw Chiksika then. He and his father rode the same horse. Steam rose from the horse's flanks. His father rode in front. His father's legs were tied beneath the horse's belly. His hands were knotted to a rope slung around the horse's neck. He leaned back against Chiksika and bounced and swayed with the horse's cadence.

Their mother let out a long wail. Tecumseh felt hot tears on his cheeks although he didn't know why—something about the sound his mother made.

Behind Chiksika came more horses, and warriors lay draped across the rumps like sacks of grain.

"Mother," Rattle asked, "why are all the men asleep?"

Tecumseh saw that his father's eyes were closed. And that he was not sleeping—his father was dead.

The brothers trembled beneath their blankets. Sleep refused them. It hung about, declining to settle, charged with the anguish of that night. Outside the wigwam, their mother shouted at Chiksika. Tecumseh felt Rattle find his hand in the dark and they breathed together, listening. They had never heard their mother raise her voice—she never needed to. People did whatever she asked.

"If you sign the treaty," she said, "your father will have died for nothing."

Chiksika was not the sharpest mind, and he was not

the most accurate archer, and he did not speak as smoothly as many of the other men, but there was something about him, Tecumseh saw, which people wanted to be near. He was strong, for one. But it was more than that. When Chiksika was around, flashing his smile and sometimes shaking out his long, black hair—which he was unreasonably vain about—everyone felt safe.

"I do not want to sign the treaty." His voice broke with exhaustion and, Tecumseh thought, sorrow. "But there is no fight left in the other men."

The elders had gathered in the Great Council House. They argued for a long time. Tecumseh tried to listen from outside. Some of the men wanted to continue fighting a man named Dunmore. Others said more fighting would only lead to more dying. Tecumseh had been turning that name over in his brain and whispering it to himself, just to hear how it sounded: Dunmore. Was this the man who had killed his father? He did not know what he looked like, but he could picture him well enough: a white devil. With flowing blonde hair and crisp blue eyes and skin pale as snow. With red lips and a tongue forked like a serpent's.

He said it now again, as an incantation against his mother's anger. "Dunmore." He crept to the opening in the wall and peered out. He could see the shape of her against the cooking fire. Chiksika stood with his back to the wigwam, huddling against a stack of woven baskets, as if wanting to crawl beneath them and disappear. Their mother set her shoulders and lowered her head like a buffalo about to charge.

"The whites want only to swallow our land," she said. "They are a hungry beast whose appetite is never satisfied. Your father knew this."

Near the fire was her hominy block. She took up the pestle, club-like, and swung it against the hollowed log. The block flew. The pestle split in her hands. She used the largest shard to pound other things then—her best skillet, the stack of woven baskets, scattering both the baskets and her oldest son, the neat row of gardening tools. Everything was clattering and flailing as her grief consumed her.

Chiksika reached for his mother and tried to gather her in his arms, cooing to her the way Tecumseh had seen him coax a spooked horse. When finally she collapsed against him, spent, he said, "I will care for this family now."

1778

Ohio Country

METHOTASKE SANG SONGS TO SOOTHE HER BOYS. She told stories about their people and how they came to be. How the world had once been destroyed by a flood. How water had covered everything. How from that devastation Our Grandmother decided to build again and send five crayfish to the bottom of the sea. These animals returned with soil from the ocean floor, and this soil became an island. And when Our Grandmother created a Shawnee man and woman, she set them on the center of this island and surrounded them with animals so they might hunt and eat. And then she created eleven other tribes so that the Shawnee would never be lonely—so that they would always have someone to fight.

Tecumseh sprinted up the hillside, his breath easy, his steps soundless. Chiksika had marked certain trees, and these were the targets. When a circle appeared, Tecumseh bashed it with his war club and ran on.

His weapon was carved from a thick root. One end

was shaved and rounded, the other worn smooth. He was only just learning its power, how much damage this war club, gifted by his oldest brother, could do.

Sometimes the targets were above his head, sometimes knee-high. Sometimes two marks came in quick succession. He had to vary his swing. He moved easily across the ground, over the pine needles and leaves and the obstacles they concealed, everything obscured by the play of light through the branches. He saw his path through the trees even as he ran, and could plan, far in advance, the most efficient and seamless way through the growth. The trick was to keep his feet moving and step lightly. To adjust his body to the roots and stones, to let his balance be something that shifted instead of something rigid—to take what the land offered and stay in control. It was important to trust himself, even if he felt himself picking up too much speed. He never missed. When his club connected, the tree exploded with bark.

Rattle, though, crashed through the forest like a boulder. He struggled with the weight of his own club, letting it bounce behind him. Sweat poured down his face. He winced as branches slashed his skin. He did not charge the marks—the ones he noticed, anyway, because he missed more than a few—but ran up to them and, hefting the club above his head, the club head wobbling as he lifted it, bumped the weapon against the tree.

"Don't stop." Chiksika clapped his hands. "Find the next mark."

Age had accentuated the physical differences among

the brothers. Now ten years old, Tecumseh was quick but also thin, like a young tree with wiry limbs shooting out in all directions. Rattle was built more like Chiksika, stout and strong, but with thick flab around his middle and none of the effortless grace of his brothers, who wondered, sometimes, how they could possibly share the same mother.

Tecumseh came upon the final mark and swung. The war club, now heavier in his hands than it had been when he started, glanced from the tree and spun off into the undergrowth, slipping from his grip. Chiksika was on top of him in an instant, screaming in his face.

"You cannot drop your club!" He cuffed him on the ear. "A warrior who drops his weapon is a dead warrior, do you understand?"

Tecumseh stared at the ground, hot shame burning like a fever down his back, under his arms.

"Find it." Chiksika pushed him in the direction of where the club had disappeared.

Rattle came up moments later, wheezing. He didn't bother attacking the final mark, if he even saw it. Chiksika wrapped his arm around him and spoke encouraging words, offering pointers on how to hold the club, to hold it loose, but not as loose as Tecumseh, whose club had gone flying off into the woods.

"It isn't fair," Tecumseh spat back. He was kicking at the brush, too furious for a proper search. "I hit every target. He hit none. And yet you yell at me."

Chiksika came to him and steadied his heaving shoulders with both hands. Tecumseh felt tears behind his eyes—angry, frustrated tears. But he wasn't going to cry. Not now, not ever.

"You told me you want to be the greatest Shawnee warrior who ever lived," Chiksika said.

"That is what I want."

"Then you must work hard."

"I work just as hard as everyone else."

"That's the problem." Chiksika poked him once, firmly in the chest. "If you want to be the best, you have to work harder than everyone else."

Methotaske told stories about how the Great Spirit brought down the twelve tribes in a basket and set them on the shore of a wide ocean. He told them they must cross the water to reach the island he had set aside for them, that was balanced on the back of a sea turtle. He put a young man in charge, and the man's name was Chillicothe.

They camped for twelve days, fasting and singing songs on the beach. On the last day, the waters dried up. The men made their way across to the far shore. Once they'd reached the opposite bank, the ocean filled in behind them so they could never return.

Chillicothe led them north. One night, as they were camping, the Great Spirit appeared to them and declared that here, where they'd laid their blankets, was home. From now on they would be called Shawnee; the river they lay beside would be called the same.

"Pray to Our Grandmother," the Great Spirit instructed. "Because I have left you here to think for yourselves."

In their hearts, each Shawnee now carried a piece of the heart of the Great Spirit. So when their hearts quickened in the night, straining to hear strange music in the woods; when their hearts pounded against their chests after a long run; when their hearts felt too large to be contained inside their bodies, so full they were with love for creation, what they felt was a piece of the Great Spirit inside them.

Chiksika was shorter than most men but stronger, too. His wrists were veiny and thick. He could grip a tree trunk and, with one hand placed several inches above the other, lift until he held himself out over the ground, his legs straight as a saw blade. He rarely spoke, but when he was around, everyone knew it. The squaws followed him and whispered about him and dreamt futures for themselves, with him, alone in their blankets. He led a pack of older boys who hunted and caused mayhem after the dances when they'd drunk too much. But it was harmless fun. His eyes were bright in a way that seemed to promise something, and that was what people trusted.

There were things the older boys knew. Tecumseh and Rattle shouldering their first quivers, dragging their bows behind. Open Door somewhere many yards back, stumbling and distracted by what they could only guess, the splintered light through the budding trees, a swollen mushroom. They learned to read a snapped twig, or a bent blade of grass, or the half-moon impression of a claw-strike in the mud and know that a muskrat had passed by. They learned to spot the different way light caught the fur of an animal through the trees. And the things that the older boys could hear that Tecumseh could not, the way living beings moved in the forest. The most experienced among them, Chiksika included, no longer followed tracks but seemed to read the animal's mind, knowing what their prey wanted even before it did, able to follow its exact route to water. To be waiting for the animal when it arrived.

The hunters glided through the woods like frost, leaving a silent chill on every branch. At the edge of a clearing, Chiksika signaled. The younger boys fell back, not wanting to miss the action but understanding their place in it, not quite trusting themselves not to ruin it.

Chiksika had ordered them not to be annoying. He said that if they kept quiet and didn't get in the way, if they blended in and didn't talk about babyish things, then his friends wouldn't send them home. Tecumseh was determined to seal himself into this pack of older boys. He would earn their respect, prove himself their equal, or their better. But Rattle worried what would happen if their mother found out. They were still too young to be on a hunt.

"Who cares what she thinks?" Tecumseh said, although of course he did care, very much. "Stop being such a badger."

Tecumseh dragged Open Door into the tangle of

brambles and honeysuckle. With Rattle they watched the others spread out along the perimeter of the dell, keeping themselves concealed in the brush. He knew the older boys' tolerance for them was part pity—their father, after all, was dead—and part loyalty to Chiksika. But their tolerance was leaf-thin. One childish joke, one misplaced step, could send them back to pulling vegetables and cooking meals with the women.

"Where are you going?" Rattle whispered.

Tecumseh silenced him. He crept forward, readying his arrow. He wanted just one kill, to make the older boys notice him. No one, not even Chiksika, could order him around. He'd prove to them just how good an archer he was, turn his rage at being treated like a child into a hunting trophy.

"We're not allowed—"

But Tecumseh had already slipped out of the bramble.

At the edge of the clearing, he squatted in high grass that was lit by a blazing column of sun. Before him, the field was covered with blue and gray feathers. The grass shimmied. A flock of passenger pigeons snapped up seeds from the thawed ground. And there were hundreds, thousands perhaps, extending a half-mile along the river basin, thirty yards wide. A river themselves, emptying out somewhere Tecumseh could not even see, it was so far away.

Some of the pigeons perched on one another's backs. The largest of the birds seemed to change color as they moved in the sunlight, flashing pink and iridescent green to bronze. The grace of these birds—the sweep of their spine, the sharp human quality of their round, black eyes—but also the power of them amassed took his breath away. The density of them stretching along the basin. Theirs was a buzzing sound: a hollow *coo-coo* that swelled with a volume he felt in his belly, which seemed to carve up his insides. A hollow pitch, an offering to the wind. Had Chiksika, who was only fifteen yards across the clearing, called to him, Tecumseh would not have been able to hear. The sound of the birds was all consuming. His blood pulsed with its rhythm.

The older boys readied their nets. Others gripped short, sharp sticks that they turned slowly through their fingers, waiting. The idea was to take the birds on the ground. It was easier that way, and you didn't lose as many arrows as trying to take the birds on the wing. Tecumseh had only the bow he'd made from a hickory sapling. He'd wrapped the bow in sinew from the hindquarters of a deer, the way Chiksika had taught him. He carried a dozen arrows, fletched with owl feathers and weighted by stone chips for the heads. He decided to shoot at only the closest targets. He didn't want to lose an arrow. Each one took a long time to make.

Across the clearing, Chiksika stood and raised his hand. The hunters, concealed, waited motionless and tense. The noise of the birds rose in volume, but all at once Tecumseh felt the inside parts of himself fall quiet and still, his attention focused and sharp as the point of a spear.

A branch snapped. Someone gave a short cry. He turned to see his brother, Rattle, stumble out of the honeysuckle as if he'd suddenly lost his balance. He fell forward into the field, and there was a moment when the other boys all looked at him as if they couldn't quite believe what they were seeing.

"Now," Chiksika shouted, clapping his hands.

But it was too late. There was a great rustling and then a high-pitched whistle as the birds were flushed. The flock lifted into the sky, darkening it. The difference was noon to dusk, quicker than Tecumseh could count, as the multitude ascended, wings thrashing, their mournful calls blasting overhead.

He fell back, paralyzed at the sight. As if the earth itself had heaved and churned at once into the sky. The mass moving created its own wind. Feathers and grass spun in the air. He was only vaguely conscious of the older boys dragging themselves to their feet, bows drawn, to fire into the black cloud. He couldn't understand how they could even move—the sound of this scattering alone was enough to pin him to the earth.

Still, birds fell with arrows in their breasts. And the horde screamed past. It must have been a mile long, perhaps more, moving overhead for an impossibly long time. He saw Chiksika reach for an arrow, string it, and let it fly. The arrow was swallowed instantly by the darkness.

He heard his father's voice then, a voice somewhere deep inside himself, commanding him to get up. He thought he heard the crack of his father's switch. And then he was on his feet again, nocking the bow.

The birds had almost passed. There were patches of

daylight now between their outstretched wings. Another moment or two and the birds would be gone without Tecumseh having fired a shot. He could not let that happen. The older boys would mock him. He would forever in their minds be as cowardly as Rattle, who huddled still in the brush, having caused the pigeons to wing earlier than they'd wanted. Or as weak as Open Door, who most likely shouldn't have been out with them in the first place. He couldn't be paired with them—either of them. He needed to distance himself and stand on his own.

Another round of arrows blasted from the treeline to his left. Birds fell. The pigeons were sparse now, the last few stragglers trailing behind the main column.

His hands shook as he drew his first arrow. He felt the sanded shaft between his fingers. He touched the point of the stone head and strung it. Narrowing his vision, he selected one bird still some ways off. It seemed to freeze in space. Other birds disappeared around it. Suddenly only the one bird hovered in the sky.

He released the arrow. Feeling as if part of himself traveled with it, soaring higher—almost straight up, he saw it was on target. The spiral fletching flashed silver as the arrow spun and gained speed. But the bird flapped its wings as if sensing the arrow's approach. One wing stroke and the arrow had passed, continuing on toward blue sky. Tecumseh watched the arrow clear the tops of the trees, watched it twist and shudder against the wind. The arrow reached the extent of its energy, a peak, and paused, the white stone of its barbed tip gleaming in the sun, before it turned, end over end. And then the arrow was coming down.

Tecumseh waved his arms. "Arrow!"

The birds had passed, leaving behind a thunderous silence. Tecumseh's warning rang out clear. The hunters dropped to their knees and covered their heads. All but Rattle, who stood a few feet out from the treeline gazing into the sky, likely stunned by the sudden light.

Tecumseh would wonder, later, if there were some things that were simply bound to happen. Maybe everything was. Call it destiny, or fate: maybe he had no more control over the flight of the arrow than he did over the sun and moon. Maybe the arrow had its own needs and willed itself to soar, turn, and fall to earth.

Rattle's head snapped back when the arrow plunged into his face. For a moment he stood, back arched, palms out, on tiptoes, greeting the clouds. The arrow shaft protruded at a right angle. He made a soft grunting sound and fell back.

The boys raced to him. Tecumseh was on his knees, his hands on his brother's belly. Rattle was alive. His chest rose and fell. The arrow was sunk deep in his right eye. But his left eye looked wildly around, stunned and terrified.

"You didn't duck," Tecumseh said, nearly weeping. "Why didn't you cover your head?"

The other boys drew near. Rattle lay on his back, breathing quickly.

Chiksika pushed him aside. "Mother is going to be very upset."

He clutched the arrow shaft. He knelt one knee on

Rattle's shoulder. Then, slowly, steadily, and without a word, drew the arrow out.

The eyeball came with it, balanced like a fleshy ball of meat on the tip of the shaft. Only a dry, red socket where the eye had been, and surprisingly little blood.

That night Tecumseh cowered at the door of the wigwam. Inside, the medicine man, Knotted Pine, knelt and chanted over Rattle's body. The shaman swayed in the shadows like a spindly, old tree bending out over a river, leaning from the bank. In hazard, yet bowing slightly at every breeze, still able.

Rattle had been forced to drink from a bottle of clear liquid. The burning smell of it filled the room. His brother complained about the taste but drank it all, almost, before collapsing into sleep. Knotted Pine then bound the boy's hands and feet in case he happened to wake. He cleaned the black hole in Rattle's face with water and lye. He rubbed honey inside the wound and blotted it with a kind of leaf Tecumseh did not recognize. The shaman wrapped his patient's face with clean linen and tied it off at the back of the head. All while muttering in the ancient language in words no one else understood.

Chiksika stoked the cooking fire. They had already eaten, or tried to, but still he returned to it every few minutes and shifted the coals around. Methotaske was there too, clutching Open Door to her. She stroked his long, smooth face and closed her eyes and rocked in time with the medicine man's chanting.

She had said nothing to Tecumseh since the hunting party returned. They had brought Rattle to her and she had cried out, falling to her knees, asking why was their family cursed, to lose their father and now her son had only one eye—how would he ever provide for a family of his own?

"He'll live," Knotted Pine said. "You should be grateful for that."

Their mother sobbed—one outburst, and then swallowed the rest. Open Door looked at her, eyes wide, upset on her behalf, not understanding why. Or most likely not, anyway. Tecumseh never knew what his youngest brother could figure out for himself. Not everything. Not most things.

Knotted Pine turned to them. "I recommend a patch. For the boy's sake. The wound will look better with time, but it will always be jarring for others."

Methotaske nodded.

He turned to go. He collected his few things, patting the knitted sash around his waist where his medicine bag hung. He grunted once and shuffled toward the door. He moved so slowly Tecumseh had almost forgotten about him before he was suddenly there, right on top of him. He realized he was blocking the exit.

"Sorry," he said.

He shifted out of the way, but the old man gripped his shoulder. "Come with me, please."

Tecumseh caught Chiksika's eye from where he stirred the coals. His older brother nodded, so Tecumseh followed the shaman into the night. It was cooler under the stars. They went around to the yard where the shadows met between their wigwam and their neighbor's.

"The loss of your brother's eye is very unfortunate," the old man said. "He will no longer be able to hunt. He will even have a hard time riding a horse at any real speed. His life has changed, and maybe not for the better."

Tecumseh nodded—he understood. He feared the old man a little. Rumor was, he commanded the rain.

Knotted Pine said, "You have your older brother Chiksika, and you have yourself. But that is all. Your father is dead. And you will no longer be able to rely on Rattle for much." He paused, as if uncomfortable with what he had to say. "It's been clear for some time that Open Door, if he reaches maturity, and I'm telling you now that many with his particular condition do not, will need a great deal of care."

The old man bent very close. Tecumseh swore he heard his bones creaking, stretching in the night air like wet, swollen wood.

"You are young, but your family needs you." He gripped Tecumseh's chin suddenly and studied his face. This made Tecumseh sweat. He wanted to run away. He had to remind himself that his father had trusted this man, and was friends with him. "Best you go now while your brother is recovering."

"Go?" he asked.

"I know it seems as if, out of everyone, your brother's circumstances have changed the most." Knotted Pine showed his tongue and dabbed the corner of his mouth with it. "But I assure you, Tecumseh, it is you who now find yourself faced with an entirely different journey than the one you woke up with this morning. I have seen all I need to know in your face: on the next moon you will go on your Quest, and when you return, you will be a man."

In Methotaske's stories, the land was made by the Great Spirit in a place he set aside for them in his heart, on the back of a giant sea turtle. The turtle was Our Grandfather. He would tell them what to do, if they asked.

The Great Spirit came down from the sky and showed the Shawnee a door. When he opened the door there was a man inside. The man was whiter even than the Americans—white as ash. His eyes were red. He was naked and uncircumcised. This was the White Spirit, not made by the Great Spirit and so not subject to his control. The Great Spirit foretold that when the Shawnee were finally settled on the island on the turtle shell, the White Spirit would wait until they were comfortable, until they had forgotten, and then try to ruin all they had built. The White Spirit and his loyal subjects were not to be trusted.

Of all the tribes, the Shawnee were the only ones to come from someplace else—the only foreigners. Having made the long journey across the dried-up sea. Having been given the island on the turtle's back. Having been trusted to think for themselves. Having been warned in advance of the dangerous White Spirit, and having been sent to the island to protect the rest of the tribes of the First Nation from him.

But the Americans were a new breed. That's what Chiksika said. They were not landed gentry, like the British; and they were not yet wealthy, like the French; and unlike the generals of the past these men had no idea who their grandparents were. They had dispensed with that Old World where-you-from. After all, Chiksika said, you had to be a little crazy to settle out here in the first place—it was those who weren't afraid, who knew how to survive, who could kill, who stuck. This new breed of man was being birthed from the same wild that had been the Shawnee hunting grounds for a thousand years. In their villages, in Chillicothe most of all, there was a kind of unspoken panic, a tension beneath every conversation. Had Our Grandmother abandoned them? Did the progress of the Americans mean she had given up on the Shawnee, that fate had turned against them? Chiksika dismissed this kind of talk. "Fate," he snarled at supper, grease on his chin, "is only as accurate as my next arrow. It listens only to the sound of my knife being sharpened. This is what the Americans believe, that fate is theirs. But they are not the only ones who can believe in destiny."

Tecumseh spent three nights in the woods. Three nights and three days. He barely slept, and then only fitfully. At night the darkness swirled around him as if he were being drawn into the breast of a menacing, black bird. Squeezed beneath its wing, he could hear the darkness breathe.

He had plenty of time to think about what happened to Rattle, what he himself had inflicted, the errant arrow and the taking of the eye. He had helped Knotted Pine use string to measure the distance from his brother's eyebrow to cheekbone. They measured too from his nose to the far side of his lost eye, and used these measurements to mark the shape of the eye-patch on a soft swath of leather. They cut the patch larger than it needed to be. The shaman formed it into a kind of cup that would give Rattle's eye a little more space. They drove holes through the leather and wound string around the boy's head and knotted it. With some trimming, the patch fit.

Now Rattle had only one good eye. If before Tecumseh had felt responsible for his brother, in the sense that he would one day be war chief—the shooting star and the birth legend that was already gaining momentum among the Shawnee bands—now he was indebted. He had caused his brother harm. There was no changing it, and there was no way to make amends. Rattle would wear the patch for the rest of his life, but Tecumseh would wear the shame and guilt of being its cause.

On the third night of his Quest, he passed several

woodsmen on a path that wound from the fork of the Little Miami River north to Piqua Town. There was no moon. He stood just off the road, in the high grass, having heard their approach. As they drew near, he slowed his breath until all of him, inside and out, was quiet and still. He waited. The men passed, chattering, their powder horns and hatchets clanging from their belts, their pale faces like soft, dull orbs in the night. Their laughter and their strange tongue wove a shroud over them that they could not see through.

They did not notice him, although he might have reached out and touched them—tapping each one on the shoulder as if to count them off. He smelled their gunpowder; he smelled the bacon grease on their fingertips. The last man wore a hunting bag across his chest and Tecumseh let the bag's leather fringe tickle his fingers. Still they did not see him. He let them pass.

He was deep in Ohio Country. He led his horse, or his horse led him. There was heaviness behind his eyes, and lack of sleep caused his eyesight to narrow and to blur. His face was blackened by charcoal to announce the seriousness of his Quest. The charcoal had begun to crack and peel with his sweat and the salt from his skin.

He began to doubt what it was he was looking for. A sign of some kind, what he understood to be a supernatural creature who might offer itself as his spiritual guide. He had questioned Chiksika about it, but his brother offered little advice.

"It is different for everyone," he said. "When you meet it, you will recognize one another instantly."

Tecumseh stopped and let his horse—still a colt—drink from a stream. Its legs were restless; it stomped and snorted and lapped at the water. Cloudy Girl was mostly white, with flecks of brown and a short, reddish mane. Although gangly, she was fast, or would be one day.

He squatted on the bank, pulling up blades of grass and twisting them around his finger until they snapped. It had been a dry summer. There were shallow pools between the river rocks. He submerged his hands and let the water flow in and out of the vessel he made with his fingers. He heard his horse whinny. When he turned again to spot her, she was gone.

He stood. In the fading light, the edges of the trees were smudged. Shadows fell across the high gulch walls, gnarled with roots and flint-rock slabs. He felt his tiredness like a thin string of needles through the center of his brain. He called his horse and listened. He had not tied her off but had not thought he needed to—she'd never bolted before. And she had made only the one startled cry.

He heard her again, this time from the top of the gulch. He did not know how she could have made the ascent: there was no obvious path. She whinnied, and he strained to look, but he could not see her. Beginning to climb, he hoisted himself forward and up on bare roots and whip-thin trees that bent against his weight but also helped him gain slippery footholds in the clay. He was aware of the quartzite dangling from his neck, the pawawka token he'd brought up from the river bottom as a child. He found it hot. It seemed to quicken in his palm, the way a dog trembled, anticipating a bone.

Magic was nearby.

He breathed in through his nose but smelled only the woods and the mud and someone somewhere maybe smoking a bit of tobacco. He listened but heard only his own breath, his own heart against his chest. Still, his quartzite trembled. The sound of his heartbeat grew louder then, and he was aware of nearby objects taking on a certain, sudden distance. All at once, an arm's reach seemed impossibly far away until he grasped for the next handhold and found it to be the correct distance from him. His arms, although they felt like his, seemed large and unwieldy tools. He was conscious of a certain, pressing quality to his sense of time. There was urgency to the air, of minutes being clicked quickly off. It was the opposite of a dream state where he always seemed to move in slow motion, as if through honey. He cleared the top of the gulch and gained his footing.

Cloudy Girl was not there. Instead there was, leaning against a tree and drawing on a corncob pipe, a man about four-feet tall. From one of the five tribes, although Tecumseh could not say which. Perhaps Shawnee, perhaps Delaware. Not a child, but a barefaced man fully grown to miniature.

He spoke English, but somehow Tecumseh understood. "You lost your horse."

He replied to the man in English, although he'd never learned it. He opened his mouth and the words tumbled out. "She's never run away before."

It was strong magic to change the way Tecumseh spoke. He found he suddenly knew the words for all sorts of things in this foreign tongue, as if the language had been locked inside him, hidden, but now had been unlocked through whatever magic this traveler possessed. His tongue strained against the sound of English; it left a sharp and bitter taste.

"What kind of great warrior loses his horse?" The man spoke quickly, firing off words.

"I am a great warrior—or I will be one day. And my horse will return to me."

"No." The traveler knocked his pipe twice against the tree. "I will take you to her."

Hours had passed, or perhaps only moments. That sped-up quality of time, a sharpness to the trees and underbrush that also seemed to hold him at a cool remove. A glance away, a glance back, to see they'd actually traveled quite a distance in the time it took to move his head from one side to the other. A mildew smell beneath the otherwise sweetly pleasant summer breeze.

His guide was short but quick. He wore beaver fur—too warm for the season. His boots were cinched by garters at the knees. The tail of his coonskin cap swung behind him, down his back. Tecumseh had to double his stride to keep pace.

"How's your brother?" the man asked. "The fat one?"

Tecumseh wondered how he could know about Rattle. "He's well. He lost only the one eye."

"A blessing then."

Tecumseh wondered. It was hard to look at his brother and not stare at the patch. It seemed to have its own mind, apart from its wearer. The leather often creased at the corner or sagged, depending on the weather, or its mood. Sometimes the patch sat crooked on his face or slipped during conversation, a slow drifting below his ear toward his jowls. Rattle still wasn't used to wearing it. He was always probing beneath it with his finger. But mostly Tecumseh couldn't help staring at the patch because it pained him, in the same way he sometimes bit his fingernails until they bled. The pain somehow felt right.

Looking at Rattle was like that. Tecumseh knew what had happened on the hunt. He wouldn't deny it; he knew he was responsible. Rattle's patch, the way he had to turn his head to see things, the way he sometimes woke howling in his sleep, these were things that were part of Tecumseh now, too.

The guide called to him over his shoulder. "Name's Jack."

He returned to the present woods, the warm night and the bare roots below his feet like bones in the moonlight. He had heard of this man. His mother told stories about him. By reputation, he was a trickster.

"Some call you 'Crazy Jack,'" Tecumseh ventured.

The man spun, glaring. "I do not like it when men call me that."

He swallowed. "But it's what people call you."

"Jack's my name." The man pushed him with both hands. "But I don't accept the bit about being crazy."

They pressed on, south. It was the direction he'd come, but Tecumseh saw none of the marks he'd left so that he could track his way home to Chillicothe. And then they were no longer in the same forest. There were plants he'd never seen before, with broad, comb-like leaves. The trees were narrow and rough, and shot straight up from the ground. They sprouted fronds at the top and clusters of round, hairy fruit. A lizard, larger than any Tecumseh had seen—and bright green—darted across the path. Everything sharp, everything glistening at its edges, as if shining with dew.

Crazy Jack grinned, toothless, his mouth a dank, bottomless cavern. "How does it feel? Talking English?"

"I don't like it," Tecumseh said. "The words are hard. And mean. There's little beauty in them."

"Get used to it." The man laughed. "Soon, they'll be speaking English all over that pretty river valley of yours."

They passed through a stand of trees and emerged into a snowy clearing. Snowdrifts lifted and curtsied in gusts of wind.

He was shirtless, and his skin tightened against the air. He felt his muscles shudder. The chill pressed on him. He felt as if he could stretch and touch the stars, and with tidy flicks of his finger, shatter them like icicles. It was nowhere he'd ever been.

He considered this man who led him over powder snow, who was now whistling and keeping rhythm with one hand slapping his thigh. The man cleared his nose and gurgled and spat into the snow, where the spittle bore a hole an inch deep through the rime. Tecumseh had once met a Delaware shaman whose spirit guide was a common skunk. It communicated through squeaks and murmurs that somehow the shaman himself had learned to replicate—he said mostly it sounded like a man trying to speak through lips that had been sewn shut. The skunk, of course, was odorous even when it hadn't sprayed its scent, and while others couldn't see the creature, they could smell it—which meant the shaman suddenly found himself with no friends and a reputation for poor hygiene. The stench of the skunk followed him and forced him to bathe three or four times a day.

Others spoke of guides who tormented the people they lived with, causing sudden drafts; poking sleeping houseguests in the middle of the night so they woke with a start; misplacing, hiding, or sometimes outright thieving personal effects. Jack, crazy or not, so far seemed passable. There was little stench to him, just that faint hint of mildew, as if he'd been left outside to dry overnight but it had unexpectedly rained. If this was his spiritual aide, well, Tecumseh supposed he could do worse.

He followed him up and over a mound of snow, slipping against the steep incline. On the downside of the slope the landscape changed again and they descended into some new, desolate place.

He had seen sand before. Once on the shore of a southern lake, and again in crumbling creek walls. But here sand stretched to the horizon. Fine and pale, the sand sifted from his feet as he moved through it.

"The white man will always be with you." Crazy Jack shouted to be heard above the swirl of wind and sand. "His morality flows one way, then another. He has no standard of conduct. The traders and surveyors want only to swindle and to steal. This is the American way. You must learn to think like the white man or he will swallow you."

Tecumseh saw no animal tracks. The trunks of the plants were forked and green and in place of leaves grew sharp, white sparks. The air was hot and heavy. He struggled for breath. It felt like a place with no future, the last, forgotten stop on the trail, where, if he stayed, he would be forever lost to anyone who ever knew him.

"Let them come." Tecumseh wiped his forehead but found no sweat there, perhaps some other side effect to the magic. "We will fight."

"Fight?" The little man raised an eyebrow. "Look around you. This desert is the future for your people. One day the white man will push the Shawnee so far west that all around will be nothing but sand and dryness and open sky. And then you will have to rely on what the white man gives you to survive."

"That would be disgrace."

"Then you must learn their language." Crazy Jack's eyes were wet, not from sadness, Tecumseh thought, but passion. "They will send men who weave words like golden baskets. Do not be romanced by their way of speaking. Listen to the substance of what they say. And refuse all offers."

They were standing then in a grove. The foliage was lush. The trees cast long shade. There was fruit on a wooden table and crates to sit on. There was a pond, and Cloudy Girl was drinking from it.

"I have led you to your horse," Crazy Jack said.

Tecumseh took the reins. "Are you my spirit helper?"

He sniffed. "Because you did not act afraid when you saw me, I will grant you a blessing."

It wasn't an answer, but Tecumseh let the man pull an upturned crate through the sand and place it at his feet. He climbed the box and stood so they were eye to eye. He produced a leather pouch and tucked it into Tecumseh's palm.

"If ever you need help," he said, "burn a little of this tobacco, and I will appear."

His eyes twinkled. Then he snapped his fingers and was gone.

1778

Ohio Country

"WAIT." RATTLE TRIED TO CATCH HIS BREATH. "Where did this creature take you?"

Tecumseh and his brother conferred at mid-field. They watched a scrum near their opponent's goal, boys and girls jostling for possession of the ball. He had returned from his Quest and was trying to explain everything that had happened to him, what Crazy Jack had shown him and predicted. The gift of the tobacco pouch.

He tried again. "The places he took me—"

"Was it the spirit world?"

"It felt like this world. But also much different."

When Crazy Jack had snapped his fingers, Tecumseh found himself alone, holding Cloudy Girl's reins, in a grove he recognized, not more than half a mile from Chillicothe. The graveyard was to the southwest. If he listened, he could hear conversation and lovemaking from the nearest wigwams.

Now a sewn, eight-inch orb of deerskin, stuffed with hair, squirted out of the pack of players. A boy booted it up-field. It skipped twice on the ground and shot into the air. The kick had good distance. Watching the ball sail toward him, he fingered the tobacco pouch at his waist. Then he touched the quartzite on his neck. The stone was still warm, carrying the residue of powerful magic.

"I don't understand." Rattle prepared to receive the ball. "I failed at the river, the day you found your pawawka token. I too have been on my Quest, only to come back after four days with nothing but the most desperate hunger and thirst. I found nothing."

The ball hung in the air, buffeted briefly by the wind, then accelerated into its descent.

"Our Grandmother hates you, brother." Tecumseh shoved Rattle aside, laughing. "That's the obvious answer."

He swept in and received the ball with his left foot. Then he sprinted toward his goal. He glanced back; several girls gave chase. And they were gaining. They came at him, fists pumping, the full sleeves of their blouses billowing and their hair untangling behind them. He was faster—or could have been. And he wanted, very badly, to win. More than victory, though, he wanted attention: as he approached the goal-wicket he pretended to stumble. This hesitation was enough. The girls were on top of him, suddenly, tackling him and dragging him to the ground. Two of them grabbed his legs, another wrapped the loose folds of his shirt in her fists and, planting her feet, pulled him down.

One of the players scooped the ball and hurled it far downfield. The other girls sat on top of him and pressed his head into the mud until he began to feel their punches and kicks recede. The blows became lighter, more teasing.

He felt hands then gripping his legs, his inner thigh, then a hand pressing against his balls. He uncovered his head: a girl named Falling Leaf grinned back at him, her hand buried between his legs.

And then the girls were off, sprinting back toward their own goal. He collected himself, rising to one knee, examining the cuts and scratches on his hands and arms. Spitting out a plug of earth that had lodged between his teeth. Wishing away the sudden swelling of his groin before he stood.

He marveled for a moment at how much he loved this game. He'd let himself be tackled, hoping the girls would oblige. And they had. But Falling Leaf had always been one of the quieter ones—he hadn't expected that from her. When he thought he could walk again without embarrassment, he jogged toward the finishing play.

He caught only the end. The girls passed the ball between them, gathered speed, and swarmed the goal. One boy stood between them and victory: Open Door. Drafted to play at the last moment because their usual goal-keep was sick, he stood frozen, arms out, legs wide. He was mimicking what he'd seen other boys do, his face calm, his lips set. Still as stone.

The girls blew past him. Falling Leaf held the ball aloft and, with two quick steps, hurled it through the goal-wicket. She let loose a war whoop—she had scored the deciding point. All of them howled and hugged one another and made rude gestures at the boys, the majority of whom were still picking themselves off the ground.

"You dummy!" Rattle stormed in, waving his arms, the weighty volume of him trembling with anger. "You're supposed to move. You're supposed to block them from scoring. How could you just stand there?"

Even as the other players left the field, Open Door still stood, hands outstretched, as if he didn't quite realize the play had ended.

Tecumseh laughed. But Rattle struck Open Door and the youngest boy fell, clutching the side of his head.

"Do you know how much I bet on this game?" Rattle drove his foot into Open Door's ribs. "And you just stand there? I've lost all my money."

Reaching them, Tecumseh did not hesitate: he punched Rattle in the face. The boy stumbled, hand on his cheek. He'd hit him hard enough to knock his eye-patch sideways. He caught a glimpse of his brother's right eye, now a hard, black crater.

"He doesn't know any better," he shouted.

"He lost my money." Rattle wept. "I should have strangled him in the womb."

Tecumseh turned to help Open Door to his feet, but his brother had already run off. They saw him disappear into the trees, leaving the playing field only a clearing again.

There was another game the brothers played where opponents tossed six painted plumb stones to see which sides came up. The stones were painted black on one side, white on the other. The shooter shook the dice in a wooden bowl and let the pieces scatter. One player counted white, the other black. The first to sixty, won.

It was, Tecumseh knew, a game entirely of chance. No one could control how the pieces fell out. No skill determined whether or not the stones turned up black or white—they did or they didn't. You did not so much play the game as the game played you. The players could only instigate an unending string of probabilities.

Even when they wagered on the outcome of a throw, which Rattle begged to do more and more often, doubling-down favors and promises and eventually things he didn't own—Chiksika's horse, their mother's heavy quilt—until he ran out of objects of value, the game failed to satisfy Tecumseh. He believed the best contests mirrored real life. That is, he did not believe the world worked only by chance. There was luck out there, to be sure, and sometimes it was with you and other times it was against you. But luck was not everything. He could not enjoy a game where he had no hope of affecting the outcome.

But for Rattle, the more stones rolled against him, the more he bet. Six stones would turn up black roughly half the time, but he failed to recognize this certainty, always swearing the next roll would bring him back to even. Always confident the fates were on his side. Always sure, despite all evidence to the contrary, things would break his way on the next throw. Next week, next month.

But Tecumseh knew it was only luck. The dice fell

out, turned up one way or another, and no one cared—not Our Grandmother, not Our Creator. Luck was its own thing entirely, a free agent. And believing that something so fickle would ever be on your side, that it could ever be counted on, was a good way to get yourself killed.

The only light in the sky was the after-glow of the sunset, like smoke drifting from a musket after it's fired.

Tecumseh and Rattle made the long, slow walk to their wigwam, among the spicy, gamey smells of the many cooking fires. Throughout the village, mothers rounded up their children and scolded them for being late. In the air twirled tiny bits of ash.

"You're too hard on him," Tecumseh told his brother. "You shouldn't say those things."

"Shouldn't I?" He turned the ball thoughtfully between his hands. "Open Door is weak. He'd starve if we didn't look after him."

"But it's not his fault you lost wampum on the game."

Rattle squeezed the ball until the thread snapped along the seam. Then he reared back and hurled the sphere, high in the direction of the woods.

Tecumseh wanted to say more. He knew that he and Rattle were drifting apart. They were losing the easy way they had with one another, how once they could finish one another's thoughts or have whole conversations without saying a word. Now it was long silences and a feeling of all energy being drained from whatever time they spent together. They no longer jostled for the largest slapjack, or to be first through a door. It was as if Rattle had conceded to the world his place in it, and Tecumseh's. Who would Rattle be among the Shawnee? That's what he was trying to figure out. The gambling was nothing but a distraction, and not a healthy one. It hid something deeper. Taking his frustration out on Open Door was another side to the same problem. Rattle was acting like a cornered snake, lashing out at the hopelessness of it all.

Tecumseh didn't get a chance to say this though, because Open Door wasn't home.

"Find him." Their mother did not even look at them when they entered, but simply turned them back out into the twilight. "No one eats until you find your brother."

But they couldn't find him. Not with family or friends; not at the Great Council House where he sometimes went to annoy the guards with questions. No one had seen him since the ballgame.

"What about the river?" Tecumseh said.

Darkness was complete when they made their way out of the village. They joked they'd find Open Door lying on his back staring up at the stars. Having maybe even fallen asleep. They began at the northern edge, at the river's fork with Massie's Creek, where their father had taken them to dive for tokens long ago.

But the banks were quiet. The horse compound, too. An old dog raised its head at their approach and, recognizing the boys, laid it back down again.

"I'm starving," Rattle said. "Our little brother, who you love so much, has cost us dinner."

"Ignore your stomach for once," Tecumseh said. "It's your fault. If you hadn't struck him, he wouldn't have run off."

"You struck me." Rattle lagged behind a good bit now, his feet refusing to keep up. He said it again, softer this time. "You struck me."

They could hear the river current carried on the darkness. Something landed, fluttered its wings, and whipped the water. They heard the steady squeak of the community well, as if someone were drawing water from it. They approached, listening. But Tecumseh heard no human breath, no shuffling feet, no sound but the rhythmic creak of tension on the well-bucket.

"I am sorry about your eye," Tecumseh said. "I haven't said so before, but I am sorry. I never meant to hurt you."

The stone wall girded a circular opening in the earth wide enough for a man to reach across, arms outstretched. A pulley system raised and lowered a bucket into the spring. The brothers came to the well often when they were younger, before they were allowed to hunt.

Rattle went to the edge and peered over. "I know."

He shouted into the hole, and his voice came back to him. He smiled at this, then laughed. He shouted again. He called his name and listened as the stones returned it to him.

"You can still do anything you want," Tecumseh told him. "Be anyone."

"You sound like Mother."

Tecumseh kicked at the dust. He didn't know how to reach him anymore, but it felt like someone needed to try. Maybe he was the only one who could.

"I've been studying a bit with Knotted Pine," Rattle said.

This was a good start, or something, at least, to latch onto. "He's the wisest man in the village."

"You know he's the Keeper of the Eternal Flame. But did you know he's the only one left? There are supposed to be two, but the second one died a long time ago, and no one ever named a new one."

"Something to aim for."

Rattle shrugged. "Maybe. I want him to teach me to divine, using the flight patterns of birds. But so far, all he has me doing is rooting around the insides of different animals, trying to read the livers."

"One step at a time." Tecumseh thought he heard real excitement in his brother's voice, and this was a positive turn. He didn't want to push him, though, and worried that if he showed too much enthusiasm his brother might cool toward his studies as well, the way he'd been turned off hunting and sport. He left the subject alone.

It was all the energy he had, anyway, because the other half of his brain was still turning over his experience in the woods, his meeting Crazy Jack. He hadn't expected his spirit guide to be human, first of all. It was much more common to discover an animal. Also, there was the matter of the English, which Tecumseh found he still knew. When he showed his brothers how fluently he spoke this foreign tongue, they were amazed. Crazy Jack had also given him the tobacco pouch. All of which made for an impressive story, and seemed important. But for now, he felt more as if he'd been initiated into something special—or something that others cherished, anyway—and had come out on the other side with little or no understanding of what he'd gone through, or what to expect moving forward.

Rattle and Tecumseh walked long arcs from the river southeast to the graveyard and back again. Further and further they pushed into the woods. The hunger in their bellies became a knot of fear.

"He wouldn't have just run off," Rattle insisted.

But Tecumseh thought their brother might have done just that. Humiliated by the ballgame, all the kids laughing at him—led by the brother he loved most—Open Door might have simply run headlong into the forest, become lost, and when he couldn't find his way out again.... No. He wouldn't imagine the worst.

"We need to think like him," he said. "Where would he have gone?"

Rattle shook his head. "He doesn't think like you or me."

"No. It's something simple."

But the moon was dropping and still they hadn't found him.

"Would he have crossed the river?" Rattle asked.

They rested on a hillside. There were rocks and naked roots and things scurrying in the darkness, through the leaves, all around them. Each time, Rattle jumped and swiveled and looked at the sound with his one good eye. Tecumseh had to turn away, so much grief overwhelmed him at once.

"He wouldn't have gone into the water," he said. "He can't swim."

Tecumseh shivered. But then something caught his eye, coming up the hill toward them. Winding through the trees. A golden, flickering light. Darting between branches. The last firefly of the year. It came to them and hovered, flashing.

Rattle rubbed his eye-patch and tried to cup the firefly in his hand. But the insect shot into the air, out of reach. It seemed to feint right, then left. It began to cut down across the hill.

"We should follow it," he said.

Tecumseh didn't argue. His brother was the expert at this sort of thing—the magical woods. After all, he'd apparently been spending all his time with the medicine men and the Keeper of the Eternal Flame. Learning how to predict the weather. Learning how to heal. If he thought they should follow a flashing bug through the woods, Tecumseh had no argument against it.

They descended to a creek bed. The water twisted between steep clay banks. They kept the firefly in sight. It seemed the farther they walked, the quicker the flash of the insect's light. Tecumseh touched the quartzite around his neck. It was cold and lay at his throat, unmoving.

The firefly stopped suddenly, turned one spiral through the air, and was gone. Thirty paces on lay Open

Door, half-submerged in the muddy creek.

Tecumseh ran to him, splashing through the water to take him up in his arms. His brother was not breathing. Looking back, Tecumseh could see the steep bank and the tracks that Open Door had made as he slid. He must have lost his footing at the ridge and fallen, tumbling into the creek.

"Let's go." Tecumseh hoisted his brother on his back. He tried to run with him, to high-step through the water, tripping against the hidden, crooked rocks. Rattle just stood there watching. "Now."

But he knew the moment he touched him: lifting Open Door was not like picking up a body that was whole, cohesive, compact. Instead, it was like shouldering a bag filled with loose and jumbled things, a sack of rocks. Like taking unbound kindling in his arms.

They hurried as best they could, carrying their brother between them, to Knotted Pine's cabin. They burst through the door and lay their brother across the floorboards. In the firelight they saw his body was caked with mud, his left arm bent unnaturally behind him. Already his skin had taken a pale, waxy sheen. Knotted Pine stood over them.

"Fix him." Tecumseh was on his knees. He tried to prop his dead brother up, as if that might help. "Work your magic and return our brother to us."

But Knotted Pine only muttered in the ancient language of the shamans and waved his hands over the boy and shook his head.

"Do something." Rattle grabbed the old man's arm. "Fix him, like he said."

The shaman put his hand over Rattle's, and with his other hand touched Tecumseh's face. By these gestures, they understood: there was nothing to be done. Their brother's body was broken. And although his heart tried to seal itself from this fact, and in sealing itself fought back powerful tears, Tecumseh knew for certain, had always known, that the river revealed everyone for who they truly were, that the Great Horned Snake waited for them all in turn, and now Open Door was dead.

The funeral took four days. They wrapped Open Door in a blanket and lowered him into the earth. Tecumseh found himself waiting for him to open his eyes. To sit up suddenly and rub away sleep with his fists, the way he did each morning. To smile and ask what all the commotion was for. But instead Open Door was put in the ground and dirt was heaped on top of him and the earth swallowed him. They buried him beside their father.

"You'll need this." Chiksika staggered to where Tecumseh and Rattle sat outside their wigwam. He clutched a bottle and encouraged them to drink.

Tecumseh recoiled at the smell. Whiskey: the fumes burned his eyes and nose.

"There is a time for the white man's drink," Chiksika said. "Now, for example."

Tecumseh had never tasted whiskey. He sipped, then gulped. Maple and ash. The overall sensation was searing. He felt warmth around his heart and passed the bottle.

Rattle drank deeply. He swallowed, swished, and drank again. "I've had whiskey before."

Tecumseh only nodded. He didn't feel like arguing. Chiksika drank and then the bottle was back in Tecumseh's hands. He closed his eyes. He saw his brother's face—the face of Open Door. Expressionless. One eye set slightly lower than the other, the strange shape of his shadow on the wigwam wall, his pinched head made even stranger and more sinister by the firelight. Forever frozen too, standing in the middle of the ball field, arms outstretched, waiting for a play to develop long after the players had blown past. Tecumseh drank again. His brother's face was smudged, or it was not quite as clear as it had been only minutes before. Another sip or two, or maybe three, and his face might be washed away completely.

Chiksika kicked at his brothers' feet. "There's something I want to show you."

He led them through the village and into the woods. The ground rose steeply. They climbed for an hour or more, saying little, passing the bottle.

The ground grew rocky, and then they were standing at the top of a cliff. Chiksika squatted; the younger boys did the same. Rattle wheezed through his nose. Tecumseh tried to take another sip from the bottle and, finding it empty, let it drop from his hand.

"Take a good look," Chiksika told them.

In the valley below, a column of American soldiers moved through the fading light. Shoulder to shoulder they marched in a current of blue military jackets. The different shades resembled a river, the darker patches revealing where the water was deepest, the lighter colors warning of shallow rocks. The men shouldered rifles. The sound of 400 soldiers marching was not steady like the beat of a drum but instead was the sound of unfurling thunder, rolling and deep, offering crests and waves. It shook Tecumseh's belly. Boots rose and fell and pounded the earth flat. Wagon wheels turned, dragging cannons through the mud.

"The Americans are at war with their Mother," Chiksika said. "It will be a war to last many years."

"They will leave us alone," Tecumseh said.

"For now, yes."

One of the soldiers shouted and the men shouted back at him. There was some choreographed movement, switching their rifles from one shoulder to the other.

"Once someone wins," Chiksika said, "they will get back to fighting Indians. Their hunger for land will never be satisfied. This is what Father believed, and it is what I believe."

Tecumseh said, "It is what I believe too."

Behind them, Rattle lay on his back, exhausted and drunk. Chiksika placed his hand on Tecumseh's shoulder.

"I promised Father I would raise you," he said. "And so I will train you to be a warrior."

Tecumseh understood. "I want to kill them all, as you do."

He saw his older brother smile—just a flash, before he covered it with his hand and looked away. "While the Americans fight their Mother, we will prepare ourselves. So when they are finished fighting, and they are tired, we can take back the land they have stolen from us. And maybe, if we are lucky, we will drive them far again across the ocean."

The army began to disappear from view. There was more shouting, a kind of call and response. Tecumseh felt these soldiers were an offense to the valley. Their marching silenced the birds, driving out all other sounds. Their smells—oil and sulfur, tobacco and sweat—filtered through the forest, carrying on the air. And it stank, this garbage river flowing past.

1780

Ohio Country

TECUMSEH HEARD THE FLATBOAT long before it came into view. He stood alone on the riverbank, in English shoes that barely fit, dressed as any white child might—as a decoy. The bait inside a trap. Behind him, hidden somewhere in the woods, were a dozen Shawnee hunters, but he felt only the expanse of river before him and the empty beach all around. There was nowhere to hide. Any moment the flatboat would come into view and he'd be spotted. The rest was up to him.

The sun cast a golden spill down the Ohio River. The searing heat had mellowed into a wet, heavy air. He heard the oarsmen singing as they steered their flatboat west, toward him, pushing closer, no doubt squinting against the slanted light, their rough voices carrying downriver far ahead of their progress.

There were scores of flatboats, every summer. And he saw plenty of surveyors in what was, by treaty, Shawnee land, their pale faces burnt red, measuring distances and calculating costs, dreaming in their sleep of tomorrow's riches. Claiming, dividing, selling land—something particular to the whites. And although he did not fully understand it himself, he knew this was the core of who they were, part of their nature, their soul.

He did not feel bad about what would happen to these men. He had been raised, after all, not to pity them. But he wished Rattle were there with him, someone he knew he could rely on. Although he trusted Chiksika, he wasn't sure about his brother's friends, those hunters now concealed nearby. He played games with them, of course, and accompanied them on hunts. Boys several years older—he knew already he was their equal on the battlefield. He could wield a tomahawk with one hand better than most of them could with two. But he was never sure they wanted him there, or had accepted him. Yes, they sometimes slipped him whiskey, and played countless rounds of Nosey, and they had described once how to make love to a woman, sparing no detail. But in the end, he knew the older boys tolerated him because of who Chiksika was, of who their father had been, and because he never complained.

But not Rattle. The older boys had spoken on that matter, and Rattle was no longer welcome on the hunt. Rattle was smart—smarter than most. But he talked too much, which irritated Chiksika, who wasn't much for wasting words.

But then Rattle was more comfortable with adults anyway, hanging around the cabins of the medicine men, Knotted Pine in particular. He didn't talk like other twelve-year-olds—he spoke like a grown-up. His sense of humor was like theirs, all ham-jokes and puns. He enjoyed showing off simple magic tricks. And the girls looked at him with such disgust, or confusion, it made Tecumseh want to hide his brother away, to protect him, to make him invisible. Better to be invisible than laughed at.

But of course the others laughed: they didn't know what to make of him. And deep down, most of the time, Tecumseh thought it was better that he no longer came along.

Earlier that morning, Chiksika's voice had yanked him from sleep. The wigwam was dark, the sun having not yet broken through the trees. His older brother knelt beside him. "We must go."

Tecumseh had untangled himself from the pile of blankets, the twisted nest that Rattle had kicked on top of him in the night. He was already dressed. He had only to pull on his moccasins and shoulder his bow and quiver. Rattle still slept, turned toward the wall. Tecumseh listened to the high wheeze of his snoring. He thought to wake him, wondering whether he should invite him too, once more. He wondered if the older boys would mind.

"Tecumseh." Chiksika called from outside. "Everyone's waiting."

But what would he say? Chiksika had invited him, Tecumseh. He had not invited Rattle. And when they talked about it, Rattle said he didn't care. So that was it, then: he would take him at his word. He would ignore the soft sniffling now coming from the corner where his brother slept. He would shut it out, blocking out too the sorrow that leapt from his heart to his throat. He ducked through the flap and into the morning air.

The older boys were waiting. Their faces were hidden in the pre-dawn, their sullen and impatient shapes barely outlined. He knew them by their voices, though.

"Are you sure the baby can handle it?" A boy named Big Jim growled. "He's young."

"I've been training him myself," Chiksika said.

Tecumseh held his head high and tried to look serious, tough. He wanted to prove what kind of hunter he could be. In a footrace, he knew he could outrun them all.

The hunting party headed southeast from the village. Tecumseh stayed close to Chiksika, still not sure which boys accepted his presence there and which might cause trouble. He felt better as dawn broke: he could see them more clearly. There was Big Jim, a snarling brawler with arms like great logs. There was Half Moon, who rarely spoke, but whom Tecumseh had always liked. And there was Sinnantha, who was white, but who had lived with the Shawnee since he was five years old. He claimed he no longer remembered how to speak English. When they stopped to rest, two miles from the village, Sinnantha reached into his pack and produced several copper tins. Inside were different colors of paint: red, green, black. He dipped two fingers and swiped them across his cheeks, leaving parallel streaks of mossy green. The other boys did the same, studying themselves in tiny mirrors they had tied to their packs with string.

The forest sharpened. Columns of sunlight bore through the canopy overhead. Tecumseh saw then that many of the boys carried war clubs and tomahawks. They slipped rifles from beneath blankets and slid long, curving knives from their leggings. They stripped their shirts and smeared paint across their chests.

"This isn't a hunting party," Tecumseh said.

It wasn't a question. He wanted his brother to know he understood. A shifting in the air around their band of hunters focused the early light, edging the outlines of the trees.

Chiksika lowered his eyes. "No."

"And Blackfish? What does our chief say?"

His older brother gripped his arm. The strength of his fingers startled Tecumseh fully awake.

"Blackfish, our so-called chief, caters to the weakest men and women in our tribe," Chiksika said. "He dishonors our father's memory. He signed the treaty with the whites. But there is no peace in my heart."

Tecumseh swallowed a blooming fear. He set his jaw to stop his chin from quivering. He determined to do this thing, whatever it was—to claim his manhood. To fight, to make war: the Shawnee rite of passage. What were his choices otherwise? Run home to his mother and his fat, cowardly brother?

"I will follow you," he said.

Chiksika released him. He opened the pack he carried. He dug inside and unfurled a spool of clothes. There was a cream-colored workshirt and canvas breeches. There was a flattened straw hat. And there were shoes, black and polished, the kind worn by the English. If Tecumseh left them unbuckled, he could fit his feet inside.

"Why me?" he asked.

Chiksika helped him dress in the English clothes, cursing when he saw how short the pants were—Tecumseh's ankles were bare.

"You've grown," his brother snarled.

"They're knee breeches," Tecumseh said. "There should be stockings."

"We don't have the stockings." He gripped Tecumseh's shoulders and stood him up straight. "Why you? You're the bravest and strongest warrior among us, little brother. Plus, your English is better than anyone's."

Tecumseh had plenty of chances to practice his new language with the traders that came through Chillicothe. By now, he could speak English better than many Americans. His diction was perfect. But standing on the bank of the Ohio, listening to the flatboat draw near, able now to pick out the individual voices of the oarsmen, some woefully off-key, he felt fear like a sparrow in his throat.

All in the merry month of May,
When green buds they were swellin'
Young Willie Grove on his death-bed lay,
For love of Barb'ra Allen.

This was different than felling a passenger pigeon. Different from ballgames or the challenge of firing an arrow through a rolling hoop. It felt at once like something he was much too young for and at the same time something he was destined for. He did not want to disappoint the older boys, and he wanted to make his brother proud. That was what he would concentrate on, and not worry about what came next. Chiksika had assigned him a role, and he would perform it perfectly. The rest was not up to him.

He wore the straw hat and the too-short breeches and the polished, black shoes. He kept the brim of the hat pulled low to hide his face—his skin.

He sent his servant to her door
To the town where he was dwellin'
Haste ye come, to my master's call,
If your name be Barb'ra Allen.

The flatboat appeared, swinging out wide into the center of the river. Tecumseh cupped his hands around his eyes—owl eyes, they called it—and the flatboat grew larger in his vision. He was surprised how quickly it moved. It drew little water. Onboard was a central cabin. Half a dozen horses were tied behind it, above deck, and in the bow was a simmering kettle. He noticed the steam rising from the cauldron as the boat made its way toward him. The wind changed and brought with it the smell of coals and smoldering pork.

His brother's voice came from somewhere behind him. "I count four."

So slowly, slowly got she up,
And slowly she drew nigh him,
And all she said when there she came:
"Young man, I think you're dying!"

Tecumseh darted from his hiding place and tore down the bank. He waved his arms and shouted out in English, calling for help. He drew even with the vessel and ran with it downriver. He imagined his voice carrying like a bird. Finally, a man came to the bow. He wore no shirt. His chest hair was so thick, Tecumseh mistook it at first for a blanket. This traveler was joined shortly by a dark-haired woman and an older man in a nightcap.

"What's yer name?" the first man called to him.

"Jordan!" Tecumseh waved his arms. "Thank you, sir!"

"Whar's your family?"

"Killed, sir." He was breathless and desperate: he didn't have to act. "All killed down in Kennedy's Bottom, Kentucky County. The Indians brought me up here, but I escaped."

The boat had slowed but so far showed no inclination of turning toward shore. It stayed in the center of the current, far from the bank. Once they reached the bend, in about fifty yards, Tecumseh would run out of ground. On board, the men whispered with the woman. They'd no doubt sworn to themselves—owing to all the rumors—not to go ashore until they'd reached their end point. And yet here was this English child, needing help.

"Please, sir," Tecumseh called out again, appealing directly to the shirtless man who seemed to be in charge. "I'm very hungry and very cold. If you leave me here I'm sure to die—by the Indians or by the weather."

The man in the nightcap kept scratching himself, as if scratching might help make up his mind. The woman wore one skirt layered over another: one blue, one green.

"You're not injun, are ye?" The man in the nightcap had a shrill voice.

Tecumseh rolled his eyes and indicated his clothes. "Please, good sirs. I'm tired of the frontier. I don't like it alone in the woods at night."

The hairy-chested man disappeared into the stern. The boat slowed against the current and came portside, drifting to the very tip of the river's bend where a rocky beach jutted out into the water.

The woman called to him. "Can ye swim?"

"I cannot, ma'am." Tecumseh acted shamed. "Bring her to these rocks and I'll jump on."

He waited for them on the beach. They were thirty yards from shore, then twenty. Then ten. He saw the flat-boat's plan, to come along the beach, snatch their rescue, and push off again into the current, quickly, touching land and then pushing back again in case Indians suddenly came storming out of the woods. One could never be too careful on the frontier. Word had spread.

Tecumseh pitied them, but he kept his distance from the water's edge, twenty paces. The boat drew close enough that he could see the holes in the old man's dressing gown, the pearl-tipped chatelaine on the woman's waist. The boat bumped against the rocks.

"Come on, boy!" The old man waved to him. "Run for it!"

Tecumseh locked eyes with the woman. She had high cheekbones and thin lips. It seemed as if she'd had a hard journey, that she was not used to this kind of living. A city girl, no doubt, from somewhere back East. She had black hair and that gleaming silver chain around her waist. His heart closed against her, and it must have shown briefly in his eyes. Because there was a flash, a moment right before, when something in her eyes changed as well, and she understood then what had already befallen her.

He did not turn around. But he knew when his brother and the other warriors burst from the woods. He knew it by the way her eyes flared with the purest expression of terror he had ever seen. As if all her nights had been haunted by visions of Indians erupting from the wild, shouting their war whoops, and now here they were, and she was awake.

Rifle fire from the bank: bullets tore through the boat's gunwales and shredded its hull. The woman fell, a musket ball lodged in her cheek.

Tecumseh closed his eyes. When he opened them again there were Shawnee braves on the beach and more higher up the bank. They shot into the boat. There was no return fire. Guns went off and the settlers screamed and the warriors hollered their war cries and in all that noise was the sound of horses being shot, the sound of hooves stomping against the deck, the heavy, crushing sound of bodies falling, a sort of shrieking, and then the most profound silence once the last horse was down and the shooting was done.

The old man lifted himself from behind the gunwale. He raised his night cap in surrender. Tecumseh heard the snap of an arrow released from its bow; he heard the arrow whistle overhead. He heard the soft crackling as the arrow entered the man's chest, splintered ribs and muscle, and pierced his heart.

The Shawnee warriors swept over the boat the way crickets swarm something dead, erasing its shape by covering it completely. Big Jim dragged the survivors onto shore: the shirtless man was not hurt. There was also a younger man they hadn't seen who was wounded in the leg. Big Jim dropped him and Chiksika tomahawked him where he fell. Once he'd taken the man's scalp, he dumped the body into the river. The other dead were also scalped and set to drift.

Tecumseh could not convince his feet to move. All around him the older boys got down to the business of ransacking the ship. They found sacks of flour, barrels of beer and corn, coffee and smoked meats, and a case of Chambers long guns with walnut stocks. There were other provisions too, and pieces of gold.

They found something else: a girl. Her hair was raven-black. Her porcelain skin gleamed in the afternoon sun. She looked like a doll—that unreal. They picked her up and passed her from the flatboat down to the waiting arms of Big Jim. He set her next to the bare-chested man. She did not weep, but kept the same wide-eyed expression, silent.

When the stores had been counted and divided, the warriors pushed the flatboat back into the current.

"We'll take the man and the girl with us," Chiksika said.

He had come up from behind Tecumseh and placed a hand on his shoulder. He glanced at the ground and laughed. Soon he was laughing so hard he was bending over and clutching his belly. Tecumseh had not moved at all. His feet, still inside the English shoes, had sunk six inches into the sand.

They bound the man, whose name was Boden, and marched him in front. They didn't bother tying the girl. There was nowhere to run.

Tecumseh caught up to her. "Is that your father?"

She looked at him with cool, green eyes, like a lizard. That's what popped into his head. A lizard, like the kind he'd seen in the desert with Crazy Jack. Smart, watchful, cool.

If she was surprised by his English, she didn't show it. "That's not my father."

"Who is he then?"

"Just some man who was supposed to get us to Kentucky County."

She was about his age. Her hair was thick and black. She had tied it back with spurweed. There were the faintest hairs along her arms. She said the other passengers had been her distant relations, a cousin, an uncle. Her father was in Kentucky County now and she had meant to join him.

The Shawnee walked quickly, but she kept pace, grabbing the hem of her dress in her fists and scampering up the hillsides and over the rocks and roots. She took quick, small steps. After many miles she wasn't even breathing hard.

He was carrying jerky, and he bit some off. He knew she must be hungry. They hadn't fed either prisoner, and wouldn't, for hours yet. "Why's your father in Kentucky County?"

"Leave me alone," she said.

"We have trouble with men from there," he said.

Since he was a boy, as long as he could remember, raiders from Kentucky County had crossed the Ohio River and pillaged the Shawnee towns, stolen horses, and shot down those who did not flee—the old and infirm. Those raiders were not warriors of the five tribes. The Shawnee might have excused them, then. Instead, they were white men, frontiersmen and traders and men battle-worn from fighting the French and more recently, the British.

"My father doesn't do anything like that," the girl said.

He had touched a sore spot. Well, so had she. Probably, he thought, raiding was exactly the kind of thing her father did.

"I've come to evangelize." She pulled herself taller, and spoke quickly. "I want to spread the good news of Jesus Christ to the savages. To boys like you."

He remembered the black book from the settlement, the one Rattle had raised against the Wampus Cat. He'd heard talk of this person, Jesus, at the trading post.

"I overheard some of my men," he said. "There is a

woman in Chillicothe who recently lost her daughter to the sickness. We are taking you there now. You will live with her and care for her as if you are her own child."

He stripped some bark from a tree and offered it to her, running the soft underside between his fingers, to encourage her to eat. She shook her head. Her hair hung now over her eyes and she walked with her head down. He offered the bark again and again she shook her head. He could hear now that she was weeping, so he left her to walk for a time on her own.

He caught up to his brother's friends and laughed about something with them, laughing loudly, hoping she'd hear him. He wanted her to notice him—to not be able not to notice him. To know that he was someone important: the Great Panther Crossing the Sky. But when he glanced back at her again, her arms were folded around herself and she was weeping openly, with no one nearby, pale and alone against the dense and unforgiving country.

That night, they made camp. When the others were asleep, Tecumseh crept to where the prisoners were being kept watch over by Half Moon and Big Jim. Not very well though: the braves also slept. He wouldn't have cared anyway—they weren't going to stop him. He found the girl and shook her awake.

"Is it time already?" she asked, sitting up.

She couldn't see him in the dark. He said nothing,

but grabbed her wrist, and yanked her to her feet. She cried out. He clamped his hand over her mouth and then dragged her into the underbrush away from the others.

Finally, he let her go. She staggered back, seemingly weighing her choices. Stay or run. The dangers inherent in both. She had no idea of his intentions.

"Close your eyes," he said. "Now, open them again."

He knew when she had by her sharp intake of breath. And even he had to smile—it was still one of his favorite offerings of the woods.

There was a long, rotted log leaning against the cliff wall. Along the top of the tree were thick rows of mushrooms and the stems glowed an impossible shade of yellow-green. In the darkness, it looked like a luminescent arc from the earth to the sky, some kind of golden path to the clouds. The longer they let their eyes adjust, the more light revealed itself. Large swaths of the forest floor were covered with radiant moss. Half-circles of cool fire strung the bases of the trees and highlighted every unfamiliar shape.

"It's beautiful," she whispered.

He knelt down beside her. He took her hand. "There is no reason for you to cry so much. You feel as if your light has been extinguished, but the Shawnee carry the one true flame. There is light in the world that you have never seen."

She laughed, though she was still weepy. "I just feel sorry for myself, is all."

"Tell me your name."

"Rebecca," she said. "Becky Galloway, of Pennsylvania."

She was tall for her age. He thought at first she was older than him, but it turned out she was a year younger. Her hair was like Shawnee hair, thick and black. When they reached Chillicothe, the women fawned over it and braided it and tied in her hair pieces of feathers and bones. The woman whose daughter had died welcomed Becky into her wigwam and gave thanks that Our Grandmother had seen fit to bless her with another child.

Becky's hair was pitch and her eyebrows were straight and black and serious. They were like felt to showcase the jewels of her eyes. So green. And her eyes challenged him, even as they poked fun. There was something about the way she looked at him that seemed instantly familiar, as if they'd known one another for years, and also full of joy. Even when she was most afraid, or feeling lost, there was something in her gaze that seemed to both ask for reassurance and to offer it.

Her arms were strong, and she was fast as any squaw. She ran, in ballgames and footraces, with abandon. Chin forward, feet flashing, sprinting across the fields. She won her share. He thought maybe she tried harder because of her race. To prove to herself, and to them, that her circumstances were not her fault. Not a personal shortcoming, being taken captive. Nothing about it that could be done.

As the weeks passed, she spoke a lot about her god and a book she called *The Bible*. It was as if she had resolved to see her present situation not as a hindrance but as the ideal solution to realize her true calling, to missionize the savages. She sang songs from her religion, those plodding, serious hymns like heavy woodblocks. She worked the fields singing. She prayed before every meal, hands clasped below her chin, eyes squeezed shut. When Falling Leaf cut her hand, working to shear the hide from a deer, Becky went to her and wrapped the wound in cloth and said words over the bleeding, an invocation of healing.

It should have made him angry. He heard rumblings from others. After all, her people had committed all manner of horrors against the Shawnee, in the name of their god. And coming from anyone else, he might have cut their tongue out himself.

He couldn't explain it, other than to say it seemed honest, coming from her. That she showed compassion to the woman who was now her Shawnee mother, and to others. And it didn't seem as if she did it to be noticed—certainly she never expected anyone to join her. Tecumseh hoped he himself might have enough strength, enough confidence, to lean upon his own gods and carry on with his beliefs if the situation were reversed, if he were prisoner.

It went against everything his father had taught him, but he felt protective of this American, Becky. Maybe because he'd seen her family slaughtered, and played a role in that. Or maybe because the very quality of the air changed when she was nearby. It thinned out, and he had to remind himself to breathe. The air changed and also the light. It wasn't that she lit up, but that everything else seemed to dim. Things he thought were important or bright turned out not to be when she was around, when they were held up against her glow.

Tecumseh was assigned the task of painting the second prisoner and readying him for death.

The American stood naked with his hands and feet bound. Dark coils of hair covered even his shoulders, as if he wore a bearskin. The black paint clumped, and the hair tangled as Tecumseh rubbed his hands through it. Still, the American seemed to understand what was about to happen to him.

"It's to be the stake for me?" he asked.

Tecumseh leaned very close, painting the corners of the man's face with his fingertips. "The gauntlet first."

The prisoner's eyes, which were blue as a robin's egg, closed and then sprang opened. "Where did you learn to speak English?"

Tecumseh said nothing.

"It was the English that made us decide to rescue you."

"A bad decision."

"It only takes one." He shook his head. "A million good decisions, and a single bad one wrecks it all."

Soon the village had gathered. Men, women, and children arranged themselves into two lines running from the Great Council House nearly a hundred yards to the creek.

At the water, Chiksika untied the prisoner's hands and feet. The crowd cheered. He led Boden to the front of the lines.

There had been gauntlets before. While torture did not excite Tecumseh the way it did the others, he also did not pity the man Boden. He would get what he deserved. More than anything, Tecumseh wished things would hurry up. It was very dull. There was never any doubt about how the day would end. It took little skill for a village to club a man to death.

He was proud of himself though, proud that he'd played his role perfectly, worn the English clothes and assumed the part of a runaway. Chiksika and his war party had taken the flatboat and the supplies and scalps and now the older boys had begun to accept him, or at least not make things so hard for him.

But something about the day was beginning to wear on him. It was not the death itself that bothered him—the white man would die, as he should. It was all the rest of it, the ceremony and proceedings, the grandstanding by the older boys who were being flattered for their bravery. In truth, Tecumseh knew the flatboat had never fired a shot.

And now the white man Boden stood alone at the head of the gauntlet. His path to the Great Council House wound slightly uphill. Three hundred feet, though, had probably never seemed farther: a Shawnee village between him and the door. Some of the women held muskets or flintlock pistols. Others held long, rawhide straps they snapped between their fists. Chiksika had promised that if the prisoner reached the Great Council House door, he would be spared further suffering.

Boden blew snot from one nostril. He twisted, and stretched out his legs, kicking them. Naked, painted black, he looked to Tecumseh like a cannon ball, round and obdurate. He cupped his private parts with both hands and settled back on his haunches. Along the lines a great cry went up, and soon everyone was shouting for the man to begin.

Rattle appeared, the first Tecumseh had seen him that day. His brother had taken a rose vine and wrapped it tightly around a short log. Tecumseh's own switch was made from hickory, and he remembered the switch his father had always carried. He scraped it back and forth across the ground, roughing it up. He stood with his brother toward the end of the double line and doubted the prisoner would make it that far. He hoped he wouldn't.

Boden shifted his weight from one foot to the other, as if measuring the distance to the Great Council House door. The crowd grew impatient and began to hiss. Finally, Chiksika came up behind him and swatted the man's buttocks with a heavy club. The blow was enough—Boden sprang forward headlong into the gauntlet.

He wove down the line, bouncing back and forth the way an acorn ricochets down an oak tree. The Shawnee struck him as he passed, launching him from one line toward the other with each blow. Soon blood was pouring from his head. Blood leapt in spurts from his body as it was lashed by thorns and brambles. The pistols the women held were loaded only with gunpowder. They ran behind him and, pressing the barrels of the guns to his flesh, pulled the triggers. The gunpowder seared his skin and left smoldering red half-circles. He howled each time.

Tecumseh admired the power of the prisoner's legs. Each time he was struck, he dug his heels deeper into the mud and took another lurching step forward.

"What's the matter, brother?" Rattle spun his thorny branch between his hands.

"I don't see the point of this," Tecumseh said. "Don't we have better things to do?"

"You're soft." He stood with legs apart, grinning. "You've got no stomach for killing."

"I don't care if we kill him or not." Tecumseh punched his brother in the arm. "But I'd rather just kill him and be done with it than spend the whole day thinking about it."

Boden stumbled toward them, arms raised, shielding his head. There was no part of him now that was not leaking blood.

Ten yards: Rattle brayed with anticipation. But Tecumseh's stomach was sour. He felt toward this prisoner what he felt whenever his hunting arrow found prey. He saw how a thing could be beautiful even in defeat—especially in defeat. All its strength bravely bowing to an overwhelming force, but not necessarily to greater courage. This man, Boden, showed the grace of something magnificent finally being brought down.

There was commotion in the line to the left. Sinnantha, the white warrior who had been raised with the tribe, broke from the lines to meet Boden head-on. He waited for the prisoner to approach, stumbling; he reared back with his war club, expecting a weak and broken opponent. But instead, the prisoner charged. Seeing Sinnantha waiting for him, Boden ran, leapt, and wrapped the Shawnee brave up in his massive arms. He landed three crippling blows before Sinnantha had a chance to swing. Both gauntlet lines collapsed. Twenty Shawnee dragged Boden to the ground.

"Get him up." Rattle screamed. "I want a chance."

"He's very brave," Tecumseh said. "A true warrior."

They stood at a distance from the horde. When the crowd parted, Boden lay in a heap of blood and mud. Two men helped him stand. He was alive, but his eyes were swollen shut. His arms and legs were bruised and bleeding. The hair along his shoulders was singed and in some places, smoking. He had fallen less than twenty feet from the Great Council House door.

"What now?" Tecumseh asked.

Rattle sighed. "Back to the beginning."

Tecumseh watched Becky spending time with the other women. Sometimes she caught him staring. But he didn't look away. He wouldn't. She didn't either, but stared back at him. Not in fear, and not, he thought, with what he had heard called desire. Something else. Something blank. Her expression seemed to dare him to take something from her that hadn't already been lost. He thought there was probably nothing left.

They walked together in the woods, not far from where Open Door had fallen down the ravine. She was gathering buckeyes in her dress. It was the time of year when cicadas began to hatch. Already he could hear the first wave screaming from the treetops. He hated cicadas. Even hearing them made his skin feel like insects were crawling all over him.

"Your god," he asked her. "What does he say about what happens when we die?"

He was thinking about Open Door. How he had carried his brother back to Knotted Pine, to the greatest of the Shawnee medicine men, the Keeper of the Eternal Flame, and how the shaman had been powerless to help him.

"We don't die," she said. "Our bodies die. But our souls live forever."

"We split in half?"

He was tossing one buckeye into the air and catching it. She snatched it, midflight, and turned it over in her hand to reveal the pale, soft spot on the otherwise hard, black shell. She pressed her thumb into the blanched eye and the shell crumbled.

"Our bodies are like that," she said. "Our spirits are who we really are. And our spirits go to live forever, with Jesus."

"The Shawnee too believe the dead travel the spirit world," he said.

She explained in detail this process of "life everlasting," but in the end it wasn't exactly what he was looking for. There was something she called a "fountain," but it seemed to be more of a symbol, or anyway she couldn't tell him where these waters could be found. And the spirit world she described was an all-white place where no rains fell. It sounded dry and lonesome to him. Nothing worth living forever for. He couldn't figure out why she talked about it so.

The Eternal Flame burned in his heart and this flame was the birthright of every Shawnee. More than that, he felt with absolute certainty that he was meant to lead his people and establish, once and for all, their home in the river valley. His life was destined, although saying those words somehow cheapened it, or didn't express it fully. From the comet that had passed the night of his birth to his finding the pawawka token in the river; from the tobacco pouch Crazy Jack had given him to the way he heard girls whisper to one another whenever he passed by, these were all part of the same magical whole that was—for reasons known only to Our Creator—his life. No one asked a waterfall why its waters roared, or an eagle why it soared higher than the other birds. This was how it was for Tecumseh too. And so his successes were no surprise to him. They were what he expected, what he worked for. Nothing more. While others stood in awe, or sang his praises, or wondered how he did such things, for him it was merely the life he lived.

He supposed that if he stopped and thought about it then, yes, he could see a difference in himself, some heightened abilities. But he never questioned them, or wondered about their source. He displayed them proudly. Most of all, he enjoyed them, and they made him well-liked. None of which he minded, all of which he accepted as properly due to him since birth.

Boden was tied to the stake. He sat cross-legged, hands bound behind him, with his feet secured to his hands by the same rope. Falling Leaf had cleaned his wounds, but still he bled freely. The hair on his body was knotted with blood and crusty streaks of black paint.

After his humiliation in the gauntlet, after the way Boden had beaten him and might have killed him if other Shawnee hadn't intervened, Sinnantha was ordered to guard the prisoner. He sat some distance away, cradling his rifle, silent and sullen. He said nothing when, later that night, Tecumseh and Rattle came for a closer look. Sinnantha did not acknowledge them but turned his head away in shame.

Tecumseh wanted to talk more with this prisoner who had shown such courage in the gauntlet. He asked Rattle to come with him. He admired Boden, but he was a little bit afraid of him too. He brought him water in a gourd. When they found him, his eyes were closed, his chin resting on his chest. Rattle snatched a branch from the ground and whipped it across the man's bare feet. Boden's eyes snapped open, and he jerked against his restraints, grunting and cursing.

"You're not so big up close," Rattle said.

Tecumseh disagreed. The man was plenty big. He knew it would be impossible to wrap his arms around that chest. The man's thighs were whiskey barrels.

And it had been his legs that had carried Boden through the gauntlet not once, but twice. On his first attempt, he had failed to reach the Great Council House door and was forced to start again. But the second time, instead of waiting for Chiksika, he had, without warning, charged suddenly into the middle of the gauntlet, passing two dozen Shawnee before they'd had a chance to swing. Tecumseh was stunned by the man's speed—he'd thought him nearly dead. But the prisoner kept his legs moving and never lost balance. By the time he was halfway through again he'd barely been touched. Sprinting, chest heaving, he veered suddenly to the right and leapt over a young boy—hurdled him as easily as clearing a log. This had caused great confusion and anger among the Shawnee, who then had to chase Boden past the horse compound to the northern edge of the village. They hadn't caught up with him until Massie's Creek. He very nearly escaped: they found him only because his arms were broken and he couldn't swim.

Tecumseh put the gourd to the prisoner's lips and he gulped it dry. He glared at the brothers from beneath heavy lids.

"What happened to your eye?" Boden's lips were badly swollen, and he had trouble forming words.

"I lost it in a fight with a horse thief," Rattle boasted. "One even bigger than you."

There might have been a grin there, in the shadows—or a wink. To Tecumseh, the man said, "Your brother here lost an eye, but that horse thief lost his life."

He ground his big toe against the dust. "That's right."

He saw the way the prisoner looked at his brother, also shirtless in the night. He saw too the way his brother's belly hung over his waistline, the way he had little titties, like a girl.

"Who was he?" Boden asked.

Rattle bit his lip. "Who?"

"The horse thief."

"We never learned his name."

Boden cleared his nose and hawked a wad of spit off to the left. "Because I know just about every trader, surveyor, and horse thief there is to know in these parts. Ain't not one of them bigger than me. It offends me to hear you say that. Someone bigger than me. Some may have bigger reputations. Boone, for instance. Maybe Kenton. But there ain't nobody bigger than me physically."

Tecumseh took two steps forward and slapped the prisoner across the face. "My brother is no liar."

The man looked up at him, working his jaw a little against the shock of the blow. They locked eyes. Tecumseh wondered what scenes played out behind those bruised and swollen lids—what triumphs or injuries, what brawls. And something else, something they shared. The freedom Tecumseh felt in the woods, the sense of purpose his body carried when he was alone among the rolling hills, flitting between the stark, white sycamore trees. He and this woodsman loved the forest the same way. They valued their freedom above all. And in Boden's eyes he saw a fading light—a light that fluttered, weakening, not from what he had endured in the gauntlet, which he would one day recover from, but from this captivity.

"You're pretty brave for one so young," Boden said finally.

Rattle stepped forward then and, saying nothing, struck the man again in the face with the branch.

"Ouch." Boden spit blood. "Would you stop that?"

"I'm not so young," Tecumseh said.

"Ever kill anyone?"

Tecumseh felt his hands shaking and put them behind him so the man wouldn't see.

But the prisoner only spat again. "All in good time, then, I'm sure."

He said he did not know the rest of the party on the flatboat that day, or hadn't known them before agreeing to escort them downriver. He sometimes hired himself out when work was slow. He hadn't lost a boat yet. Before that day.

"I feel responsible for what happened to those people," he said.

They could hear shouting from the Great Council House. Inside, the elders debated Boden's fate.

"What's your name?" the prisoner asked.

Tecumseh told him.

"You know they're talking about me in there." He lifted his chin. "They're deciding whether or not to kill me."

"You're a criminal," Rattle said. "An enemy of the Shawnee."

"We both know that ain't strictly true." The white man shook his head. "There's some say the Indians stole from us first. That it was you started all this."

Tecumseh stood, positioning himself between them. "The elders will decide your fate."

Boden's eyes were fully open. "Let me go."

"I cannot."

"Free me now. I won't forget you."

Later that night, curled against his younger brother in their wigwam, replaying the conversation in his mind, Tecumseh trembled at the memory. He had wanted to set the man free. And that part of him was much bigger than the portion of him that wanted to see Boden burned or run the gauntlet again—or see him dead, lying in the muck. The woodsman showed him something he also recognized in himself. How they both drank freedom like walnut milk; how all that kept them moving was the fear that if they ever stayed in one place too long, all familiar parts of themselves would vanish.

In the end, the elders decided Boden was property not only of Chillicothe but of the Shawnee nation. They agreed to let him live, and took him to Wapatomica where all the chiefs could discuss his fate, and, if they so decided, execute him somewhere more central to the Shawnee tribes.

Rattle was smart, maybe even smarter than Tecumseh. But he was obsessive too. When a thought or an idea grabbed hold of him, he wrestled with it, and it alone, until either he figured it out or dismissed the riddle as unsolvable.

At night, grasping for sleep, the brothers listened to the last crackle of the fire logs and now, well into summer, the steady rise and fall of cicada song. The hiss of green wood heating up, the sharp splinter, then the collapse of splinters turned to ash, giving way. Above this, the insects calling to each other like someone laughing between their teeth.

"She says her people live forever," Tecumseh said. They were talking about Becky, who seemed sullen now that Boden, her last tie to her white life, had moved on.

"No one lives forever," Rattle murmured, close to sleep. "Nothing."

"She says her people do. Eternal life. The body is a buckeye shell."

No response.

"What about worms?" Tecumseh rolled halfway over and slugged his brother in the back. "When you cut one in half, and then again, the worm doesn't die, but multiplies."

"Water."

Tecumseh knew then he had him. "Say again?"

"Think about water. A river, frozen with ice. When the ice melts, it becomes water. When I drink from the river, in spring, the water from that river becomes part of me. And then I piss it out. Does the water change, or does it simply transform?"

He pulled the blankets up to his chin, nestling in. "Isn't it water, no matter what?"

"Or caterpillars." Rattle spoke now, clearly. "Or..."

Tecumseh was still grinning when he fell asleep. It was mean, perhaps, to set Rattle's mind spinning, knowing full well his brother would now be up all night, considering this issue of existence. But he loved Rattle for exactly this reason, his single-mindedness, his brain at full gallop. Ask enough questions, and one day he might come up with the answer for the one thing they both desperately sought.

There were locusts every summer, but there seemed to be more now than ever before—more than Tecumseh remembered. Knotted Pine said it was the seventh year. That's why there were so many. That's why, stepping out of his wigwam into daylight, their noise slammed against him fully, as something solid. How so many thousands of insects could sound together like that—a deafening hum that sustained one pitch, one song. Some of the men made up melodies leading to and away from that singular, irritating note, comic stories about being hungry. It was common to roast cicadas on the end of a stick.

Tecumseh hated them. He wouldn't admit it, but he feared them a little. More than any brave should. He could almost shut his ears against their thrum, and if he kept his head down he didn't see too many. When he did glimpse one, crawling along the underside of a branch, upside down, or diving toward him silhouetted by the sun, he shivered as if against a sudden draft. He tried not to show it, but he hated the cicadas and prayed each day for them to all finally die off.

He found Becky planting squash in the far fields. There were no other women close by, and he was glad. She wore deerskin now like the Shawnee. She went barefoot, and her hair was tied into one long braid.

"Have you seen my horse?" He called to her, hurrying past as if intent on some other task.

She blew an errant strand of hair from her face. "What kind of great warrior loses his horse?"

It reminded him of meeting Crazy Jack, and he felt embarrassed. He whistled, pretending to search for Cloudy Girl, and then stepped along the careful, planted rows.

"Winter squash?" he asked.

"You know it is."

"Do your people eat squash?"

"Crookneck pudding," she sighed. "Or pies. Alongside alamode beef. Or in turkey sobaheg..."

She was making piles of dead locusts as she crawled along, burying the seeds. "Like Pharaoh in Egypt."

He didn't understand.

"*The Bible*?" Sweat dripped between her eyes. "God sends locusts, like these, as punishment."

He dropped to the ground, crossed his legs. He lay back, resting on one elbow. "Your god involves himself with everyday affairs?"

"It's why we pray."

He watched her working, saw how her fingers were black from the soil and there were trails of earth up both her arms. "What is it you pray for?"

"Deliverance." She exhaled. "To see my mother and father again."

He thought of his own father, dead. "You'll still think of them every day. Even if you never see them again."

She stopped planting and glared at him. She was squinting, a mean look. She might have said something, but didn't. She went back to her careful rows.

"Besides, look at you," he said. "Wearing animal skin. Your hair in braids. Barefoot. You're practically Shawnee."

She leapt up from her place in the dirt. She snatched the hoe and came storming toward him. He sat up quickly, wondering if she meant to strike him. The thought was almost funny.

"I'm wearing animal skin because my dress finally wore out, and I can't exactly stroll down to the tailor for another." She marched past him, beyond him. "And my hair's in my face because it keeps the sweat out of my eyes. It's hotter than sin."

At the edge of the field was a hickory tree, full and lush and green. She stopped beneath it and cocked her head, listening to the branches hum. She raised the hoe, and he saw then what she meant to do.

"No." He scrambled to his feet. "Please."

"And I've always gone barefoot."

She swung the hoe above her head, into the branches.

All at once the tree erupted with locusts, bursting from the foliage. The tree was green and then Becky swung and the tree was black with insect bodies, and this dark cloud lifted into the air like a spiraling storm. He dropped to the ground, covering his head. The swarm dove and then crashed into him. It was like braving some strong wind. Wings whistled past, screaming in his ears. He felt them in his hair and on his skin. Through it all, he heard Becky laughing.

When the cloud thinned out, he looked at her. She too had dropped to her knees, trying to catch her breath, pointing and laughing.

"It isn't funny." He rose, brushing grass from his arms.

"It is very funny," she snickered. "It really is."

It was a new sensation for him, being the butt of someone else's joke. Even when he'd taken Rattle's eye, no one had laughed. But this—this was new. It was something he felt in his gut. The shame of being laughed at was physical. And desperate, caught between the need to try and explain himself and the irrepressible urge to run away. As, he supposed, Open Door had the night of the ballgame, the night he'd fallen into the creek. It was one of the more frustrating sensations. He found he couldn't look at her.

She came to him instead. She picked a cicada up from the ground and offered it to him. It was still alive, rubbing its clear wings together.

"They're disgusting, that's all," he said.

She smiled, as if she guessed the truth. Then she pinched the bug's wings together and held it like that, dangling. With her other hand she grasped one of its front legs and pulled. The leg came away from the body, and as it did, the head popped clean off.

"See?" She brushed the carcass away. "There's nothing to be afraid of. Just make sure you pull its left leg. Pulling off the right leg just makes it mad."

Knotted Pine's face was deeply creased, the skin dry and tough. It was a mask of brittle bark, and it jutted out from beneath the bearskin he wore like a wide, bulbous knob on an ancient tree. Tecumseh wondered whether he had always resembled a pine or had he grown into the name over the years, fulfilling its destiny. He couldn't have looked like this as a younger man, although even then his name had been the same. So he had become his name, then. That was something people did.

The shaman strained his neck and opened his eyes wide. "I am disappointed in you."

There was a fire going in the center of the room. Ashes swirled in the draft. Tecumseh eyed the deerskin hanging in the doorway and wondered about the room behind it, the sacred fire of the blue flame that burned without fuel. He wanted very badly to see the flame again. His eyes kept flicking toward the doorway, imagining the purity of that eternal light, the stone wrapped in animal skin.

"It's only a game," Rattle said.

"Only a game?" Knotted Pine reached into the air above his head and seemed to snatch something out of it, something invisible in midflight. "Your mother tells me you are in great gambling debt."

Knotted Pine had summoned both boys and now they sat around the fire. The old man seemed to want to talk about how reckless Rattle had become at dice. Tecumseh knew his brother was in debt. He had no idea the extent of it.

"We are a scattered people." Knotted Pine opened his mouth and shut it several times. It seemed very dry in there, inside his mouth, where his tongue moved like a turtle head. "We've no land to call home. We are dependent on ground that belongs to the Delaware, or the Miami, or the Potawatomi. We move here and then there, as treaties move us further west.

"We are protection for the other tribes, who think, 'If the Shawnee are here, the whites will not attack us.' Well, half the Shawnee would now make peace with the whites, the other half would fight them to the death. And of the half that would make peace, half favor the Americans, the other the British."

Tecumseh wasn't sure what the point of this was, or how it related to his brother's obsession. He was anxious to go and shoot his bow and arrow; he was anxious to go and see if Becky was working in the fields.

"With no land to call our own," the elder said, "we will always wander. Divided. Scattered. Lost."

He slipped his hands from beneath the bearskin. He flung blue dust into the flames. The fire burst, brightly. Both boys leapt back. The flames began to congeal and then became a twisting column that reached toward the crossbeams and the thatch-bark ceiling. At four or five feet the pillar began to churn as more colors appeared in its folds: orange and yellow and red. Streaks of color that appeared and then withdrew deeper into the burn.

"When a Shawnee dies," Knotted Pine said, "we lose a part of ourselves—an arm or leg. For the Americans, death is not so important. One dies and more appear. Like a lizard who loses its tail and quickly grows it again. But not the Shawnee. We cannot replace ourselves as easily as that."

Tecumseh rubbed his eyes and gazed into the seething fire. Scenes formed in the colors, half-realized figures stepping out of the smoke and flame.

"One Shawnee is worth five white men," Rattle said. "That's what our father taught us."

Knotted Pine grunted. "Pucksinwah was a wise man and a great warrior."

In the fire, an image of the moon passed over an image of the sun. The Great Council House shook and trembled and collapsed. Horses drowned in a bloody river; the upturned face of a white woman wailed in the moment she was scalped. The brothers saw Pucksinwah shot from his horse.

"No more, please," Rattle begged, covering his eyes.

Tecumseh knew the histories of the great leaders who had come before: Cornstalk and his sister Nonhelema; Blue Jacket and Black Hoof, who had won plenty of honors on the battlefield; his own brother Chiksika who was now war chief of the Kispoko band of Shawnee. He knew their accomplishments. Their stories were all he thought about.

He wanted to be those men. He wanted to surpass them. And now, one by one, they appeared to him in the fire. Cornstalk, with red feathers in his headdress like sharp, long talons: he was there and then muskets fired and he fell, unarmed, murdered by militiamen at Fort Randolph, under truce. Tecumseh knew the story and saw it now unfolding in the flames. The scene changed: a man he recognized as Black Hoof stepped forward, but he was much older than Tecumseh knew him to be, with a shock of white hair and a creamy ascot tied at his throat. His mouth was moving but Tecumseh couldn't quite make out the words. The chief raised his hands and forty geese erupted from his fingers, a rush of honking and feathers and the fierce pounding of wings. The geese took formation and circled, predatory. From their perspective looking down Tecumseh saw a panther splayed across the earth, larger than the earth, but dead, blood pouring from a wound in its side. The geese honked and chattered and swooped and then were gone.

"You must protect one another!" The shaman shouted above the roaring fire. "One brother's debt is the other's debt. The future of the Shawnee people is on your family. The time for games has ended. Find us a home, Tecumseh and Tenskwatawa. Find us a home, gather our people there, and defend it."

It felt as if the medicine man's voice was everywhere at once—even inside of him. Tecumseh closed his eyes and opened them again. He was met with the image of Open Door, buried in mud up to his armpits, having slid down the gully and stuck. He heard his dead brother calling for him and he leapt from the floor, reaching for him. But the shaman called out in words he did not recognize and the column fell and soon was a regular cooking fire again.

They didn't taste like much, cicadas. When they were roasted in a fire. They were gone the moment he put them in his mouth. Tecumseh thought he'd feel the legs between his teeth, or worried the hard wings might get stuck in his throat. But no. There was really nothing to them.

Around the fire, the older boys turned locusts on long spits. Trying to fit as many on one stick as they could. Trying to see who could eat the most. Chiksika had a tree branch, thin and green, longer than an arm. He threaded cicadas onto it, steadily, pushing the other bodies along. Big Jim held a branch forked like a serpent's tongue. Both tines were shiny and black with insects. They fought the sticks like swords and then plunged them into the flames.

"What a pest." Big Jim spat into the coals. "These bugs are proof Our Creator hates us."

Chiksika laughed. "How can you say that when we have all this abundance?"

He plucked a charred cicada from his own stick and popped it into his mouth. He chewed with his eyes closed, slowly, as if savoring the taste.

Sinnantha, who claimed he remembered eating bugs all the time back when his white family first came to the wild country, called out from across the fire. He opened his mouth; Chiksika tossed a burnt cicada in a high arc over the flames. Sinnantha threw back his head and caught the cicada in his mouth and swallowed.

"You're disgusting." Tecumseh put his elbows on his knees.

Big Jim waved a cicada under his nose, making buzzing sounds. Tecumseh swatted him away.

"What's the matter?" Big Jim mocked him, looking grumpy. "Don't like the taste?"

"Actually," Chiksika smiled, "I think my brother here has developed a taste for something else."

Big Jim wiped his mouth. "Do tell."

"White meat."

Tecumseh knew what he meant. The other boys laughed. He sat up and punched his older brother in the arm. "I don't."

"You have been spending an awful lot of time with that girl," Big Jim said.

"Be-cky," Sinnantha sang. He clutched his hands beneath his chin, batting his eyes. "Sing me another song about Jesus. Please?"

Tecumseh went for him too, but Chiksika pushed him back. His skin burned—more humiliation. And behind it, a swarm of anger. He'd said nothing about Becky and still they'd stuck the knife where it hurt most. Where it hit truth. He wanted whatever he felt for Becky to be his secret, to share it with no one.

"Have you ever been with a white woman?" Sinnantha

was tossing back handfuls of cicadas—he'd taken some of Big Jim's.

"Once." Chiksika put Tecumseh in a headlock and pulled him close. "Close your ears, little brother: in Detroit, I lay with a white woman. She was my first. An older woman who had a thing for red skin. At a saloon. I went outside to piss and found her there, waiting for me. She wore nothing beneath her petticoat. It was all over very quickly. I remember she kept licking my ear. Little flicks of her tongue, during. This made it hard for me to concentrate."

All the boys roared with laughter.

Finally released, Tecumseh stood, straightening his clothes. "That's disgusting."

"Cicadas are disgusting." Big Jim smiled. "Sex is disgusting. Everything is disgusting to Tecumseh tonight."

"It's none of your business."

Sinnantha, who seemed able to make piles of cicadas materialize out of thin air, he had so many, threw one and nicked Tecumseh's ear. "Tell us you've at least kissed her."

He hadn't, although sometimes at night he let himself imagine it. He'd leaned close enough, once, to smell her breath, its heavy wetness, and imagined his breath touching hers. But he couldn't find an opportunity. He couldn't think how to get from here to there. Just a kiss—he wasn't even asking to couple. He thought he was probably too young for that, anyway, and really he still couldn't see how it was all supposed to work. Now this ear licking was another angle to consider.

He'd seen her by accident the day before. Close to

dusk, hoping to find her finishing in the fields. Instead, he heard her voice in the creek and saw her bathing there. He hid himself. He hadn't meant to come upon her like that, although his first thought upon turning away was that he wanted to see more.

He looked again. Her back was to the shore. Her body was silvery and slick. There were impressions on either side of her tailbone. Her hair was down and she was singing, *Nae woman in this whole world wide, sae wretched now as me.* Steam rose from her flanks and around her, a last sliver of sunlight on the creek, cutting across her hands as she stretched them and then bent to wash.

He ran somewhere more private and jerked himself off in no time at all. He'd seen naked women before, of course—even girls his own age. But there was something about her there in the water, like a fish, a quality to her nakedness that seemed both dangerous and charged and made his member frighteningly hard. The river, he remembered, revealed everyone for who they truly were—maybe her, maybe him.

"I'm not surprised you fucked a white woman." Tecumseh wouldn't let the other boys glimpse his vision, or his aching desire. "You never did have any standards."

His brother's friends made cat-calls and laughed.

"Everybody fucks white women," Chiksika grinned. "It's all they're good for."

"Not me." Tecumseh looked at them each in turn so they knew he meant it. "I'd rather fuck a horse than dirty my cock in a white girl."

The boys exploded with laughter, shouting, cheering—some fell off their logs. Chiksika reached over and tousled his hair and pulled him close again. He'd made his oldest brother proud.

"I'm glad you won't miss her then," Chiksika said. "I was worrying on how to tell you."

"Tell me what?"

"We're taking her to Fort Dunmore tomorrow."

Big Jim lay down his forked branch. "Turns out, the Americans pay good money for captives."

Was he, as Rattle said, only water? Subject to heat, cold, rocks, wind—never choosing what he became? Or was the choice, in the end, really his? He felt able to choose. That his destiny, his actualization, was something he could grab onto and ride. There were choices in everything. He had a mind and body. He was different from water. He could choose.

He was awoken that night by a grip on his big toe. He swiped at whatever held him in the dark. Whoever it was hoisted a lantern, and he recognized the flushed face of Crazy Jack.

"Did I wake you?" The traveler apologized. "I've brought you something."

Tecumseh's pawawka token lay at his throat. He glanced at the pile of blankets where Rattle slept. No magic then, and not a dream.

Crazy Jack passed him a market wallet. Tecumseh shook it out. There were clothes inside, a polonaise and skirt.

"What do I want with a dress?"

"It's not for you, boy." Crazy Jack slapped him on the head. "It's for you-know-who."

"She's leaving tomorrow."

"She's going back to her people. And she doesn't have a thing to wear."

Crazy Jack was gone then, disappearing into the night, leaving a dress behind and a dank, mossy after-scent. Tecumseh risked losing face if anyone caught him with it—he certainly couldn't give it to her outright. So he slipped to her wigwam and placed the linen bundle at her feet, where she'd be sure to find it when she woke.

The next morning, he and Rattle watched Chiksika and some of the other braves lead Becky from the village. She wore the new clothes, and they seemed to fit her. The flounced skirt swept away from her waist and made her hands and feet seem tiny and fragile as sparrows, although he'd seen those same hands dig planting rows through solid earth, and those same feet kick a ball farther than most boys. Now, though, he saw her differently. He was aware of her being a girl, as if for the first time—someone of the opposite gender, and all the mysteries that went along with that.

"There's something about her, isn't there?" Rattle said. "Despite what Father always said about her people."

"Filth," Tecumseh said. "If she brings us money, fine.

But it's better not to have her here."

The woman to whom she'd been given wept openly and loudly. Some said it was wrong of Chiksika to make her lose her daughter a second time. But these were difficult days. Every tribe was doing what needed to be done, and the Shawnee were no exception. Personal feelings couldn't be put ahead of the common good.

Becky was waving to someone in the crowd. Tecumseh stood with arms folded, squinting back at her, watching, before he realized she was waving at him.

She called his name and broke from the others. She threw her arms around him and kissed him on the lips, pushing them apart with her tongue. He'd never been kissed like that: hard and warm and wet. He thought maybe she pressed her chest against him as she whispered in his ear, her breath hot and even more arousing than her kiss had been. "Thank you for the dress."

His skin was scalding hot, all over. How had she known the gift was from him? He said nothing but stood watching her leave. She tossed a smile back in his direction and was gone.

"I hate you," Rattle said.

"I don't know what that was about."

"No, stop. Speaking only makes it worse."

Chiksika turned and winked once more before he too disappeared into the trees. Tecumseh sniffed his collar—he could smell her there. Lye and honeysuckle and the rich, musky, barnyard smell of earth.

1788

Northwest Territory, formerly Ohio Country

People sometimes said, "I will try to do this" or "I will try to do that." But for Tecumseh, there was nothing worth doing that wasn't worth doing better than everyone else. To try meant leaning on some sliver of hope that things would work out as planned, according to your efforts. Instead, he simply believed he was the best. Whether shooting arrows or reciting well-worn Shawnee legends around the fire, he envisioned the achievement and then made the success real. It mattered to him, whether he won or lost. He didn't like to lose. It mattered that he shot the largest bobcat or bagged the most squirrels. It mattered to him that he rode in front, just behind his brother Chiksika, when they galloped into battle. Let no one wonder who was next in line, or whether Tecumseh might one day lead his own war party.

That others didn't always feel the same meant nothing to him. What were they to him, if they weren't trying to win? Teamwork, collaborative effort—these things mattered only as far as they supported his singular achievements. They were like the frame of a wigwam, there to brace him against foul storms and ensure his status endured. Fair play and participation had little intrinsic value, the way a hoe was merely a stick with a sharp edge until someone used it to till the ground.

Sometimes, in the middle of the night, he'd sit up, head rushing, with a sick feeling in his stomach as if he'd misplaced something or forgotten some important chore. The fear—the certainty—that someone else was working harder, or devoting more hours. He would accept no equals. Let others carve out their success wherever they might; they could fight over the scraps he left them.

His father, for example, was considered a wise and courageous man among their band of Shawnee, perhaps even by other tribes in nearby territories. But no enemy still trembled at his invocation, and certainly no white man. He had achieved some status as war chief, but his victories were not great, and no one sang songs about his deeds. In fifty years, or less, he would be forgotten.

To be remembered. This is what drove Tecumseh, the spark of gunpowder inside of him that propelled him from his blankets each morning.

Others might persist—Blue Jacket, for one. Already, the myth around him was large, and he was still alive, with time to add to his history. He had led the resistance in Dunmore's War; he had fought well alongside the British in their struggle against the Americans. But Tecumseh determined to eclipse even him.

That was the goal, the point of it all: to become the

greatest man among men—the greatest Shawnee. So that in fifty years, a hundred, or three centuries from now, when another great man rose up, shamans and scholars would say, "Yes, this man is great, but he is not as great as Tecumseh." He would set the standard by which all other men were measured. Anything else would be failure. And so his rivals were not his peers, the other men under his brother's command. He did not compare himself to Big Jim, or care if Sinnantha treated him with respect. He was already greater than them. But Blue Jacket, Daniel Boone, those men were already turning themselves into legends. These were men Tecumseh hoped one day to surpass, as sometimes the moon passes over the sun and shrouds the world in darkness.

It was blasphemous to even think it, but still he wondered if immortality, life everlasting, wasn't man's ultimate aim. How much death had already touched his life, and how much more would come? But to find a way to live forever, to walk like a god. To be remembered, to persist. What aim was higher than this?

"So you want to be chief then?" Rattle was trying to understand. He was fanning out a pack of Hardy playing cards. The cards expanded and then collapsed again in his chubby fingers.

"Chief?" Tecumseh spat. "There's no power in being chief. Who remembers them? Chiefs sit and get fat, while entertaining guests. They play nice with the white man. They die and are replaced while others fight their battles for them."

"What then?"

"Tell me." Tecumseh leaned closer. "Have you ever seen Knotted Pine bring something back to life?"

"There are stories." Rattle fanned the cards and offered them to Tecumseh, who took one. "Trips to the spirit world, and those who return. Show me."

Tecumseh revealed the Queen of Spades. "I'm talking about something greater than celestial wanderings. Not to die—that would be real magic."

Rattle took back the card, and seemed happy with it. "I've never seen something like that."

"But the Wampus Cat," Tecumseh pressed. "She's immortal."

"Not immortal." He was shuffling the deck again. "She might be able to die. But she's not of our world, or part of the physical realm."

"It felt pretty physical to me, when the cabin was shaking."

Rattle shrugged. "Well, she's not not of this world, either."

"But how did she get here in the first place? Where did she come from?"

"She's always just...been."

Immortality seemed to be reserved for monsters and ethereal tricksters, like Crazy Jack, mythical beings who flickered back and forth between this world and the next. It was such a waste. All the Wampus Cat did was terrorize settlers. Crazy Jack, at least so far, was humorous and occasionally thoughtful, but no real help in any practical way. And yet he was blessed. Immortal. Was that kind of longevity inaccessible to man?

Tecumseh wanted a say in how he would be remembered. He wanted a say in whether or not he would one day die. Rattle had never seen something like that, which meant Knotted Pine had most likely never spoken of secrets that deep—or dark. But that didn't mean it wasn't possible.

Tecumseh stuck his oar against the bank and shoved off. His bark canoe wobbled and took on water. It drifted out into the Licking River, pulling starboard against his rowing. He cursed, paddling against the current. But it was like riding a drowning cow. Each time he shifted his weight, more water poured in over the sides. The canoe seemed intent on turning circles.

He spat. "Who makes a canoe such as this?"

As the newest member of his brother's war party, the other braves had drafted him for this task, to be a decoy, like so many years ago when they took that first flatboat on the Ohio River. They had given him the canoe and made him shove off, and now he feared he might drown before he saw any action. It was all part of their hazing, to keep him humble. But knowing this didn't make his present situation more bearable.

"Try not to move so much." Crazy Jack reclined against the bow, feet up. "If you wanted it done differently, you should have made it yourself."

Tecumseh's token was buzzing around his neck and his hands and underarms were strangely dry, which meant Crazy Jack was invisible to everyone else, most likely. His companion fingered an unlit cigar, one gaitered leg propped over the side of the vessel. He wore a red Highlander's coat that must have dated back to the war with the colonials. It was badly faded and fell open to reveal his fleshy paunch.

On the far bank, Tecumseh saw the scouts' signal. It was time to get moving. "We'll sink before this is over."

He laid his paddle across his lap and bailed water with his hands. He didn't think the canoe had even been sealed. It was hastily made and packed with an empty case of whiskey and several sacks of coffee and sugar. He hoped to give the appearance of a warrior returning from a successful raid.

"It's your weight making us sink." Crazy Jack peered inside the case of whiskey, but finding it empty, made a show of being disgusted.

"Ridiculous."

"It's not me that's got the fat brother."

Tecumseh picked up the paddle again and swung it through the tide. "You could help."

"You're doing fine."

"I thought you were supposed to be an aide."

The traveler shrugged. "This is one of those, leave-a-good-enough-thing-alone type situations."

They were drawn into the confluence of the Ohio

River. They turned south, downstream, and did not look back. But Tecumseh saw the first boat in the flotilla out of the corner of his eye. The scouts' signal had been precise. Heading toward them now, close behind them as they paddled, near enough for him to see an oarsman stick a finger in his mouth and fling a tobacco plug into the water, were three keelboats. He dug hard. He heard the oarsmen begin to shout and knew they had been spotted. They were fifteen yards ahead.

Tecumseh thought of that first morning, when he had stood on the riverbank and waved to a passing flatboat, how Chiksika had dressed him in English clothes and taught him to call for help. His pants had been too short, his heels not quite fully in the black polished shoes he wore. It had felt like a child's game. But years had passed and still he found himself terrorizing other pioneer families who dared make the treacherous journey downriver. He wondered what it all added up to.

It was no challenge to slaughter these pilgrims, most of whom were ill-equipped to handle life in the wild. Plus, the frontiersmen had grown smarter. Now the keelboats traveled with a raft tied to the hull, so that if someone flagged them from shore they needn't put the craft at risk. Tecumseh was proud that his playacting had brought this about. But Chiksika had devised a new technique that flattered the settlers' swelling confidence. It meant using Tecumseh as bait.

Two rifle shots rang out.

"Paddle." Crazy Jack covered his head.

"I am paddling."

"Paddle harder."

Tecumseh feigned surprise and turned to look upstream. He waved his arms, acting frantic. He made a big show of spinning the canoe back the way he'd come, against the current, as if to escape again up the Licking River where the bulky keelboats could not follow. But his canoe was sluggish and did not respond. The window between the mouth of the Licking and the front keelboat was quickly closing. He cursed his floundering vessel as a munitions ball burst the hull and exited cleanly out the other side.

"This is the last time I listen to them," Tecumseh cursed. "Some plan. Some canoe."

"We will make it." Crazy Jack glanced back at the keelboats, and recognizing their nearness, began paddling as well.

"No. We will die without honor, and they will write comedic songs about us."

"We could always swim for it."

The keelboats slowed. Onboard, men took turns firing, using the bark canoe for target practice. Tecumseh heard them taking bets on who could nail themselves an Indian. He paddled across their line of fire, staying low, flinching each time the sugar sacks absorbed buckshot and exhaled small clouds of white powder. He saw debris in the river, a gnarl of limbs and vines, and on the lead keelboat a man in a white hat and several dogs that barked after each rifle blast and snapped their jaws below the rails.

At the man's side was a boy with only one arm. He had a toy pistol and took careful aim, winking. His empty sleeve was tied in a bow. He pulled the trigger and made gunshot sounds with his lips.

Tecumseh searched inside himself for the sudden rush that always came with combat. But as he drifted past the lead boat, as the shouting of the oarsmen grew more feverish, as he listened to the sound of ammunition whistling overhead, he felt empty.

Something had been nagging at him and now it defined itself: was this gambit, this foolery, what his father had died for?

His canoe attained the mouth of the Licking River. All around him went up a piercing Shawnee war cry. Rifle fire burst from the trees along the bank. The volley crashed over the flotilla with a tidal force. Frontiersmen pitched forward into the water or flung backward across the decks, dead.

A second barrage: twenty Shawnee warriors erupted from the forest, swinging tomahawks. They leapt into the river and moments later the three keelboats were overcome.

Tecumseh stopped paddling. Against the Shawnee swarm, the remaining frontiersmen panicked. Few even had the presence of mind to shoot. They leapt into the water and tried to swim away, praying the current would carry them quick and far. But the raiding party took their own places at the bow of the lead boat and fired at those who fled. Soon blood floated in pools at the confluence.

They killed forty-five whites and took seven prisoners, all children. The flotilla surrendered her riches: one ton of gunpowder in fifty-pound kegs; two tons of lead bars; bullet molds; two boxes of new flintlock rifles; and Spanish silver.

That night there was a celebration. His friends seemed glad for the day's haul—and it was a fine haul, by any measure. But Tecumseh found no pleasure in any of it.

Chiksika included Tecumseh now in every conversation. He was learning what it meant to lead, the endless stream of questions asked by those who followed and the unending string of decisions that had to be made. He wondered, at times, if anyone thought for themselves, or if they looked to Chiksika for everything.

"Do you ever doubt yourself?" he asked his brother in private.

"Never," Chiksika said. "Someone must make the decisions. If someone else has a better idea, let them speak."

Chiksika had pledged a dozen warriors to reinforce the Chickamauga in the South. The Chickamauga were at war with American frontiersmen. The war had lasted nearly fifteen years. Their chief, Dragging Canoe, had sworn to fight the Americans against the advice of other chiefs. He led a few hundred warriors camped near Marion. Chiksika had volunteered his men for a season, maybe more if things fell right.

In the Tennessee River Gorge they found mountains that, unlike the rolling hills of home, slammed dense pine forest against the sky. The streams were clear and crisp when Tecumseh slurped water from his hands. It was not the murky tide of the Ohio River but a clean current that polished every stone and pebble and flashed sunlight back to itself.

Tecumseh felt closest to his brother at times like this, when they were the only things moving in the early morning woods. They crossed below a limestone cliff-face, their feet light and quick through the heavy fog.

There were often periods of silence between them. Hours unfurled without either man saying a word. Chiksika was not a man who shared the Shawnee passion for chatter. But moments such as this, their bodies in motion, moving toward action with strong warriors behind them—these were the easy moments.

He touched the eagle feather in his hair. Double-tipped in white, fixed to his ear by a gold medallion, the feather trailed to his shoulder. This announced his rank as full warrior, by all rights able to lead a raiding party of his own. All in good time. For now, Tecumseh was his brother's soldier, nothing more.

Chiksika raised his hand. Behind him, each man froze. He gestured and made a whistling sound. "Do you hear it?"

Tecumseh heard the forest. The cackle of crows overhead. The wind in the leaves. Somewhere behind him a squirrel clattered down a tree trunk and rooted through the underbrush.

"I don't—"

But then he did: the unmistakable sound of men laughing. They were somewhere farther down the mountain. He shook his head, impressed by his brother's ears. Tecumseh had to listen very hard to hear the laughter even now, standing still. Chiksika had registered it running at three-quarters speed.

They made their way down the sloping pine forest. Soon he could make out distinct words. The men spoke of measurements and money. They spoke in English. By listening to their voices he counted four and then five. Then six.

The Shawnee came upon the edge of a clearing so rapidly that they almost stepped out in plain view of the men. Catching themselves, they dropped behind a fallen tree. There was a sodden field, and in its center an enormous boulder with a clean, flat top. It was an impressive piece of rock, nestled there on the ridge, taller than any man. Four woodsmen lounged on top of the boulder like lizards in the sun. He now counted five more in various positions of repose along the ground, lying in the grass or leaning against the pile of furs and pelts. The breeze picked up. He caught the scent of Virginia tobacco.

"What do you see?" Chiksika asked.

"Woodsmen," Tecumseh said. "Eight muskets. One long gun."

"Very good, little brother." Chiksika clapped him on the back. "We'll make a warrior out of you yet."

He flushed with pride as his brother laid out the

approach. They would encircle the boulder, then tighten their circle like a noose. They would use only tomahawks and knives. Otherwise they might shoot one another in the crossfire.

"We could lose an eye that way," Big Jim snickered.

They ribbed Tecumseh then. Everyone still remembered the misfired arrow that had taken Rattle's eye.

In the clearing, the traders passed glass jars of clear liquid and made sour faces when they drank. They chewed the ends of their cigars. They were becoming boisterous. Likely they'd been up all night. Silently, the Shawnee spread themselves along the perimeter. Tecumseh settled in behind a wide, tall pine and waited for his brother's signal.

He swallowed the discomfort in his stomach. His bowels were always in great distress before a raid. His belly smoldered with tiny embers and sometimes a little flare leapt up and singed the back of his throat. It was usually okay once the action started. He never thought about it once his body was moving.

He heard a rustling. He peered around the tree trunk. A man approached, one of the woodsmen. He wore a red beard and a brimmed hat. The front of the hat was smashed up in front. His matchcoat was belted at the waist and pinned at his chest by a medallion. He was shorter than Tecumseh and older by thirty years—the oldest of the crew.

Tecumseh tried to draw himself closer to the tree, imagining himself part of the soft bark. But the man was walking straight for him. A scalping knife was in his belt. Tecumseh pressed against the tree and tried to keep out of the man's line of vision. There was nothing to do until Chiksika gave the signal. There was nothing to do but wait.

The woodsman came right up to the tree. Tecumseh could hear him breathe, the way he sucked snot out of his nose and spit. He stopped so close that Tecumseh would have only had to reach around the tree with one arm to unlace his boots. He waited as the man wrestled with his breeches. Then an arcing, yellow stream shot out from the far side of the tree, landing so close to Tecumseh that spray hit his foot. The man's urine steamed and hissed against the pine needles.

Tecumseh only slipped his moccasin out of the splatter, the softest rustle of nettles, but that was enough. The man made a kind of grunting noise and stepped forward. He strode a full yard past where Tecumseh crouched against the pine. It was as if the man felt him then, some animal instinct that sensed the presence of another person without seeing him. He turned. Tecumseh met his eyes. The woodsman opened his mouth to warn the others, and that was all.

Tecumseh sprang forward, tomahawk twirling. He gave the war cry. A wide swing buried the head of his tomahawk in the old man's groin, where one of his veined hands still held his trouser button. The man exhaled as if all the air had been sucked out of him. Tecumseh spun the tomahawk and brought it up over his head like a hammer, driving the iron through the old man's skull. The woodsman bled from both wounds then, a wide arc of bloodspray as he twisted and fell.

Hearing the war cry, other braves burst from their hiding places, accelerating and closing the gap of lawn. A span of time passed, enough for only one breath, and they were upon the woodsmen then: the distance was closed.

Tecumseh was no slower. He dashed from the trees, pounding his fist against his chest and shouting. He sprinted across the grass and hauled himself to the top of the boulder. He swung his tomahawk. Blood flew in ribbons from a young hunter's neck. A second man in a faded tri-corn hat lunged at him with a knife. Tecumseh sidestepped and, as the man stumbled past, thrusting, pushed him from the rock. The man followed his battle-worn cap over the side and into the waiting arms of Big Jim, who held him down and slit his throat.

There was only one woodsman then on the rock. He was leveling his long gun to fire when Tecumseh slammed against him. The rifle went off; Tecumseh wrapped up the man in his arms, tasting the rank odor of his unwashed parts. Their feet slipped on the limestone, on the fine silt and gravel, and they slid together. Falling, Tecumseh pushed his elbow into the other man's throat. When they hit the ground, he felt the snap of the neck.

And then it was over. All nine woodsmen dead. Tecumseh had killed four.

Big Jim helped him to his feet. "Leave one for us next time."

But something caught his eye—his brother, Chiksika, lying on his back at the edge of the clearing. When he reached his brother's side he found a musket ball had entered through his chin and splattered his brains against an ancient pine.

They buried Chiksika in the high, pure Tennessee hills.

Tecumseh felt a crushing guilt. If he'd tackled the woodsman sooner, or differently, the man might have never gotten off a shot. Now Chiksika was dead, and there was no one to care for their family.

"You'll lead us now," Big Jim said.

They shared a pipe in the darkness.

"I do not want to be chief," Tecumseh said.

"Nor should you. Leave the glad-handing and politics to those who cannot fight."

He breathed in the cherry smoke. The cloud reached inside of him, down his throat and then curling up into his nose to settle somewhere behind his eyes. It mingled with the sadness there, the drifting and uneasy grief he felt in every limb and most of all, in his heart. It coaxed feelings from a deep place inside of him, where he hid them: how he felt each time he looked at his brother, Rattle, and remembered who was responsible for his one eye. How the last face he saw before going to bed each night was Open Door's.

"It's my fault," he said.

Big Jim gestured for the pipe, impatient. "No."

"I did not wait for the signal."

"That unlucky man pissed on you. What were you

supposed to do?"

He felt the urge to sob and tried to swallow it, to cram his sadness back inside again. "My heart is full of rage. Each day a little more."

"Let us return to Chillicothe," Big Jim said softly. "We'll rally our allies. The Miami. The Delaware. Our war has just begun."

There were some whites who were friendly with the tribes, who could move between worlds. One trader in particular was always in Chillicothe before the harvest. He camped on the edge of the village. Outside his tent he hung his many wares: badger pelts and coon skins; mink and silver fox tails; cast-iron skillets; sharp, shimmering knives; and half a dozen pistols that he unfurled, upon request, from a long, blue-cloth roll. Children were forbidden. Many grown men avoided him too. There was too much temptation with the whiskey and tobacco and the trunk marked *curio* which, when opened, revealed a pile of treasure: sea shells and gold chains and bronze cups and twinkling jewelry and tokens that sparkled and shimmied in different kinds of light.

Tecumseh knew he would find his brother here.

At the camp, a fire was going. The smell of chocolate and rising dough. He discovered Rattle near the cooking pot.

He dispensed with any formal greeting. "You can't be

bothered to meet your brother on his return?"

Rattle sat cross-legged, examining a bear-claw necklace. "Welcome back, brother."

"At least you could have shown your face. For mother. For our sister-in-law."

He would not mention Chiksika, not yet. Not here among the white man's treasures.

"I'm sure our warriors were warmly greeted for their heroic and supernatural demonstrations of strength," Rattle said evenly. "I'm sure I'm sorry to have missed it."

Tecumseh did not blame Rattle for the man he had become, or for the things he was never taught, or for what was overlooked in their family. Those mornings Tecumseh found him passed out drunk at the well, or in the graveyard, or sometimes lying half in and half outside his wigwam, snow blowing in through the opening in the hide, he knew it was not his brother's fault that he did not know how to behave. For twenty-one years, no one had raised a word against him.

But the sarcasm was something new. The callousness. Rattle seemed absent even when he was right there in front of him.

"I have news," Tecumseh said.

But he was interrupted by a voice from the darkness, a face stepping forward to be recognized in the firelight.

"Come in, come in," a man said. "Plenty of room for customers."

It was not the trader Tecumseh had expected. But he recognized the voice: Crazy Jack. The little man wore red, candy-striped stockings and a mauve riding jacket. He twirled a cane and stepped lightly around the fire.

"Your brother was just admiring my bear-claw necklace," the trader said.

Tecumseh was relieved Rattle could see Crazy Jack—that the trickster hadn't chosen to hide himself this night. This relief took the edge off the deep irritation he felt when he otherwise considered his brother, which more and more he was trying not to do.

The trader extended his hand, reaching above his head. "Name's Jack."

Tecumseh shook the hand, peering down. If the trader recognized him, he gave no sign. It was certainly him—the sparkle in his eyes when he tipped the brim of his hat, mischievous and all-knowing, confirmed it. But why pretend?

Tecumseh's own eyes fell upon a bowl filled with small, polished stones.

"Found those in a cave not far from here." Crazy Jack grinned. A full set of teeth shone back at the brothers. "Have one. On the house."

Tecumseh took a stone in hand, measured its weight. It was the size of a bird's egg and just as smooth. He pocketed the marble. "Your teeth."

"Advances in tooth science," the trader beamed. "Swindled a dentist in Iroquois country into making me a full set—from the finest hippopotamus ivory."

"I don't know what that is."

"A fierce beast the hippo is," he explained. "Lives below

water and above. Killed many a man. Mean as a sunburn." He scrounged in a wooden trunk and produced three tin cups. A bottle followed. "Spruce beer?"

Tecumseh nodded and joined his brother near the cooking pot. Each man raised a cup and drank.

"To mastication," said Crazy Jack. "To chewing one's food."

He asked after local affairs, how the hunting grounds had changed, what new treaties were being negotiated with the Americans, about the rumored unrest in the Shawnee camps, that a faction wished to continue the troubles with the settlers.

"You speak pretty good English," Crazy Jack said.

Had he winked? Tecumseh wasn't sure.

The trader leaned forward to get a better look at him. "You ain't one of them whites-turned-Indian now, are you?"

He let himself be examined in the firelight. Satisfied, the trader leaned back and, laughing, poured them all another drink. "So what did you bring to trade with me?"

"We have nothing," Tecumseh said. "I came only to find my brother."

"Everyone's got something." Crazy Jack licked his lips. "What about your knife?"

Rattle wore a long, curved hunting knife. For what purpose, Tecumseh didn't know—it had done nothing more than shell walnuts since their father had given it. Still, it was an excellent knife, one that had skinned hundreds of pelts and, he guessed, more than its share of scalps during

Dunmore's War.

"His knife is worth more than your necklace," Tecumseh said.

"See anything else you like?"

"I will not part with my knife," Rattle said.

Crazy Jack sighed. "Then we are at an impasse."

He turned his attention to the pot. He stirred with a ladle and scooped out three steaming clumps of dough from where they'd been simmering in the chocolate sauce. He let them cool on the ground. They ate. The dough was shockingly sweet and disappeared on their tongues.

Rattle said, "I could read a fortune for you."

The trader laughed. "I have no interest in my fortune. A man knows too much about what lies ahead, he's liable to stop working hard."

They sat for a while, licking their fingers.

Crazy Jack said, "We could play a game for it."

"I like games," Rattle said.

"That is, if there's nothing to trade, we could wager."

Tecumseh shot his brother a look but was ignored.

"I will win your game," his brother said.

The trader grinned and bowed graciously. He never sat down. While standing, he was their equal in height. He drained his cup and gestured for theirs. He turned the three cups upside down so they formed a line in front of him. Then he reached into his breast pocket and produced a marble like the kind he'd given Tecumseh, except that his marble was golden and shone in the firelight. He rubbed it between his thumb and forefinger before slipping it beneath the center cup.

"Where's the marble?" he asked.

"The middle," Rattle said quickly.

"Very good." He picked up the cup and revealed the marble. "Now watch."

He began to move the cups, slowly dragging them back and forth across the dirt, switching the positions, feinting, then trading places again. After a few deliberate movements he asked, "Where's the marble now?"

Rattle pointed. "Beneath the cup on the right."

Crazy Jack raised an eyebrow. Then he lifted the cup on the right. The marble was there.

"Excellent." He began to move the cups again, this time faster. Sometimes he slid them forward, sometimes back. When they stopped, Rattle again guessed correctly.

The trader sat on his haunches. "I am no match for someone as quick as you."

"Do it again," Rattle said.

But the trader was reluctant. "I don't have much time for games, much as I do love them. But if you were to place a wager..."

Rattle stood and puffed out his chest. "I bet this war knife."

He had taken it from its sheath, and now he held it out. If the trader noticed its worth, he did not show it. "And if I lose?"

Rattle kicked at the jewelry display. "This bear-claw necklace. And a crock of beer."

Crazy Jack nodded once and set to work. He placed

the golden marble beneath the center cup. Then he began to move the three cups much more quickly than he had before. He used both hands when earlier he had used only one; his hands moved independently of one another, shooting out from his sides. The cups swapped places. They made a soft clinking sound as they brushed past, as his left hand passed a cup to his right even as his right hand pushed one forward and brought it back and then spun it again into the center of the dance. He mumbled to himself, keeping rhythm with his lips. The rims shaped the dirt. And suddenly all were still, three cups lined neatly before them.

"Where's the marble?" he asked.

Rattle never hesitated. He pointed to the center cup. The trader flashed his hand and turned the center cup over: nothing.

"Impossible!" Rattle roared, scattering the cups with his feet.

But Crazy Jack didn't flinch, only held out his palm. "Your knife, please."

"I won't give it to you—I'll kill you first."

The sparkle was gone from the trader's eyes. He squatted in the dirt, palm out. Rattle, in all his mass, could have fit the man inside his belly. He looked as if he might swallow Crazy Jack whole.

But the trader's eyes were black as the cast-iron pot. "We had a deal."

"My father gave me this knife."

"Then next time you'll be more careful what you

wager."

Tecumseh had seen enough. He grasped the quartzite that hung from his neck and broke the string. "Take this instead. It's magic."

"Tsk-tsk." The trader eyed the stone, then reached for it. He rubbed it between his forefinger and thumb. He held it between his teeth, examined it against the firelight. To Tecumseh he said, "Do you still have that tobacco pouch I gave you?"

Before he could answer, Crazy Jack disappeared. The trader, the kettle, the furs and trunks and tent and horse and wagon all were gone, leaving only the empty hickory grove and the brothers alone in the gloaming.

Tecumseh was constantly reminded of their childhood accident, the misfired arrow and Rattle not looking away but instead looking up. The arrow coming down as if this were its sole purpose, as if Tecumseh had sanded the sapling and fletched it only to one day deprive his brother of sight. Even now, pranksters would sneak up on Rattle and, as he was in the middle of a story, or just as he was about to take some food—when he least expected it—and clap him on the side of the head or stick a wet finger in his ear. Rattle never saw him coming, because of the missing eye. And the other men always laughed as if it were the first time anyone had ever done that to him. Sometimes Rattle would complain, or bark, but usually he just walked away.

He was mild, unless he'd been drinking. Tecumseh knew no one else whose character changed so completely under the influence of alcohol. Sober, Rattle was a glob of unbaked dough that was interested in herbs and spells and ancient, half-forgotten stories—stuff few people cared about. He could spend the day not talking to anyone, following his own lines of study. He was the kind of person you saw and then immediately forgot.

But drunk: something heavy seemed to settle on his brow, and his one good eye became hard and focused. It looked right at you, made accusations, even if you turned away. He would lean forward a little, and his head would nod, and that good eye would sharpen as if looking ahead, as if seeing the moment when the conversation would end and the fists would start flying.

He loved to fight. He would wander the village in the late hours, hollering. And sometimes a warrior would oblige. For someone who loved to brawl, he was never any good at it. Tecumseh couldn't name a time Rattle had gained the upper hand. Mostly his opponent just beat him until he was lying face-down in the mud, and he'd wake up a few hours later and crawl home to his wigwam. His missing eye left him vulnerable.

Sometimes Tecumseh would find him passed out in the bushes or struggling to right himself against a tree. Those nights, he would lead his brother home, sometimes supporting him as they walked, sometimes wiping vomit from his chin. His brother complaining the whole time about how much his eye hurt—not his good eye, but the absent one.

"I can still feel it in there," he'd say. "It hurts me every day."

Now he kept his one good eye on the ground like a child who knew he was to be punished but whose parents wanted to drag him out of sight first, to avoid a public shaming. Inside his wigwam were empty liquor bottles and half-eaten cakes, discarded hunting shirts and woven garters. Mice scattered as Tecumseh gathered blankets to make a place to sit. The air was stale with dried sweat and unwashed bedclothes.

"Brother," Rattle began. "I will replace your token—"

Tecumseh swatted him on the back of his head. "Shut up."

His brother caught himself against the wall, against the hides and patchwork bark. For a moment, the entire structure swayed and leaned with his weight. He clamped a hand over his eye-patch, as if it were the eye's fault the room was spinning.

It wasn't so much the loss of the token that bothered Tecumseh, although he hated to part with it. He felt betrayed by Crazy Jack, who he thought was supposed to be his spiritual guide. Once the trader's tent had disappeared, Rattle found he was too drunk—he could barely stand. Tecumseh draped an arm around his shoulders and half-carried him home. Now Rattle shuffled to the right, then to the left, wringing his hands. He was worried. Well, he should be.

"What kind of man are you?" Tecumseh spat. "You do

not greet your brother when he returns? I come home to find you gambling and then must right your wrongs?"

Rattle wiped his mouth. "I never asked for your help. I don't want it."

Tecumseh thought his brother had gained weight. His face was fleshier, his features watery. His lips blubbered when he spoke.

"Chiksika is dead," he told him.

This seemed to sober Rattle for a moment. He staggered to the table and braced himself there. He grimaced, as if feeling pain in his gut. He allowed a bubble of air to pass through his lips.

"I am sorry for that," he said.

"I killed the man who shot him," Tecumseh said.

Rattle busied himself cleaning up. He dragged a dirty skillet from one corner to the other. He picked up a shirt and, sniffing it, tossed it to the floor again. Finally, he began to laugh. A snicker at first, then more.

"Funny." He laughed through his nose. "You've been waiting your whole life for this. Our whole lives. And now, it's here."

"I don't know what you mean."

"You'll lead us now. My older brother—older by two minutes, maybe less—is finally a Shawnee war chief."

"I would rather Chiksika were here. Or father."

"They chose you, you know." Rattle stumbled across the room, wagging a finger. "From the very beginning, they chose you. Tecumseh, the Great Panther Crossing the Sky. First-born, the very same night a comet passed overhead.

Tell me, brother: in the womb, did you shoulder me out of the way so you could be first out of our mother's cunt? Was your ambition that great, even then?"

"Speak about our mother like that again," Tecumseh warned, "and I will kill you."

But Rattle only sneered. "You found quartzite in the river that morning. I found nothing. Our father soothed my heartbreak with lashes from his switch. I was so jealous I could hardly breathe."

"Our Grandmother sends us what we need, at the time when we most need it."

"You shot out my eye!" Rattle clasped his head with both hands.

But Tecumseh took three steps across the room and grabbed his brother by the collar. Despite his mass, he hoisted him off his feet.

"So you lost an eye." They were face to face, and Tecumseh's spit was flying. "Because you didn't have the sense to look away. And you've used it, ever since, as an excuse for what you've become. Or what you've not become—for refusing to become a man. The way you simper. The way you let others care for you. Let me tell you something, brother, it was you who killed Open Door. Your bullying, your teasing."

"You've got no right to say such a thing."

"I will not."

"Take that back this instant."

Spit traveled between them, tongue to lip, tongue to cheek. They locked eyes, and Tecumseh had the thought to strangle him, to put him out of his misery. No one would miss him. Even their mother would one day forget him.

"You killed our brother," Tecumseh said. "And you'll carry that the rest of your life."

Something seemed to stir then deep inside his brother's belly, so that his entire body began to shake. When finally the scream let loose, he broke Tecumseh's grip. In the next moment he had unsheathed his knife.

Rattle charged, blade high. Tecumseh merely sidestepped. Rattle flailed and stumbled, the knife sweeping off to the left. Tecumseh placed his hand on his brother's shoulder and pushed, just a little, as he passed, but it was enough to send him crashing through the table to the floor.

The space lay in shambles. Rattle, face-down, was motionless. His shirt rode up his back, revealing great mountains of flesh around his waist, the hairless expanse slick with sweat, the pale stretchmarks on his brown skin.

"Get up," Tecumseh said.

His brother didn't move.

"Stand up, you coward."

He kicked him. Rattle grunted, exhaled, and after a long moment, began to snore.

Tecumseh wiped his hands. He stood the broken chair against the wall. He dug through his brother's bedding until he found a half bottle of whiskey. He stood in the center of the room, over the body, taking one long swallow after another. Then he set the bottle on the table. He slipped the cleanest-looking blanket from the tangle of bedclothes, snapped it open, and lay it gently over his brother's body.

"Sleep well, Tenskwatawa," he told him. "In sleep at least, I hope there is peace."

1795

Northwest Territory

NO ONE NEEDED TO TELL TECUMSEH that life had changed. It was rare now to see a buffalo herd. In his youth, the skies were filled with passenger pigeons so thick they hid the clouds. Now their flocks were frail and unimpressive things.

He had seen white hunters set fire to the woods to smoke these birds out. They scattered grain, soaked in alcohol, which made the pigeons drunk. In the white man's cities were heaped great piles of dead birds. Old women sat at the foot of these grisly mounds plucking fistfuls of feathers, from daybreak to supper bell. It was, he thought, an insatiable hunger that drove them, like a funnel cloud consuming everything in its path.

Now Tecumseh had been summoned. Sixty miles northwest of Chillicothe was the Place of the Devil Wind. The Eternal Flame protected the Shawnee from the errant, twisting storms that spiraled across the prairie there, but still they gave the place wide berth—other tribes simply refused to cross the land at all. There was something different about the air, about the way the wind blew. It was dangerous and unpredictable. It seemed to defy the things the Shawnee knew elsewhere to be true.

It had always been wild land, uninviting. But now a man named Jim Galloway—Judge James Galloway, the messenger had called him—had established a settlement, the Americans' most northerly push into what was once Ohio Country, and sacred Shawnee hunting grounds. As was his right: the recent battle at Fallen Timbers had broken a loose confederacy of tribes. In the aftermath, a new treaty ceded all land north of the Ohio and south of the Little Miami rivers to the Americans.

Many important chiefs had signed this new treaty, but Tecumseh had not. That is why Judge Galloway had invited him to where the wind bucked and kicked in whorls, and the rain sometimes seemed to shoot up from the ground. The Americans wanted him to sign the treaty. They needed him to sign. Tecumseh now led a Shawnee war party larger than what his father had led. He had traveled to the Southwest Territory and as far west as the Great River. The tribes respected him. The British respected him. Perhaps the Americans respected him too, but they needed his signature on their paper. Without it, there would never be peace.

The Galloway home presided at the edge of a wide meadow. A servant woman welcomed Tecumseh inside. She had a pinched face and bent severely at the waist. He waited in the front room while she fetched the judge. There was an iron stove and four wooden chairs pushed against a table. There were otherwise no decorations of any kind, except the books.

He had never seen so many. Entire walls were shrouded by rows of thick leather volumes with gold trim. Above the door; above the fireplace in the kitchen; on shelves built specifically to hold them—stacks of books used as furniture to put things on.

It made him nervous. He could speak English well enough, and understand its conversation, but he could not read or write. So many books, together in one house, disclosed a type of person he wasn't used to dealing with—a scholar, someone who spent too much time alone with his thoughts. Someone for whom the world revealed itself in many nuanced shades. Mostly these government men were men of action. You met, traded blows, and then you knew what you had. But men who read books were unpredictable. They couldn't be counted on to see reason. Often, they were slaves to their emotions and to some individualized sense of right or wrong.

"The ceiling is too low," he grumbled to himself. "I can't breathe."

The walls were pale yellow, the curtains white. He brushed his head-feathers against the rough-hewn rafters, pacing slow, tidy circles around the room. Eventually he was joined by a young boy, the woman's son, Tecumseh guessed, who wanted to get a look at the Indian. He appeared from behind the stairs and leaned against the wall. He watched him, whistling softly.

Tecumseh let his hands wander over the books. Their bindings felt like tightly woven thread. He chose one that was tall and ribbed along the spine. He opened it, overwhelmed by its pulpy scent. Across the pages were printed small black words.

He wondered what these books contained. Stories, such as those passed down by his own people? Of gods and spirits? Or were they tales of war, of heroes, of nation-building? Books about the value of land, and how to steal it from others? Dishonest books; books that taught you how to swindle; books that taught you how to make liquor, rifles, armor; books that instilled their readers with a sense of entitlement? And maybe they were religious books after all: there was certainly a god in these pages. A god who taught that if you wanted something you took it, or pretended to ask for it and took it anyway. These were valuable lessons—how the white man lived in a world where there was no negotiation, where he laid out the terms and if you agreed, you became friends. If you refused, he expressed displeasure and sent you home. No matter what you chose, the white man just did what he wanted anyway, in the end.

"Do you know Thomas Paine?"

A voice from the stairs. Tecumseh turned to see a man who could have only been the judge take the last two steps and swallow the lower room completely. Some men were born large; others carried themselves with great bearing. The judge was both: a massive physical presence. He stood well above six feet and had to stoop a little to avoid knocking his head against the crossbeams. His white beard, marked with streaks of silver, was knotted wool. Dressed formally in waistcoat and stockings, his skin was pink around the cheeks as if he'd recently gotten sun. His hands, though, were soft and clean. So were his black-polished shoes.

"I do not read," Tecumseh said.

"Do not?" The judge grinned. "Or cannot?"

They shook hands. The judge's paw absorbed Tecumseh's own. He found himself shuffling to the right and to the left, trying to find some corner of the little room that wasn't consumed by his host's girth. It was like being trapped in an outhouse with a bear.

"We're not much for ceremony out here on the frontier," the judge said. "Shall we eat?"

In the dining room each man sat at his place setting. Whale-bone china with blue and gold trim; spotless cups and heavy cloth napkins; silver that reflected Tecumseh's broad nose and sturdy chin better than his looking glass. The judge seated himself at the head of the table with Tecumseh to his right.

The walls felt very close, then closer, as if someone were turning a crank to contract what space remained on the periphery of the judge's elbows. Or perhaps, Tecumseh thought, the room was shrinking—or they were growing, swelling, getting too big for their chairs. The servant woman entered and poured water. He wished silently for her to open a window. He shifted in his seat as she leaned over him, unsure of the proper manners. He could see down her shirt; he could smell the almonds and honey she had rubbed into her skin. He dropped his napkin, bent to pick it up. He couldn't settle his eyes on any one thing. Pale, severe faces were flattened behind frames and hung on the wall. The charger sparkled and seemed to challenge the ivory gravy boat to a duel. At the far end of the table, a chiseled vase had been stuffed with purple leaves and wispy flowers. He'd never been so uncomfortable.

He reached to touch the quartzite around his neck but did not find it there. Odd that after so many years he still reached for it, still expected to sometimes feel it quiver at the base of his throat. He'd never realized how much he relied on it before he sacrificed it for his brother.

"Cozy?" the judge asked.

Tecumseh swallowed. He leaned on one elbow, tilting away from his host. He needed to speak first or risk being overrun.

"Before we begin," he said, "you should know that I have no intention of signing your treaty."

The judge plucked a wedge of cornbread from the basket. "I'm sorry to hear it."

"I do not want your meal spoiled by unrealistic expectations." He was impressed by how calm his voice sounded, muffled by the square-hewn walls. "I am here as a courtesy to the Shawnee chiefs. Nothing more."

Galloway shrugged his broad shoulders. His jowls wobbled, and the chair joints ground beneath him. He had an honest face, Tecumseh thought. He could see how others might believe they could trust this Kentucky politician, even if he himself could not.

The judge snapped his cornbread in half, scattering crumbs on the tablecloth. "They told me you spoke excellent English. Where did you learn it?"

He looked at his hands. The edges of his nails were black with grime and chewed through. He placed them under the table. "It is something I have always known."

The servant appeared then with her son trailing behind. They delivered soup bowls. Tecumseh put his nose to the dish and inhaled parsnips, apples, and a warm, tingling spice he could not name. He watched Galloway seize his spoon and glide it through the soup, churning his elbow like a mill wheel to deliver the food to his mouth.

"I was a private in Dunmore's War," the judge said. "You're familiar with it?"

Tecumseh named the spice for himself: sumac. "I was only a boy."

"Hard to call it a war, I suppose. Just a series of skirmishes really. But I was there at Point Pleasant." The judge coughed into his napkin, swallowed something unpleasant. "I remember that morning, we planned to move out at sunrise. Just before dawn, a friend and I thought we'd catch ourselves a turkey. Something for the journey. We were sick of the gruel and hardtack the army was feeding us. So we went foraging. And we had ourselves a line on one beast of a bird. We chased him into the underbrush. Really plunged in after it. And I remember, there was this thin fog still clinging to everything, fine as a spider web. And damned if all at once that fog didn't lift, the sun broke through, and we come up short in the face of three-hundred Indian warriors, faces all painted, ready to ambush us."

Tecumseh stopped eating and felt his muscles tense.

The judge went on. "We forgot all about the turkey. My friend took a rifle blast to the chest and fell dead. I ran off, back toward camp. Damn Indians caught us by surprise, no mistake. It took us a long time to get ourselves together. The chaos of interrupted sleep, everyone thinking maybe they were still dreaming. The Indians overran us, and things looked pretty grim."

The judge dug around in the bread basket again until he found a piece of the loaf that seemed a bit more burnt than the others. He dunked this in his soup and swallowed it.

"We made our stand." He spoke with the mush still in his mouth. "We put up makeshift breastworks and fought the savages for quite a while. Quite a while. In fact, now I'm remembering, somebody a bit famous died in that one. Who was he? Some Indian. One of yours I think, a Shawnee. One of your great war chiefs. His name—is gone if I ever knew it. Anyway, a rifle shot slammed him to the ground like the hand of God. And I suppose it was exactly that, in its own way."

It was Tecumseh's father, of course, who the judge was referring to. And he wasn't so naïve to think the judge didn't remember his name. It was part of the game, part of the negotiation.

"Most of the Shawnee chiefs have signed my treaty," the judge said.

"And most Wyandots." Tecumseh laid his spoon aside. "The Miami. The Delaware."

"So I don't actually need your signature, do I? Your chief, Black Hoof, has already signed."

"Black Hoof does not speak for all Shawnee."

"Little Turtle, Blue Jacket." The judge shrugged again for emphasis. "All have signed. Your people believe the chiefs are God's representatives here on Earth."

Tecumseh leapt to his feet—he would not be lectured on Our Creator, not by this so-called judge. "They do not speak for me."

The judge didn't move, but continued spooning soup between his wet lips. Then, as deliberate as raising a hymnal, he slid his napkin from his lap and revealed a coach pistol.

Footsteps then—Tecumseh spun, his hand already dropping to the knife on his belt.

The door swung open. A young woman, not much older than twenty, strode barefoot into the dining room. She was carried upon the airs of a billowing blue and white dress. The dress was clasped at the neck. Her black hair was gathered by a string and draped over one shoulder. If she noticed tension between the men she did not show it. Instead she slipped along the wall and placed a kiss on the judge's cheek. Tecumseh had never seen anything so breathtakingly clean as this woman, whoever she was.

The judge's mistress? He didn't know. She was too young to be his wife. But he couldn't feel his hands. He was overcome with a sensation of being lifted out of himself—he had to grip the table edge to keep himself secured to the ground. It was as if her entrance brought with it the first promise of summer, the first strawberry from the field, a blast of warm air that put hunger and cold behind him. The room expanded very quickly then and he found he could take a full breath for the first time. Her eyes were green jewels.

The judge grunted. "My daughter, Rebecca."

And then he recognized her. Galloway, Rebecca. The Becky from his youth, who had spent a season as a daughter of the Shawnee. Tecumseh bowed his head. He should have introduced himself, but his voice had been swallowed by his heart.

"This is the great Tecumseh," the judge said. "The Panther of the Shawnee. The one I was telling you about."

She acted impressed. "How d'you do?"

Her eyes lingered a moment too long, he thought. Did she recognize him?

"Will you sit?" she said.

He hadn't realized he was still standing.

"We were just discussing the trouble with the Indians," the judge said. "About whether or not Chief Black Hoof speaks for them all, in matters of state."

Tecumseh felt his nose twitch. He glanced at Becky. He kept hearing her voice, the soft vowels and swallowed consonants. *How d'you do?*

"Politics?" She fanned her napkin across her lap. "How ghoulishly boring."

"About that." Tecumseh twisted and untwisted his

own napkin. "Perhaps it would be prudent for you to walk me through the terms of your treaty once more. I am not confident that I fully understand its finer points."

The judge whipped his napkin from beneath his belly and plunged it into his collar. Rebecca sighed, squaring hers on her knee.

"Nothing would make him happier, I'm sure," she said.

But Tecumseh would not look at her—he could not risk even a glance. Sweat rolled down his back. He ate dutifully, eyes lowered. One more glimpse of Rebecca Galloway might cause his chair to sprout wings and launch him through the roof into the evening sky. At any moment, he might take flight.

He remembered nothing of what the judge talked about at dinner. His host blathered at length and without interruption about what was generally referred to as Dunmore's War, more than twenty years ago now. On and on about the role he played and how the war had come to define the territories for the new America. He paused only to inhale more food, heaping story upon story that featured himself as the hero.

Later that night, standing outside his tent, watching the sky turn from pale blue to silver to black, Tecumseh could not remember any of the judge's words because they meant nothing to him. The treaty was nothing, too. All he could think about was Becky, who went by Rebecca now.

There was fear in his gut, and this wasn't something he'd felt before. He kept opening and closing his hands. He thought surely she recognized him, but then maybe not. So many years had passed, and she had been with the Shawnee so short a time.

He ducked inside his tent again and snatched the water pitcher. He dumped its contents and headed up the path toward the house. His body pushed forward even as his mind raised objections. But his feet knew what his heart wanted, and led the way.

She would be asleep, of course. The hour was late. But he needed to try and see her again, to hear her say *good-night*, to ask if she remembered him—and if so, what then? Whatever feelings he had for her long ago came rushing back to him so quickly and with such force it was as if they'd been stored inside his heart all this time, and now, seeing her again had broken loose the dam. His mind was flooded with memories of her, which were also wrapped up in emotions from that time, his first flatboat raid, the rawness from losing Open Door, how he and Rattle were still everything to one another, then. All of this centered around her presence in Chillicothe that summer. She was the hub of that time in his life, a time which had been important, and now he was staying on with her father for who knew how long.

But reaching the door, he couldn't bring himself to knock. Doubt stopped him: he was being too obvious. The ploy was transparent, this errand of needing fresh water. She'd see right through it. But then he wanted her to see through it.

He cursed himself, feeling his resolve wither at the thought of facing her, forced to make conversation. He felt panic, even as the dread of not seeing her made him desperate. More than likely, he reminded himself, the servant would answer. More than likely he wouldn't see Rebecca at all.

He dropped his chin. The pitcher dangled from his fingertips. He turned from the stoop.

"May I help you?"

He spun, knowing her voice before seeing Rebecca Galloway holding open the door with one hand and clutching a blanket around her. The moon was bright. He could see her clearly. Her ears stuck out a little from where she'd tucked her hair behind them.

"I've just come back from the barn," she said. "I was checking the horses. The night may still bring a chill."

How to reply? Words like horses and abstract discomforts meant nothing to him. These were things men had invented for themselves to try and make sense of the world. But they didn't explain this, what he felt. He stood there gaping.

"You're the one they call Tecumseh," she asked.

"I am." He praised himself silently—he'd managed two words. Two syllables.

"My father has trouble with silence. He feels a great compulsion to fill it."

"And yet he owns so many books."

"The books?" Her eyes shone. "The books are mine. It was my one concession for coming north with him. He had to let me bring all of my books."

His tongue was a dead fish in his mouth. He tried to sort out some words to say but found that he could not. He wanted to hand all of his words to her at once and let her select her favorites.

She indicated the water pitcher. "Empty?"

"Yes," he said. "I'm very thirsty."

He wondered at himself, what a hopeless case he was, pleading thirst.

She took the pitcher from him. "Wait here."

The door shut, and she was gone. He stood looking at the chipped white paint, the hasty mortar slopped around the frame. He would wait all night if that's what she required of him. The servant Sabreen would find him here tomorrow when the sun rose. When Rebecca did finally return, he didn't know if it had been minutes or hours.

She passed him a full pitcher. Their hands brushed against one another in the exchange, the knuckles of his forefinger tingling against the veins and ridges on the back of her hand.

"Thank you," he said. There was a long pause. "Well, good night."

He turned from her. He hated himself at that moment. How many romances had been strangled in infancy by those three words—*Well, good night.* Three doomed syllables were all he could manage, he who could hold conversations with himself for hours on the hunt. No one could talk like a Shawnee, and here this Galloway girl had struck him dumb.

But she called him back. "I hope we won't find many cicadas here."

He turned. She was smiling at him, and it was that same smile, full of joy, but that also seemed to challenge him a little. "You do remember."

"Of course."

He swallowed. "I wasn't sure—I knew who you were, the moment you entered the room. But I didn't know, I wasn't confident, you'd remember me. It was so long ago."

"I knew you immediately," she said. "I've been looking forward to your arrival. I think about that summer often."

He nodded, and looked away, and then both of them seemed to be searching for something else to say. His mind was empty. He couldn't find words in either language.

Finally, she asked, "Do you read?"

He held the water pitcher with both hands, close to his chest. "No."

"I can teach you to read."

He bowed, savoring the formality of it, the way he'd seen the pale lords do. "I would like that."

She laughed, her voice trilling. "You needn't bow to me as if I'm a lady. We'll start tomorrow. Then we'll see how ladylike I can be."

Awake that night in his blankets, he considered her prospects. Rebecca Galloway, daughter of a Kentucky judge. Rebecca Galloway, alone with her father on the frontier—

her father and a platoon of American soldiers on loan from the government, to protect the Galloways during negotiations. She didn't go near them.

"Too coarse," she had said at dinner. "Every time I see one of them, they whistle. Is that how they expect to get a girl's attention? Whistlin' to me like I'm a dog of some kind, or a horse?"

Tecumseh thought but didn't say yes, that was exactly what the soldiers thought of her. A piece of flesh, but better than the downtrodden women who trolled the edges of the camp looking for "work." But she also was the apple of her father's eye, a bargaining chip to be married off somewhere proper when the time was right, when it suited him politically. A soldier wouldn't be good enough for his daughter, to say nothing of a Shawnee brave.

But Tecumseh's thoughts—his dreams—were running away with him.

Her prospects were less than if she'd been a "savage," as she still referred to them—some Shawnee women became chiefs. At the very least, Shawnee women shared the work and so shared in the decision-making. Shawnee men honored their wives and treated them as equals. Not like here, among the whites, where the women cleaned the houses and cooked the meals and bore the children and raised them while the men—while the men planned and fought wars, he supposed. He could see how that would take up a lot of their time.

The next morning, she taught him letters of the alphabet. She made different sounds for each and paired the letters in combinations and then made new sounds for those.

She handed him a piece of slate. He held it like something precious. She gripped his right hand. Her touch sent lightning up his arm. She forced a piece of chalk between his fingers. His fingers cramped against the pose she held them in.

She laid the slate piece flat across his lap. "This is how you write."

The chalk scraped and shrieked as she directed it, as he left long, white trails on the stone.

"A," she said. Then, "B."

They were leaning over the slate board. Arm in arm, almost—holding hands, or her hand on top of his, their fingers knotted around the chalk. He risked a glance: her eyes were full of concentration, squinting over the board. Beautiful in her singular devotion to this task, how she'd sworn to teach him to read and write.

In the afternoon, Judge Galloway showed him maps of the Northwest Territory. He drew lines across the maps that divided white territory from Indian. Tecumseh took the quill and drew another line farther east.

"This is where the border was drawn after your Dunmore's War." Tecumseh licked the quill and made the line thicker. "Now you want it here. Tomorrow you want it somewhere here, in Miami country. Too far west for us."

But his host raised his hands and pleaded innocence. "I have the assurances of the U.S. Government. Everything west of here will be Indian land in perpetuity."

Leaning over his slate board, his fingers dusty with chalk, he breathed the same small pocket of air, tasting Rebecca's breath, not so much the fragrance of her breath as the essence, the way he knew she would taste if their lips met. She studied the marks he made and guided his hand. He felt as if all his energy, some whirlwind of feeling, were wrapping itself around them both and cocooning them.

She wiped his board clean. "Try again."

Her breath in his nose; the dry smell of chalk; the ash still lingering from last night's fire. The smell of a book when she opened it—the sweet redolence of the pulp. He gave himself over to it, how quickly the library became his entire world, how it seemed as if the air around him was infused with her, that every breath he took, everything he touched, was somehow hers too.

Sometimes she would be instructing him and studying the book they shared and he would forget about the lesson and watch her, the way her mouth formed the words, how the freckles on her nose and cheeks clustered and then expanded when she smiled, the delicate skin at the top of her ears and the way her ears stuck out a little—she was always tucking her hair behind them.

"Books," she told him, "are the superior art form, in my opinion. Books help you to travel. In a very real way, they help you see the world. They remove you from the suffocating little box of your life—my life, anyway—to live as someone else for a while. To live somewhere else."

He had always thought the English language harsh and ugly sounding, but it was beautiful when she spoke it. Her voice found grace notes and accents he had never known were there.

"And you do it alone, you know," she said. "The way I imagine this book is not the same way you imagine it. Reading is private. I like that about it. Whereas the opera, or the theatre, spell everything out for you, and don't let you imagine anything."

Days turned to a week, ten days, a fortnight. He saw Rebecca each morning for lessons. With the judge, he hid behind rituals. His host took every seventh day off in deference to his god; he called it *Sunday*. Tecumseh did not complain but instead took every seventh day off as well, a day the white man called *Wednesday*. Along with every other Saturday and plenty of holidays too, depending on the shape of the moon and the taste of the wind. The judge knew nothing of the Shawnee—only how to fight them. He feared Tecumseh enough to let him take as much time as he needed. And the Shawnee warrior sometimes cited certain customs and traditions that were foreign to his host. When there wasn't one convenient, he invented one. In order to explain why he could not meet with the judge on a particular day, in order to extend his stay. Wednesdays were for hunting; every other Saturday a day of leisure. Judge Galloway held religious services on Sunday mornings on the narrow front porch of his home.

The drums had started up again. In the field, six drummers and four fife players plodded counter-clockwise around a muddy circle. The drummers flicked their wrists and the drum-heads shook in rolling patterns that unfurled a physical sound. They set Tecumseh's heart pounding. This, below the steady fife melody, piercing and melodious, was undeniably the sound of war. Everything about battle was wrapped up in it: the relentless rhythm, how the tune seemed to reflect on lives that were fated to be sacrificed. These patterned assemblies, the Americans never tired of them.

Tecumseh snapped his tent-flap closed. His time here had let him observe—and hear—the ceremony and routine of the American military. The fife and drum corps played when the army woke; they signaled when they should go to bed. They announced each meal, and told the company when to gather in the yard, and they played other times too. They never quit. As if, collectively, they might forget to do these things unless the instruments reminded them.

The day was fading, but Tecumseh felt restless. He couldn't go and see Rebecca, not without raising suspicion. But he couldn't suffer the clamor from the army camp a moment longer. Outside, the music stopped. A man barked orders. There was the crunch of rifles being shouldered, of men straightening themselves for review. Tecumseh took a breath, hoping the silence would endure, but the man cried out again and the soldiers shouted back and the music returned.

He hurried from his tent, across the fields and into the forest. There was a creek, he knew, and he thought to follow the creek and clear his mind—to be outside without books or lessons, to feel wind on his cheek. To be away from the army camp and its pollution. He found water and walked along it, pulling leaves from their branches and setting them to drift. Before long he thought he could almost be back in Chillicothe, at Massie's Creek, looking forward to supper with his mother and Rattle, who, if he wasn't too drunk, might perform some sleight of hand to make them laugh.

"Don't feel lonesome, boy," a voice said. "Your old friend Jack has come to see you."

Further up the bank, Crazy Jack knelt beside a stash of ginseng roots. Whether by coincidence or some plan, Tecumseh didn't know.

"An incredible harvest," the traveler said as he approached. "Some of these must be thirty years old."

The tubers were thick, their tendrils long. Collected, they looked like broken fingers and knotted hair. Crazy Jack rinsed each root and rubbed away the soil marks until the skin was polished white.

"Found them not a hundred paces from here. Had to be careful not to pick too many."

By now, Tecumseh was accustomed to finding Crazy Jack suddenly and when he least expected it. In mundane moments such as this one, especially. His appearing now might have been predicted, had Tecumseh thought about it. He was not surprised. The little man wove in and out of his life, inquiring about this matter or that, making idle chatter, but not, as a rule, offering much counsel. And he'd never offered to return the pawawka token. Tecumseh wouldn't mention it though. To do so would be weak. And after so many years, he was still unsure about the true nature of their relationship. There was nothing to compare it to.

He picked up one of the tubers. The forked root had a human shape, four long wisps flailing from a knobby, central tube. "You must have twenty pounds of ginseng here."

"I'm going to need help carrying it out." Crazy Jack rubbed his chin. "Would the judge let me dry these in his barn?"

"The judge hasn't warmed up to me yet."

"You're an acquired taste."

"Am I?"

Crazy Jack shrugged, and went back to cleaning the roots. The Shawnee considered them medicine. Their human shape meant they were good for the entire body. Knotted Pine, the shaman, ground ginseng in a mortar for tea.

"How about the girl?" the traveler asked. "You two are close."

"I don't know what we are," Tecumseh said. "I am beginning to think I'm nothing more than her pupil."

Crazy Jack snapped a plug from a smaller root and offered it. "When you are anticipating the moment of romance, eat this."

"Romance?" He eyed the strange plant. He put his tongue to it once, gently. There was a fresh smell. Its skin was slick. "There are…complications."

"Nonsense." Crazy Jack dunked a ginseng root in water and shook it. "All the parts on a white woman work just like the parts on a squaw. I don't see any reason for you to be conflicted about this."

But Tecumseh had plenty of reasons. Their skin color, for one—they did not match. There were also the awesome and frightening and wildly unpredictable emotions he felt from one moment to the next. And there was the memory of Chiksika and the memory of his father, and the fact that he feared betraying their honor were he to ever act on what he felt for this woman, Rebecca Galloway.

"Although," here Crazy Jack paused and made eye contact, "I should tell you, there's no one here you can trust. Not the girl, and not her father. You're on your own, son. Don't forget."

It wasn't complicated in the end. There was a window open in the library. Somehow, that's all Tecumseh could think about. The window was open and there was someone outside—the servant woman picking herbs or a soldier sneaking off to smoke behind the house. He could smell tobacco burning. It cut through the clean, hyacinth scent of Rebecca's hair.

They kissed. Their hands roamed freely over one another, and moved naturally, as if their hands had only been waiting, patiently, to explore one another's contours and the places no one else had ever touched. The slate fell, the chalk crushed to powder somewhere on the settee, beneath their tangled limbs. He kicked a short stack of books from the couch to the floor. Her lips were eager and pliable, and he knew for certain what his body had long suspected: he had been in love with this woman since he was a boy.

But there was someone outside the window, and then there were two people talking about the weather, a man and woman, and how the judge was out in the fields surveying land. Tecumseh heard these things through the open window as his touch left white-dust fingerprints on Rebecca's dress. His hands unbuttoned the clasps as she yanked his shirt over his head and placed the flats of her hands against him. He wrapped his lips around one pink nipple, her breasts in his hands, and he put his lips to one and then the other, not wanting the left to be jealous of the right, teasing them rigid with his teeth.

The judge argued he did not need Tecumseh's signature at all. The other Shawnee chiefs had signed the treaty; he was merely extending a courtesy, a gesture of goodwill because, as a Christian man, he did not want to see any more killing—not of Indians and certainly not of whites.

"No," Tecumseh said. "You invited me here because you are afraid of me. You know that I have taken the lives of many pale skins. You know that although I am not a chief, the Shawnee live in a state of war. That I command a great army.

"You white men hide behind pieces of paper that you know we cannot read. You make promises but keep them only so long as they're convenient. Then you break your promises, and when we complain, you write up a new treaty with worse terms.

"So you are right. You do not need my signature. Your treaty is valid without it. But you do need my signature if you ever want peace."

He was growing bold. He was surprised at his ability to tell the judge what he felt. He was surprised to find that although the judge feared the Shawnee, Tecumseh did not fear him.

His pants were off, and she was fussing with the hem of her blue linen dress, hoisting it above her waist. He glimpsed the black hair between her thighs before she pulled him toward her and they fell back along the settee, one of her pale legs tossed over the maple-trimmed back. She still wore her boots.

He watched in the mirror, how she offered herself to him. How her hands pulled him close; how he was lifted bare-chested onto her; how the honeycomb light through the open window fell across them. He entered her, pushing as deep as he could go. Her eyes flashed, like emeralds catching firelight, and she took all of him—clenching, gasping.

"You're beautiful," she told him. She touched his nose, his ear, his hair. "You're beautiful. You're beautiful. Beautiful."

They lay in the lengthening shadows, half-clothed, enjoying the newness of their bodies pressed together. She traced the outline of his neck with her fingertip; he touched behind her knees, the two hard lines of cartilage there. They held their arms side by side in the dying light and compared the color of their skin, his so dark and hers pale. They still had not moved to close the window. They listened to the first crickets.

"Why did you come here?" he asked her.

"Father needed someone to help," she said.

"But your mother did not. Or your sisters."

"The rest of my family has no taste for adventure."

"Is that what this is?" He kissed her hair. "You've come to the frontier for a taste of that great American magic?"

She shifted in his arms, buried her face in his chest. Then she looked up at him, mischievous. "They say there isn't any magic left."

"Not true." Tecumseh pulled her close. "You just have to know where to look for it."

The judge invited him to walk the fields. Trees had been cleared. The land was ready for settlers. With Tecumseh, the judge was taking a different tack, more human somehow, more diffident, more familiar. He had been there six weeks.

"I'm going to stay on here after you and I are finished." The judge walked with his hands clasped behind him, putting on the airs of an aristocrat. "I'm going to build something grand. A city to rival the cities of the East."

Tecumseh nodded. "This land north of the river is fertile. It will support a large population."

"The main avenue here." The judge spread his arms and gestured right and then left. "A bank. A trading post. The mayor's mansion, of course."

Tecumseh could tell he was drunk with the vision of his city-to-be. He believed it was his calling—the pinnacle of his life's work. Men could be so grand. The judge thought he was the first human to walk this acreage, that he had found it all on his own. Tecumseh resented his thrill of discovery. The judge did not deserve it. He hadn't found anything. He had merely stumbled upon a good piece of land that the Shawnee had thrived on for centuries. And yet it was a special gift of the Americans that they considered nothing found until they found it for themselves. It was their one legacy.

"I am searching for the best description." Tecumseh squinted against the sun. "At first, I thought the whites were like ants. Industrious as insects that build their houses deep underground. Wasting nothing."

"And what do you think now?" the judge asked.

"You are not like ants. In truth, you are like mold."

The judge laughed. "Mold? Are you sure that's the word you're looking for?"

"Yes." Tecumseh set his jaw. "Mildew. Mold needs a host to thrive, and sucks life out of its host until it crumbles, rotted. Instead of preserving or nurturing that which gives you life, you consume it and move on." He closed his eyes. He inhaled the early summer fragrances of grass and sweat. "This place will be no different. You will consume it too."

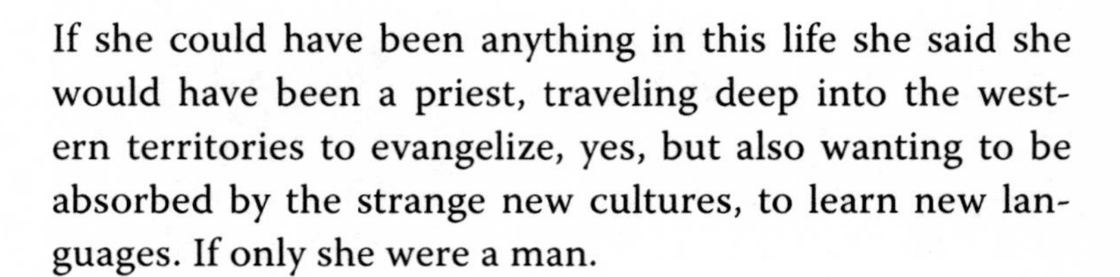

If she could have been anything in this life she said she would have been a priest, traveling deep into the western territories to evangelize, yes, but also wanting to be absorbed by the strange new cultures, to learn new languages. If only she were a man.

"For a while I believed that if I learned to do things as well as any man, I'd be granted the same privileges." They stood in an alcove on the bottom floor of the house. There were shelves with many colorful candles; there were framed images of white men in robes. Men she referred to as *saints*. There was a large metal cross and smaller wooden crosses mixed in with the candles. He understood the Galloways considered this room sacred somehow. "You know, run faster, shoot farther, learn to ride—all those things I tried to do better than the boys my age. But I know now that will never be. They'll never consider me equal."

He realized this was something they shared. That peace between the Americans and the tribes made it seem as if they were equals. But the whites would never truly see it that way. The Shawnee would never be considered equal, any more than women would one day be allowed to be priests.

"This is where you worship your god?" he asked.

There was incense burning. A thin trail of smoke rising from a glass vessel. The smell was spicy but comforting.

She dipped her fingers in a water bowl and crossed herself. "Yes."

"Odd."

"Oh?" She shot him a playful look. "And where do you worship your god?"

He gestured toward the door, toward the wall. Meaning here. Or there. Everywhere.

"All that land, who do you think owns it?" she asked him.

He shrugged. "Your father would answer differently than I."

"There is a right answer," she said. "The answer is this: no one owns it. My father calls himself a Christian, but he doesn't understand. Jesus never owned property. In fact, he persuaded his followers to give theirs away. But my father, all he does is collect. Purchase."

"Consume," Tecumseh said.

She shivered, despite the stuffiness of the cabin, the trapped heat. "It doesn't strike me as very Christian, is all."

When they met each day for lessons, they closed the library door but kept the window open, as if the open window showed the world they had nothing to hide. It was not, of course, the world that needed convincing, but Judge Galloway. They feared what he might do if he found out. With the door shut and no breeze through the window, the house so quiet Tecumseh could hear mice scurrying beneath the floorboards, sweat beaded down the center of his back as he examined the day's lesson plans, or tried to. She would read to him, enunciating each word.

But all he could think about was how much he wanted to taste her again, to inhale the heat of her, to feel her hair against his tongue, her lips pressing against his chest. The lessons never lasted long. Their lovemaking retreated from its initial, primal urgency into something more gentle and probing but no less eager.

Finding her one morning—surely she had lost track of time—by following the sound of her voice around back of the house, moving quietly until he could listen from the other side of the bath stall:

It was na sae in the Highland hills
Och on, och on, och rie!
Nae woman in the country wide
Sae happy then as me

And understanding only every other word, it seemed. Phrases such as *na sae* were unfamiliar to him, another language perhaps? But the melody was haunting. And it seemed familiar somehow. A memory tied to it, some distant surge of desire. Rebecca's voice climbed and dipped and climbed and then dropped from some great height into something that sounded like sorrow. Tecumseh followed the story anyway—the story of a brave man, Donald, who'd gone off to war, leaving her behind:

I was the happiest of a' the clan
Sair, sair, may I repine
For Donald was the brawest man
And Donald he was mine

He followed the sound of her voice to where the washbasin sat behind two plank walls. He breathed in and peered around the side: Rebecca knelt with her back to him, dipping a cloth into a water bucket. Her shift was rolled down past her shoulders, and she took the wet cloth and wiped the back of her neck, behind her ears, down her arms to the wrists, leaving her skin glistening. He was back at the riverbank in Chillicothe watching Becky wash to this same song:

Och on, Och on, O Donald O!
Och on, och on, och rie!
Nae woman in this whole world wide
Sae wretched now as me

It was as if she were unlocking him: her hands opened pleasurable parts of his body that he had not known were there—that he had not even imagined. With a touch—to his knee, to his earlobe—he felt his body flood with need, a rush of blood to his groin, a cool wash inside his head. He was, as in the play she read to him, a "votary to fond desire." And this sensual opening outward was somehow part of the English words he was learning to recognize on the page. To understand that *votary* meant "one who is bound by a religious vow" was one thing. To be able to say the word and hear it and to use it in context—that was communication.

But then to learn by Rebecca's careful instruction that this word had a shape, that the letter *v* meant his mouth made the sound at the beginning of the word *votary*, and to admire the comely shape of the *o* and *a*, separated by the stern, proud *t*, and the word itself finished off by a playful *ry*, making it seem not only a noun—something that acted—but also a verb—the action itself. It was a beautiful word. *Votary*. It was his favorite now.

And he was hers, and she was his, and he supplicated to her lessons each day as her devoted worshipper. "If I am your votary, and you are mine, then we are *votaries* to one another," she whispered, using the backs of her fingers against his neck. "I am a votarist. You are mine." All the while his body—no, deeper than his body, his skin, his muscles, his blood—responded to her touch.

And sometimes it took only her voice to summon that now familiar tidal wave of longing, the irresistible urge to take her, or have her take him, to be taken by one another...there was a word for that, there had to be, and he wondered what it was, what shape it might take, or how in the same way her touch unpeeled from him layer after layer of flesh and bone and also the barriers he had built around himself in order to survive, each word had layers of meaning, too—there was the word's flesh, what most people meant when they used the word, but there were other meanings. How *thirst* meant "a craving, especially for liquid," but could also mean "a strong desire for success," or *ambition*.

The judge was hosting a dinner party for some important men from Philadelphia. The house was suddenly swarming with servants—they seemed to materialize out of the fields, like cicadas hatching. When Tecumseh arrived for his lesson, he and Rebecca found no privacy. In every room the staff was polishing silver or rooting through storage crates or arranging flowers on every available flat surface.

"This is not an environment conducive to learning," Rebecca declared, loud enough for the house to hear.

She announced to Sabreen that they were going outside to study. She said fresh air would bring perspective to that day's lesson, something she called *English Sonnets*. She proclaimed the house was a circus, unfit for schooling. And as easily as that they were out the front door, slate and chalk and a stack of books tucked beneath their arms. They crossed the field and there was no one to follow them, no chaperone, everyone absorbed in preparations for dinner. Soon they had claimed the trees, and soon they had slipped beneath the canopy and then could no longer be seen from the house.

Tecumseh reached for her. Rebecca squirmed from his grasp and dashed deeper into the woods.

The forest floor was covered in bright green carpet. The trees were dense. In the shade, sweat cooled on their arms and legs. For more than two months now during his stay at the Galloway home, Tecumseh had carried the tension of the negotiations and of spending so much time between four walls, beneath rafters and a roof. This tension now flittered away, as if his mind could suddenly relax again and stretch and play in the branches overhead.

He caught Rebecca by the wrist. She laughed and pulled him into her.

"I did not know your people worshipped the sun," he said. It was something he'd been meaning to ask her about.

"Worship the sun?" She blew a wayward strand of hair from her face. "What gives you that idea?"

"The day you keep as holy—when you gather to worship your god. Is it not the sun's day?"

She kissed him on the cheek. "You have it partly right."

But she did not explain the rest. Instead she took his hand and led him deeper into the woods. They headed downhill, away from the sun. Shagbark and sycamore became clusters of pine. They came into a circular enclave, cleared but for two fallen trees. She dashed into this empty ring and turned to him and dropped her dress from her shoulders. Her bare flesh was a shocking and irresistible thing beneath the pines.

They made love loudly, with only the birds to hear them. She moaned as he put his lips to the place between her legs and arched her back and pushed against him as if to drive his tongue deeper. The salt-taste of her rose in his nostrils and soon she was shouting out. He had never seen her like this—not in the serious air of the Galloway home. He continued his duty, stroking and urging her on, but it was also terrifying how the ecstasy consumed her, how it seemed to wrap them both up in a spiraling storm.

When they had finished, the woods seemed quieter than before. They lay on their backs and pressed their heads together and clasped hands and arranged their fingers into different shapes: a church, a mouth, a rabbit.

"Could you live here, d'you think?" she asked him. "Among us, I mean."

He exhaled slowly. "Wear an ascot? Go to church?"

"You wouldn't have to go to church."

"No," he said. "I would lose the respect of my people."

Although he held her, it was as if he watched her recede from him until she was a great distance away. He realized then what she meant.

"Do you think you could live among my people?" he asked.

She tried to meet his flippancy. "Live in a teepee? Dress squirrels each night for dinner?"

They were both silent then for a long time.

"No," she finally said. "I don't see myself ever being part of that world."

"I think you made him angry, comparing him to mold," Crazy Jack said.

The traveler now had thirty or forty pounds of dried ginseng packed into saddle bags. He was strapping them to his horse, first one side, then the other. He planned to sell the ginseng in the many Shawnee villages.

"He shouldn't be angry about that," Tecumseh said. "If he thought about it, even for a moment, he would see that it was true."

Crazy Jack probed the recesses of his mouth with his finger. "He's been patient. I would have sent you home long ago."

"He is afraid of me," Tecumseh said. "He will let me stay here as long as he thinks we are making progress in our negotiations."

"And how much longer, exactly, do you plan to keep up this charade?"

What Tecumseh thought but didn't say was that he would stay as long as it took to convince Rebecca to return with him to Chillicothe.

Crazy Jack had a handkerchief filled with red berries. He tied the corners of the handkerchief and tucked the bundle into the waistline of his trousers. The red berries, he said, were the ginseng seeds. He had a place in mind, back home, where they might do well.

"Agriculture," the traveler winked and snapped his reins. "That's the future."

She was not waiting for him on the porch the next morning. Most days, he found her perched on the steps, book in hand, unable to keep herself from smiling as he came up the walk and stood at the foot of the stairs. Arms wrapped around her knees looking down at him. Her eyes seeming to weigh the carnal against the intellectual, and whether there might be time for both.

But she was not there this morning, and she was not

in the front room when he let himself in.

It surprised him how carelessly he opened the door and crossed the threshold. When he had first arrived, the house felt small and formal and stifling. The stove pipe that rattled in the wind; the odd angle of the door frame between the dining room and library; all those obdurate books. And now? Learning to read hadn't taught him to love these objects. Practically, he saw little value in them. Heavy, immovable, they weighed down their owners with knowledge. He couldn't wait to be free of their exhausting gravity.

Or so he told himself. There was a harder truth. One that he resisted. He was getting accustomed to this life, to herbal tea served on patterned china. To mutton. To the fragrance of wood chips in the stove. To having a pitcher of water an arm's reach away at all times, even at night, in bed—to beds. To rope-bound mattresses filled with straw. To the harsh Americanisms made beautiful by her voice, and the secret thrill of recognizing their patterns on the page.

There was a half-inch of fat now around his mid-section that wasn't there when he arrived. He had not thought about the hunt in weeks. He had not fired an arrow or spun his tomahawk or even ridden his horse, really, since before that. At home they would be making preparations for the harvest.

Had anyone asked, he would have said, "Of course I am miserable here. Cooped up inside all day hidden from the sky and from the love of Our Creator." He would have said he could not wait to return to Chillicothe, to his people, to their familiar ways. But the truth was murkier than that. Part of him was adjusting to the Galloway home just fine.

He found Rebecca in the library. "Cock a doodle do! What is my dame to do?"

They had been working on this lesson the previous day; he had been practicing. He delivered it in his best Queen's English, meaning it to be funny.

Rebecca stood near the settee. She turned toward his voice. Only when he was fully inside the room did he see the judge in the far corner, one elbow propped on a bookshelf, cigar in hand.

Tecumseh caught himself. He flushed with shame. Rebecca stepped aside to reveal a second man, seated on the couch with one leg crossed over his other, holding a teacup and saucer. He was Tecumseh's age. He wore white pantaloons and a blue army coat. His black hat was propped on the arm of the settee.

Rebecca curtsied, formally, and turned a circle through the room to stand behind the couch, off the guest's shoulder. Her meaning was clear: Tecumseh was not to act overly familiar toward her. There was something at work in the room, something he couldn't quite name.

"Tecumseh." The judge's voice boomed. "I'd like you to meet Lieutenant William Henry Harrison, of Virginia."

Tecumseh brought his heels together and gave a sort of awkward half-bow that also seemed a kind of salute. He had no idea what the protocol was.

"Charmed, I'm sure." The lieutenant made no move to stand but offered a slight tip of his saucer before he sipped.

"Tecumseh has been staying on with us. How many weeks?"

"Fourteen," Tecumseh said.

"As we...negotiate." The judge stamped out his cigar. "You see, I'm trying to get his mark on a little piece of paper, but he doesn't seem to want to give it to me."

Tecumseh looked at Rebecca, hoping to catch her eye—eager for some recognition or acknowledgement of what they shared. But her face was blank as the slate board they wrote his lessons on. This was some new side of her, all business. And she was beautiful as she performed her duty. It was her birthright, having been born the daughter of a politician.

"Lieutenant Harrison is being transferred to the Indiana Territory," she said.

"He serves as *aide-de-camp* to General Wayne," her father added.

Harrison sniffed. "So we have something in common."

"And what is that?" Tecumseh was looking at his shoes: he did not know what this meant, *aide-de-camp*.

"It appears both of us will be moving soon."

So that was what this was—another negotiating tactic by the judge. "The Shawnee have not decided to give up Chillicothe."

"They don't have to decide anything." Harrison examined his empty teacup and set it aside. "The writing, as they say, is on the wall. You can't possibly stay now that the treaty has been signed. You won't have a square acre left to piss on."

Tecumseh searched for the word: this Harrison was a bit of a *prick*, wasn't he? His manners suggested someone who had been raised proper. A slight drawl on certain accented syllables—refined Virginia. Preening on the settee with one leg draped across the other, smirking. His lips were narrow and slick. His nose was hooked, so in his features there was something of a trout snared by olfactory bait.

There was a long silence. Then the judge laughed about something quietly, to himself. Soon Harrison laughed too, lightly at first, then heartier. Tecumseh didn't know what was so funny. Both men were laughing from the belly, and he felt sure they were laughing at him, but for what he didn't know. He reached up and touched his nose—quickly—and wiped the corners of his mouth. He glanced down: all his clothes appeared to be in order.

"It's your expression," the judge wheezed. "Not a thing you can do about it, of course. It just struck me."

Rebecca caught Tecumseh's eye then. She mouthed the words, "Just go."

"Lieutenant Harrison." Tecumseh straightened. "What brings you to the Galloway home?"

The laughter trickled. Harrison shook his head slowly, feigning sadness. His nose the tired tolling of a clapper. "There are drawbacks to a life of service that leave me little time for company as fine as Ms. Galloway's. I am left no time—no time at all, really—for those quaint customs society still allows a man and woman of a certain age. That is, courtship. Which is how one gets to be as old as I am and finds himself still a bachelor. I would prefer, of course, to settle down."

Tecumseh had only been partly right. His presence was amusing to them not because of the treaty but because the judge suspected something innocent, a crush perhaps, and they found great humor in the idea that a Shawnee brave might consider himself a suitor. The judge, of course, had no idea the extent of his daughter's relationship with Tecumseh. And this was why Rebecca did not want him here. Tecumseh had interrupted a chaperoned affair.

He kept his eyes cold and unfeeling, his expression as empty as hers, as if he were negotiating the price of flour. She was looking at him too, frustrated in her attempts to read him. She was most likely wondering what sort of game this was. Good. Let her wonder.

"This woman would make a fine wife," Tecumseh said, as if the matter were suddenly settled. He kept his pronunciations stiff and formal, meeting the men's expectations of him. "She has thick hands that will be good for working the fields. Her hips are wide. She will no doubt bear you many children. And she is plain enough so as not to draw the eye of other men. She will be faithful to you, that is certain."

Harrison roared with laughter—he couldn't help himself. Rebecca was ashen. Tecumseh smiled, satisfied.

"Child-bearing hips," the judge sighed. "A Galloway family curse."

"I agree with what you say." Harrison caught his breath. "But that is not how our people live."

The judge cuffed his shoulder and leaned over the

back of the couch. "This is what I've been telling you. The savages are far behind us in many ways."

"Rebecca will not be working in a field." Harrison spoke to him now as if instructing a child. "Not like your squaws do. She deserves to be kept like a rose. She is a flower. I intend to keep her pressed firmly beneath glass. She'll want for nothing, work for nothing, raise our brood." At this he lifted his damp wrist and Rebecca moved for it, took his hand. "I will keep her in the manner of a society woman. I intend to govern one day, and I will need her by my side."

Tecumseh swallowed something huge—a peach pit, a small rodent. "She will no doubt take to that lifestyle quite well."

Harrison grinned. "Then we agree on one thing, anyway."

"Because of the books," Tecumseh said. "She always wants to stay indoors with her books. They are your only competition, Lieutenant."

The men laughed.

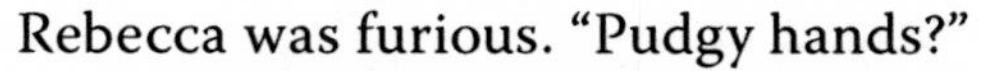

Rebecca was furious. "Pudgy hands?"

Tecumseh found her behind the barn. A kettle was going over an open fire. The air reeked of boiled animal fat.

"Thick hands," he told her. "I said you had thick hands."

Somehow he had escaped the library, wriggled free of the judge and Lieutenant Harrison. He had escaped with all of his parts intact. Or, he had at least made it out the door carrying all the broken pieces of himself that had scattered when his heart exploded like a mortar shell.

Now Harrison was gone, along with the judge. Surveying land to the west. Tecumseh had not seen Rebecca for three days.

"And what was your impression of William Henry Harrison?" she asked him sharply.

"He does not fear Indians the way some do."

She stirred the pot with a long, wooden spoon. She used both hands. Crows circled, cackling. He counted thirty at least. Behind them, he noticed the color of the sky, a sickly yellow. Black clouds framed the birds against the sallow canvas.

"And what was your impression?" he asked her.

"A gentleman." She shot back. "At least his fingernails are clean."

Tecumseh knew she had her role to play, just as he did. But he was finding it hard to think straight. His head was alternately besieged by rage and hopelessness, the rage returning as he remembered her reaching for Harrison's hand.

"A man as pretty as he should keep his fingernails clean," he said. "His vanity is great."

She stalked away from him. He followed her into the shed. Inside was an ash hopper. She scooped water from a bucket and ladled it over the ashes collected at the top of the shoot. Lye dripped steadily through a spout into a bucket below.

He saw it clearly now. Perhaps he had grown accustomed to living in the white man's world, but they would never allow him to settle here. He would never have what Harrison and the judge shared: a code of conduct, a history, a common upbringing that framed every reference and made them trust one another instantly. Tecumseh would always be an outsider. And he would rather hurl himself from a cliff than live his life in a hopeless attempt to disprove that singular truth.

"Harrison will be governor one day." She went outside again; he followed. Fat drops of rain had begun to fall. "He is a born politician. A war hero. What are you compared to that?"

She was only lashing out at him, like a cornered snake.

"There is peace now," he said. "And peace makes the white man grow fat."

"There will be war again."

"Of course," he said. "Because peace is what men like Harrison promise with one hand while stealing our land with the other."

"But war is bad for us," she said. "For you and I."

She reached for the spoon again. He grabbed her arm. "I will never leave you."

"You are always leaving me," she said. "You're leaving me even as you're standing here."

He shoved his hands inside her petticoat and grasped the eyelash-thin shift, groping the curves of her breasts and hips. But she pushed him off.

"I don't exist only for you to paw at your leisure," she said. "Now leave me alone. I've work to do."

It was raining now, a steady rush from the sky. She headed toward the house. Tecumseh followed. Thunder rolled in the not-too-distant trees as they entered the front room and shut the door behind them.

"What have I said?" he asked.

She turned on him. "Shame on you. Asking me what I think of William Henry Harrison and 'what kind of man is he.' Like this is some kind of game to you, as if all of us are just playacting. But I'm tired of living in two worlds. I feel like I'm being pulled apart at the wrists. So I won't tell you anything more about him. Don't think I don't know what this means: that you'll be departing soon, abandoning me here."

Tecumseh felt dressed as any turkey—denuded and de-feathered. "I understand this feeling. Of being caught between two worlds."

"How could you?" she asked. "You've never made a concession in your life. You're not as conflicted as all that."

"Then come with me." He reached for her hand, but she recoiled. "Come with me to Chillicothe, and then to wherever we go."

"Why would I?" Her eyes looked out at him from two inky wells. "You don't even have a home. Is it your plan for me to wander? Like Moses and the Jews?"

"Your home is with me."

"Why would I trust a savage?"

"Because I love you."

They looked at one another. Both of them had clenched fists. Both were breathing heavily. There was nothing to say.

Sabreen appeared then with her son and two of the field hands. "This storm is bad, ma'am." She held the boys close to her. "We're going down to the cellar."

Tecumseh was aware then of the rain on the roof and against the windows. He'd been shouting to be heard over it, the steady roar like waves against a beach. He went to the nearest window and looked out. The sky was dark, and clouds seemed to be turning swiftly back in on themselves, curling.

"Go," Rebecca told them. "We'll be down directly."

Sabreen guided the children outside and, flinching against the heavy fall of rain, scampered for the cellar door and disappeared through it. Then it was only Tecumseh and Rebecca alone in the house.

"You love me." She stood looking at him, hands on hips.

He dropped the curtain. "I do love you."

"If you love me, prove it."

She threw open the door, or it was yanked open by the wind. She steadied herself with both hands against the doorframe and stumbled into the yard. Chasing her to the entrance, Tecumseh shielded his face against the spray. He could see the peak of the barn and the weathervane, a copper dove, spinning so quickly he could not tell its tail from the olive branch it carried in its beak. Twenty feet from the front stoop, Rebecca stood covering her face and trying to look back at the house.

"You say you love me?" she shouted. "Come and get me!"

Lightning split the sky from cloud to grass. The air felt like some living thing as Tecumseh clawed his way through it, toward her. It was not dark as night: it was dark as only a storm such as this one could be. Dim, but also everything infused with yellow light. Small dirt clouds kicked up and were quickly tamped down by the air. He felt like he could smell the rain and whatever it was that caused the lightning. There was a spark to it.

He was halfway to her when he looked up and saw it clearly bearing down from behind the barn: a funnel cloud, black and heading for the house. This was why the Shawnee kept the Eternal Flame. It was their sacred bond with the Cyclone Man. Tecumseh did not fear him. But he also did not wish to test him.

He covered the rest of the distance between them as lightning flashed again and somewhere behind the barn a tree—an entire tree, roots and all—went sailing up over the eaves, end over end, into the clouds. Rebecca's back was turned, but she must have heard it. She spun and saw the tree fly as if taken up by a great hand. She fell to her knees and Tecumseh was there to catch her.

"Cellar!" He shouted into her ear. "Move your feet!"

But she wouldn't, or she was physically unable. The air was being sucked past them in the direction of the funnel cloud. He felt a great pull on his body and had to dig his heels into the ground to avoid sliding toward it. He scooped Rebecca into his arms and it seemed she was barely breathing. Unconscious from shock.

Carrying her now, he ran for the cellar door. His vision

narrowed until it focused only on the doors and their iron handles. Debris, caught up in the wind, bit and kicked his skin. Shutters pulled free of the house and were whisked away. He could only hear the relentless drumming of rain that seemed to cover all registers of sound. He had never been more aware of the frailty of his own body.

He made the cellar. He slung Rebecca to the ground. He pounded on the wooden doors until they leapt beneath his fists. But they did not open. He saw the funnel cloud above them. The yard was gone. It was only cloud. He beat the cellar doors. He screamed for those who were safe below. He kicked, and shouted, but no one came, and in the end, he could not blame them.

Birds. He could hear them. Or one bird, chirping. He opened an eye. A male cardinal preened on the shingles above the front door of the Galloway home.

He closed his eye again.

The house was still standing.

Something else: he still had his hearing, and his sight—in one eye, at least.

That was two somethings.

He was alive.

Still with eyes closed he wiggled his toes. He counted his fingers. He was on his stomach; he propped himself up now on his elbows and only then, when he was fairly certain he was alive and intact, did he open both eyes fully.

He was in a wagon, the one the field hands used to cart goods back and forth. There was a thick layer of hay beneath him. He spit some out, wiping his mouth. He couldn't see over the sides. When he sat up, he felt dizzy.

But for the shutters, the house appeared untouched. Across the yard, the barn was missing half its roof. Its doors were gone. Chickens and two goats and a pig scampered about, pecking, rooting. The ground was mud and tree limbs, but also bits of shingle and wood shavings and tattered cloth.

"Tecumseh."

He turned. Rebecca was beside him. She lay looking up at him. It was as if they had made their bed here and were now just waking up.

Neither of them hesitated. It was some undefinable elation they both felt then, coming to amidst the wreckage of that devil wind. He reached for her and she for him and his mouth met hers and their tongues wrapped around one another as they embraced.

"Don't you see?" she gasped. "This is what you were meant for."

"Quiet." He clutched her breasts, and her body arched toward him, straining for him beneath his hands.

"We survived because of your god," she said. "Your Creator is the reason we're still here."

He spun her onto her stomach. He hiked her shift around her waist and buried his teeth in her flesh. He held himself with one hand and with his other braced against the wagon wall. She gripped the wagon to steady them and groaned as he pushed into her.

His body met hers. The pace was quick. It seemed to be what they both wanted. It seemed the only logical response. Both of them filled with fear but also disbelief. They had survived.

There were times for making love.

This was not one of those times.

Her head was bowed. He clutched a fistful of her black hair. Her body shuddered, then again. He looked up: the front door of the house was open. On the threshold stood the servant boy, the son of the Negro woman, in torn britches, wearing no shirt. He was watching them, for how long Tecumseh didn't know. He didn't care. Rebecca writhed against him. He had to hold her around the waist to stay inside of her. She put her hand over his. She looked back at him, her eyes two green flames. Tecumseh focused on the house again. The boy was gone.

Tecumseh too—exploding against her, both of them crumbling in the hay after, breathless.

"The boy." He was nearly choking. "I think he saw."

"Who?"

"Sabreen's son."

Rebecca laughed and kissed him hard on the lips. "I don't think that boy can even speak."

"But if he tells—"

"Don't worry, Romeo." She cooed to him. "He won't."

"A miracle." The judge went room to room, inventorying all that had not, after all, been lost. "The very hand of God spared our house, our lives. It is His will to see this city built."

On this, Tecumseh agreed. Our Creator had spared the house and the lives within. Because of an ancient pact between Cyclone Man and the Keepers of the Eternal Flame. For no other reason had they lived.

He paced the distance to the army camp but found it abandoned. There were smoldering, circular trenches in the earth where the soldiers had made their fire pits. There were picket lines and toppled earthbags and the detritus of human waste. But the platoon itself was gone.

Luck or chance, he would not use these words to describe what had happened to him. He did not believe in them. They were words made up by those who could not grasp success for themselves. That the world did or did not sometimes turn against him—this was not something he ever considered. And wouldn't now. Despite knowing how unlikely the storm had been. Despite not remembering quite how it was he ended up in the wagon with Rebecca beside him.

He had been pounding on the cellar door and realized, with certainty, that no one was going to rescue them. All around had been the roaring wind and the hard rain and the sickly light and then suddenly it was cool and dark and still and dry. The rest, before he woke, was blank.

The army had moved on. Scared, no doubt, by the devil wind. He doubted the judge would be swayed. Protected or not, with Tecumseh's signature—or not—he had planted his massive feet with an eye toward staying on.

He heard then footsteps moving quickly through the grass. He slipped his knife from his belt and crouched, listening. In a moment, the servant boy appeared at the edge of the field, trembling from the autumn chill or simply from fear.

"What do you want?" Tecumseh growled.

The boy stammered. "The judge requests your presence."

So he could talk, after all. Behind him, the sky was turning pitch. The fields and woods and even the house in the distance were melting into a soupy gray. It seemed not a single lamp was lit.

"Tell your judge that Tecumseh sleeps," he said, "and that I will visit him in the morning."

He turned, dismissing the boy, but the servant grabbed his shoulder. His eyes were wide. He was holding something behind his back.

"Show me," Tecumseh said.

The boy uncurled his fingers. In his palm was a lavender ribbon. Tecumseh recognized it as Rebecca's—not that day, but perhaps the week before he'd pulled its length from her charcoal tangles of hair. What had become of the ribbon after?

He snatched it from the boy. "Tell the judge I will see him now."

This is what Tecumseh was considering as he made his way toward the house: the very fact of Rebecca's existence cast doubt on many things he'd always believed were true. They had been spared from the storm. Because of their love for one another; because Our Creator smiled upon their union. And if this was so, then it was possible for the Shawnee to live in peace with the white man.

He was thinking too about Boden, the white frontiersmen from his youth, who ran two gauntlets and begged Tecumseh to help him escape. About all they shared, about the light that died in him as his captivity wore on. There were white men he admired: Boden was one.

Perhaps there was something to admire about the judge, too. Recounting their past conversations, Tecumseh might describe him as a brave man with vision, if he was trying to flatter him. A gifted orator, or thought he was. The father of the woman he loved.

It was this last bit that was most important. Did Rebecca not owe half of who she was to her father? Hadn't he made her, or a portion of her? Exactly half?

Tecumseh stood before the front door. He closed his eyes. There was no need to knock. He had lived there long enough now to enter unannounced, and yet he hesitated. What part of himself did he need to quiet, to forget, in order to come to peace terms with the judge? He had buried two brothers with his own hands. He had watched his father be lowered into the ground. But he would need to bury them each in his heart, before meeting the judge tonight, if there was ever to be peace.

His hand pulled the rope and the door swung open. The front room was dark. The gilded script on the bound volumes glinted in the moonlight. The soft glow of a lamp down the hall, from the library. The judge would be there.

Peace in and of itself held no value, peace for the sake of peace. It made no sense for there to be peace if the Shawnee suffered, if other tribes endured hardships only so their leaders might clap one another on the back and congratulate themselves that the troubles with the whites had ended. Under those circumstances, Tecumseh would wage war with his last breath.

But there was a different kind of peace. He could imagine it; he could almost grasp it. A peace that was more evolved than any before—a harmony. Where no one suffered, where there was accord among the tribes, and the whites came and went, and settlers cherished the intrinsic value of the land. There was a kind of peace that represented the highest form of human ambition, the most fully developed human spirit. It was this kind of peace he would work to achieve.

He found Judge Galloway in the library. There was a bottle of brandy. The judge swirled his glass as he spoke. The alcohol licked the inside walls of his cup.

"Sit," he said.

Movement to the right: Sabreen was there, returning the swing-arm and the kettle that hung from it to their places over the fire. Odd for her to be in the library. The judge always took his late-night drink alone.

"You may go," he told her. "You've done your duty."

The woman did not meet Tecumseh's eyes but slipped past him in that narrow room, her knees brushing the settee and moving it a little. And then she was gone.

"Please," the judge said. "Sit."

But Tecumseh preferred to stand. The judge did not apologize for the late hour. He made no mention of it. Instead, he offered a drink, which Tecumseh declined.

"Suit yourself." The judge filled up his own glass and replaced the bottle.

The library window was open. He tried to read his host's mood but couldn't. Galloway was as he always seemed: massive, solid, lethal.

"Do you know what I did for work before I became a diplomat?" the judge asked.

Tecumseh shook his head.

"I killed Indians."

Tecumseh felt the heat from the fire, noticed the unused hooks on the swing arm, the fire stoker propped against the hearth. Its iron handle was forged into a spiral. He was not afraid of men like Galloway. Brave men bled the same as cowards, in the end.

"Not only did I kill Indians," the judge went on, "but I made it my duty to track them, stalk them, and when the time was right, murder them. I slit their throats. Ear to ear. Death that way is clean and quick. Not like the butchery your people make of dying, the torture and the dismembering. A nasty business. And that's how I made my fortune. Killing. Indians."

Tecumseh could smell the fumes of his brandy. "I

am glad to hear this. Because you certainly did not make your fortune negotiating treaties. I have been here three months and still we are no closer than when we began."

The judge grinned, so broadly and honestly that Tecumseh thought for a moment this was all an act. But then his eyes narrowed, and his face grew dark.

"You have been here quite a while," he said. "And what have you been doing with your time?"

Candlelight shone from the tin sconces. The judge patted the back of the settee and let his hand rest there, where Tecumseh and Rebecca had made love countless times. The cushions were soaked with their sweat and fluids. Sabreen's earlier presence in the room now made sense. Her son had seen them, had witnessed Rebecca and Tecumseh in the act. He had told his mother. And his mother had told the judge.

"Before you had pubic hair," Judge Galloway said, "I was fighting Indians. I was there when General Clark led us across the Ohio River for the first time. Early January, the sun running like an egg yolk in the sky. No clouds. Eleven hundred of us—the Fayette County militia and a host of volunteers, all itching to get ourselves a scalp.

"We marched for a week. We marched and saw not a single Indian. Our supplies ran low. We thought we'd be able to replenish our stores at the first Shawnee town. But the Shawnee were like ghosts. They saw us coming, and they packed up their things and were gone. Disappeared into the trees.

"Hell, they became trees, for all we knew. It seemed

a devilish magic. So we marched north, turned west, marched south again. Marching in circles. The land so dense and unyielding that each day was the same as the last. The same terrain. The same unreachable horizon.

"We were near-starved when we finally came upon a village. They must have seen our approach. They hoisted an American flag. We asked Clark of course, what should we do? But he never wavered. He ordered us to attack.

"We hacked them to pieces. Man, squaw, child. We were famished from our march, and so we set upon the food stores first. Pots of stew, some kind of Indian mush. Their women squealed a little but let us eat. And once our bellies were full, a kind of craze overtook us. Each and every man. I remember a colonel by the name of Grady. Stood there with his sword out. Just waiting. And when a group of women ran by, he chopped them down.

"The male Indians we just ran through or shot in the back as they fled. The chief, Moluntha was his name, stood in the very center of the yard in his official-looking, white robe holding a copy of the treaty he'd signed with us earlier that year. I can still see him: standing in a pool of sunlight, his people dying all around him, holding up that worthless piece of paper as if it would protect them. Holding it high like an admonishment. We paid it no mind.

"The Shawnee still raided our settlements, long after they'd signed that treaty. They still stole our horses. They still hijacked our boats. They needed to be taught a lesson.

"I found a man alone inside his tent. Sitting in his teepee in the middle of the floor with his legs crossed. When

I came in he looked up at me as if he'd been expecting me. When he smiled, I saw he had no teeth.

"Blood is intoxicating. The first splatter always takes you by surprise. There's something inside you that turns from blood, that is repulsed by it. Some survival instinct. But when you see blood again, and again, when all around you men are killing other men, something takes hold. You want to kill too. You want to see blood too—you want to cause something to bleed. It's as if a part of us that we always keep locked up suddenly becomes free. Blood lets loose the thirsty monster you've been carrying inside your entire life.

"I took three steps and hacked the Indian across the face. He toppled over. A glorious spray of blood painted the hides. And then with my knife I knelt down and took his scalp.

"I suppose a part of me was surprised to see that underneath that Indian's hair and bone, his brains and blood were the same as ours.

"Outside again, I showed some of the boys the scalp I'd took. We laughed about it. And then we heard this moaning. A mournful, pained sound coming from inside the tent. I'd hacked that Indian through the face and taken his scalp but well, he wasn't dead yet.

"So I needed to go back inside and finish the job. But one of the boys stopped me. I can't remember his name—clean-shaven kid, seventeen years old if that. He wanted to have some fun. He struck a match and lit that teepee on fire. And we stood there, guarding the entrance, in case the Indian tried to make a run for it. Those flames got hot quick, and they reached pretty high. So hot we had to take a few steps back. And before long you couldn't hear the moaning anymore. Couldn't hear nothing but the fire."

The story seemed to be finished, or the judge was through telling it.

"Why am I sharing this story?" The judge seemed to fill the room, as if by spreading his arms and giving just a little shrug, he might shoulder the ceiling off its joists.

"I understand the moral well enough," Tecumseh said. "It is the same as every moral in every story about the white man. Never trust a pale skin to keep his word."

"No." The judge put his fist through the wall. His hand disappeared inside the plaster, up to his elbow, kicking up a small, white cloud. The entire room shook with the force of the blow. "The meaning is this: if you ever touch my daughter again, I will not only scalp you. I will cut your off your dick and make damn sure you choke on it. I will light you on fire and piss on your ashes. And relish it. I may be a diplomat now, but by God I just can't help it: I still love killin' Indians."

In battle, there was always a moment Tecumseh thought of as the decision point, the moment he perceived that conflict was unavoidable and made inevitable all events that followed, to the death blow. There was before, and there was after, and in between was the moment everything shifted, when he realized a fight was coming. The ground would buckle and flatten out again; he felt somehow taller, a burst of energy through his spine. It was as if he could smell the thunderbirds circling.

And he felt it now, in the library with the judge. One of them was about to die.

Tecumseh was quicker. He lunged for the fire iron, gripped its handle, and reared back with the hooked rod high over his head. But he could not cover the distance in time. From somewhere in his housecoat the judge produced his coach pistol. He cocked and fired. Tecumseh had taken one step or maybe two before the gun went off.

He stood holding the iron. He clutched his gut. A sharp, burning pain suddenly sucked the breath out of him. The judge lowered the smoking pistol. Their eyes met, and Tecumseh was relieved to see nothing personal in his expression. This was just another death, for both of them.

Rebecca burst into the room. Her black hair flowing behind her. She called for her father and the judge turned.

Tecumseh dropped his weapon and bolted for the open window. He hurled himself through head-first, into the blind safety of the night. He dropped three feet to the ground, landing hard, but Crazy Jack was there, helping him to his feet, as if he'd been waiting for him.

"Are you hit?" his friend asked.

Tecumseh gasped. "We must go."

Crazy Jack had their horses saddled. As if he'd known.

They rode hard, putting distance between themselves and the house. It was many miles before Tecumseh remembered he'd been shot. He dropped his hand to his stomach, gingerly at first, and touched warm wetness where his belly should have been. All at once he felt exhaustion like heavy stones on his hands and feet. He lost grip of the reins and slumped until his cheek was resting on his horse's mane. Propped like that, nearly prone in his saddle, he remembered his father laid out across his brother's mount, returning from the battle that had taken his life. How his younger brothers had gaped, not understanding, and how Tecumseh stood holding the snail he'd brought home to show his mother—such a childish thing to want to do, when so much terror and grief surrounded them. He looked forward to seeing his father again, and Open Door, and Chiksika, and so many whose lives had been taken from him.

The horse stopped when Tecumseh slid and tumbled to the ground. He closed his eyes and then he felt hands moving across his chest, rolling him onto his back. He opened his eyes and Crazy Jack was kneeling over him, groping in his haversack. He heard a sound like glass paper being run across rough wood and the thought occurred to him that it was his own breath in his ears, shallow and full of sand. He began to lose consciousness, his eyes closing again, and then Crazy Jack slapped him fully awake. The traveler produced a clear bottle and removed the stopper. He held it to Tecumseh's lips and the taste was fennel and something a bit grimy beneath it. He felt the liquid all the way down his throat and then, peering the length of himself, saw what looked like a fine mist, purplish in color, begin to rise from his wound, where Crazy Jack was applying pressure with both hands pressed flat against his abdomen. It seemed like the man was trying to tamp down the mist, to cork the places in Tecumseh's body where the lavender clouds seeped through.

Crazy Jack made a disappointed sound through his teeth. He tore a long strip from Tecumseh's shirt. Then he withdrew a muslin bag from his pack and untied the string. He plunged the torn cloth into the bag and covered both sides with sugar, then packed the cloth into the cavity of the wound. Tecumseh felt as if a dozen knives were being pressed into his stomach. He felt their tips as high as his throat, as low as his knees, and the pain seemed to concentrate, to build up a kind of pressure, and then explode—out his ears and nose, through the bottoms of his feet. A cold sweat then all over his body, the world around him shifting and swaying and then suddenly coming into focus again.

Crazy Jack cleared his throat, working on something wet and large. "It's a funny thing about spittle, my boy," he said, pressing, coaxing, the mist away. "A great many cultures consider it sacred. Including our own."

Again from his bag he produced a mortar and pestle and spat into the bowl. Then he dumped white powder from a vial, followed by a yellow mash. "Ginseng powder and smashed apple," he said, adding a handful of black apple seeds which he ground into a paste. Then, using two fingers, he scooped the gummy substance and spread it across the wound.

Which is all Tecumseh remembered before he lost consciousness.

Tecumseh woke to find that Crazy Jack had made camp. Dawn was not far off, and he wondered if the traveler had been up all night, standing vigil. There was no fire, but Tecumseh was warm beneath a pile of bearskins. Only a few months ago this had all been Shawnee hunting grounds. Now he wasn't sure whom it belonged to.

He sat up, flinching. A warm, prickly pain danced across his lower half. He touched his stomach and found the tightly wound cloth. He asked after the lead shot, but the traveler only laughed. "The healer gets some compensation, doesn't he? How much will it fetch when I tell them I pulled it out of the great Tecumseh?"

It seemed a small price to pay for what his friend had done for him—rescued him, saved his life, healed him fully.

"Some luck, you standing right outside the window," Tecumseh said.

"I thought you didn't believe in luck," Crazy Jack said.

He considered. "I don't know what else to call it."

"You just can't stand to admit when I'm right."

He wrapped his arms around himself. "I am thinking of moving our people to the Indiana Territory. Perhaps the Miami will let us settle their land."

"That means appealing to Little Turtle."

"There are things we might offer him to make it worth his while."

"You'd be his protection. A border against the whites."

Gone were the peaceful visions of only a few hours

before. The notion that peace was somehow the wish of Our Creator. It still might be true that conciliation was closest to his image. But it was not the world Tecumseh had been born into. There might be peace one day, but he no longer believed he would live to see it.

His mouth was dry. "It is in our blood. The violence—the war. There will never be an end to it. I see that now."

Crazy Jack mumbled something in reply. He was making preparations for sleep, moving slowly now that Tecumseh was awake, heavy-lidded and numb-tongued. Tecumseh said nothing more, but allowed his friend to crawl beneath the blankets. He had earned that much, and more, and soon he was snoring.

Tecumseh had wanted to explain why he would return to the Galloway home, as soon as he was feeling strong enough. But he didn't need permission, and anyway, when his friend woke to find him gone, he would know.

Tecumseh figured that once a man had shot you through the gut, there was nothing left to fear from him.

Dawn broke over the Galloway home. He had not slept. Without waking his companion, he had saddled his horse and gone. He'd reached the Place of the Devil Wind before the rooster crowed, with darkness still clinging to the trees. It gave him time to hide.

He waited outside the back door, off the kitchen. When the servant boy emerged, as he did each morning, taking out the chamber pot, Tecumseh snatched him by the wrist and held a knife to his throat. The basin spun to the ground. He covered the boy's mouth.

"How old are you?" Tecumseh hissed.

"Seven," the boy said, muffled.

"If you were five years older, I'd slit your throat."

He felt something wet and warm on his leg. He looked down. The boy had pissed himself.

"The judge ain't here," the boy said.

"I'm not here for the judge."

The urine was pooling at their feet, soaking the earth.

"You know who I want to see."

The boy nodded. Tecumseh released him, and the servant disappeared inside the house.

Tecumseh picked up the chamber pot and shook it out. Then he leaned it against the stairs to drain. He stood beneath an elm, out of sight of the kitchen. Soon the door banged open and Rebecca was there, barefoot despite the chill. She hurried down the steps. No one had ever run to meet him before—someone so desperate to greet him that running seemed to be the only way.

She found him beneath the canopy. She leapt into his arms and covered him with kisses. His neck and cheeks and hands were wet from her lips.

"I thought you were gone." She buried her nose in his neck. "I thought my father had shot you—that you would die. That I would never see you again."

"You needn't have worried."

She pushed back from him. "I saw him shoot you."

"You didn't," he said. "You came in after the shot was fired."

"He was standing so close."

Tecumseh showed her the packed wound, the torn shirt. "He didn't miss."

She pawed at him and wept and put her hand on his stomach, on his skin. "I don't understand any of this."

"What do you remember of the tornado?"

She shook her head, rubbed her eyes. "You were pounding on the cellar door. I was barely conscious."

"We were up there," he said. "In the storm cloud. Do you remember that?"

"I..."

"Think. Try to remember."

"Yes." Her eyes were closed. "It was somehow quiet in the cloud. And very still. And we were floating."

"We were spared."

"You were spared," she said.

"Listen." He held both her hands. "The Shawnee will be leaving Chillicothe."

She dropped her head. He inhaled the scent of her, just washed with honeysuckle.

"Come with us," he said. "Be my wife. Bear me seven strong warrior boys."

She released a sob then. He cupped her face and tucked her hair behind her ears. He wanted to fold her up and pocket her, to carry her back to Chillicothe and then to Indiana, to keep her with him always.

"No one marries for love," she said. "Not out here. They

marry because it's practical—because there's no one else the right age. Affection—is not for us to consider. I wanted to be different. I thought it would be different, for us."

"Then I have lied to you," he told her.

"No."

"I told you there was magic left in this wilderness. But there isn't. Not anymore."

Her hair was in his face as she shook her head. "The soldiers."

"Cleared out."

"Something else." She swallowed, and grabbed his face and held him there so their noses touched. "They are heading north. My father has decided not to wait."

He pushed away from her. "What are you saying?"

"Your village—your family. They're in danger."

He didn't listen to the rest. He sprinted to his mount and kicked; in another moment he had her at full gallop, heading home.

1795

Northwest Territory

HE WAS TOO LATE. Chillicothe was overrun.

The ground showed clearly the tracks left by horses and men. The Great Council House was open. Inside, ransacked. Throughout the village lay shards of wood and torn fabric from the wigwams, and cooking equipage, and blankets and other personal effects, as if the Shawnee had grabbed what they could and scattered. The horse compound was empty. His own mount wanted to go no further, smelling, perhaps, the redolence of animal fear. The American army had come upon the town only hours before, a day at most.

A small, wolf-like creature prowled the ruins. Overhead, vultures turned loping spirals. A tree, filled with crows, erupted. Their shouts echoed back across the river, which seemed to lie still, as if the current paused to mourn this moving-on, and to say goodbye.

Confused tracks headed west and north. The tribe had been warned in advance of the army's arrival, then, with time to flee. The deeper, slower tracks moved north—the way the army had gone, he supposed. It did not appear as if the Americans had followed the retreating Shawnee.

Relieved, but grief-stricken: it was here he had come of age. Fallen in love, buried his dead. In the cemetery, he tied off his horse. There were fresh graves, but not so many. He walked carefully along the low mounds, the dry earth, the land washed by the blood of so many great Shawnee warriors. His father's grave, and Open Door's, side by side. They would be forgotten, built upon, bricked over. Progress burying what had already been buried, by his hand, and in his heart. Soon, perhaps already, they would be lost to history, beneath the falling leaves, season after season. There would be no one left to tell who came after what brave and lovely souls were buried here.

He saw then the bear-claw necklace. It was draped across a forked stick at the head of a fresh grave. He knelt beside it, handling the tooth as if it were something fragile. How well he knew this necklace—he had bartered his pawawka token to save it, once. He felt sorrow in his depths, like something that needed to be expelled from him, and he let out a howling cry that came back to him from the far riverbank.

It was Rattle. The grave was his. No one had sent word, and he wondered why or why not. The army bearing down, no time to do anything but pack what they could and run. The grave itself seemed hastily built, a few stray ashes from the fire they'd burned as an offering. The sticks laid over the gravesite not as orderly or placed with as much care as Tecumseh would have preferred, for someone who shared his blood. The grave should have been loaded with heavy rocks to protect against animals. This was suddenly his only thought, and it was of the foremost urgency. He would not weep, or pound his fists against the earth. No—he would make his brother comfortable, properly, befitting their lineage.

He set about finding enough stones to secure the grave, wondering what stories his family told as the body lay in wake four days: many of the tales, he knew, would not have been kind. Rattle was so often lazy, mean-spirited, and bullying, and acted as if the world owed him something. All of that was true. But if Tecumseh had been there he would have found nice things to say, loving things. He hoped someone had.

He rocked the stones back and forth from the places they had stuck in the river mud. He grunted and heaved them sopping up onto the bank, thinking no longer would their mother wake him in the middle of the night, crying and frantic about how Rattle had yet again gotten himself into a brawl and begging Tecumseh to convince one man or another to spare his life. No longer would he have to endure his brother's simple magic tricks, cover his gambling losses, or confiscate his liquor so he could sober up enough to eat and wash and maybe rest. Yes, all of that was gone, and although he could barely let himself think it, perhaps they were better off without him. The boy who had turned back the Wampus Cat also was gone—and surely this was a loss. He who had sat at the feet of the great medicine men, who knew all the Shawnee legends and who, even as an adult, would take on a childish innocence while reciting the creation myth, the introduction of the albino man, the turtle-back—it was always these stories that gave him the most joy.

The way he died—it was hard to speculate. Picking a fight with the wrong man, someone who didn't know him, his ways, who didn't tolerate him as someone of local color and instead took offense. A sip of bad whiskey, or passing out drunk on the riverbank, at low tide, and eventually drowned. It was one of these, or something else, but in the end they were all the same.

"I hanged myself, brother."

Rattle stood at his gravesite, draped in heavy bearskin. Tecumseh dropped the stones he carried and fell to his knees.

"I come only to lay my brother to rest." He wouldn't look at this ghost. The less he spoke to it, the better. To even say his name would invite his spirit to never leave the earth. Rattle had suffered enough in life—let him go.

"I'm no spirit," his brother said. "I'm as alive as you."

He came to him and showed him the deep red burn around his neck. Tecumseh touched it, ran his finger along the grooved scar, the cool, rigid skin.

All of it felt real. "Why?"

"You're my brother, and you love me, so you ask me why," Rattle smiled, sadly. "When the question is not *why*, but why did I wait so long?"

Tecumseh set his jaw. He hadn't known the depths of his brother's despair, or had only glimpsed it. So focused on his own path, he had failed to see how his brother needed him—or someone—to pull him out.

"You were dead?"

"Falling Leaf found me where I'd hanged myself at the well," he said. "It took four men to cut me down, to carry me and lay me in my grave."

He shook his head. "But who's below the earth? The sticks are untouched."

"Who knows? If it makes you feel better, you can say it is the old me down there, the dead me."

"And now?"

"I have returned, brother."

Sunlight on the water, blue skies, all the colors of the trees on full display, the many shades of yellow and red and brown, so many there were not names for them all. It was odd to be speaking with his brother in a setting as serene as this, his brother who had apparently died and now returned. Rattle had lost his eye patch somewhere between this world and the next. Tecumseh tried to look in his one good eye, but found himself stealing glances at the purplish crater where his other eye had been.

He couldn't get his mind around it. He had seen amazing things in his travels. He'd once seen a woman with two heads, one on top of the other, in a performance ring in Fort Washington. People paid for the privilege to view her. He had seen twins whose bodies had not separated at birth, who walked together like a spider in a twist of flesh and limbs. He had seen a blacksmith hammer out a padlock and chain small enough to be worn by a grasshopper. But that Rattle had never really been dead, only sleeping—he had never heard of anyone coming back from something like that.

"I was not sleeping," Rattle told him. "And it was no trick. I was dead."

Tecumseh laughed, incredulous. "Now that you've been to the Spirit World, you must be full of wisdom."

But Rattle only looked mournful. "I never saw Our Creator's face. But he was with me. There was a glow. A warm, golden glow, and it was him. There was no arguing with the things he said."

There was something different about his brother. Days without food or alcohol perhaps, his skin had shrunk a bit to fit his bones. But also, something in his manner had changed. The brashness was gone. He spoke quietly. He seemed empty, as if he no longer carried the anger or shame, the self-conscious rage. He spoke in the way of a man trying to understand what he had just been through.

"On the other side, I was surrounded by a straw-colored cloud," Rattle said. "The firm presence of Our Creator enveloped me. I felt something like his hand, his fingers, touching my lips. And then my mouth was gone. I was staring at my own mouth then in the hand of Our Creator. But it was not the full, red lips I see each day in my looking glass: my lips were twisted and bruised and blackened. Inside my mouth were rotted teeth.

"'Did I create you thus?' Our Creator asked me. I couldn't answer—he still held my mouth. But even when my mouth returned to my face, I felt a burning, sticky sensation but found no words."

He described how Our Creator had grabbed him by the ears, and then his ears were in Our Creator's hands.

"He wouldn't have had hands," Tecumseh challenged. "You said he wasn't human."

"No—not hands then." Rattle thought for a moment. "Still, when the cloud needed to reach for something, this was what it used. Its hands."

When he touched the spaces where his ears had been there were only hard, brittle scabs. And his ears in Our Creator's hands were black and gnarled things, like tree roots curling in a fire.

"'Is this why I created you?' Our Creator asked me. 'To hear only gossip? To wait until the lies you spread return to you as truth?' And then he crushed my ears in his hands, and they crumbled like burnt leaves and blew away in the wind."

He was short of breath. He put his hands to his chest and gasped, flinching as if a great pain pierced his heart. Tecumseh moved to help, but his brother waved him off.

"He reached inside me then," he continued. "Our Creator stretched out his fingers—that's the only thing I know to call them—and put them against my chest. And then his fingers slid inside my chest, the way you can slide your fingers between hewn logs when the cement is wet. He pushed until his hand was inside me. His hand and then his wrist. And then I felt him grip my heart.

"I knew that he would kill me. I knew he would squeeze my heart until it burst.

"And he began to squeeze. And to massage. He said my heart was black. That my heart was blighted and diseased. And I felt the worst parts of myself, my anger and fear, pour out like black liquid, pouring out every part of me. In its place, honey. A warmth, a shimmer—the very first spark of life. The very first spark of flame before it explodes into fire."

They had walked a long loop beside the river, past the stables, and back to the cemetery again. So many thoughts, and so many emotions—impossible to sort them all out. Starting with Rebecca: in one night their desperate need for one another had been replaced by something melancholy. The grammatical tenses she was always drilling into him—Rebecca and Tecumseh were now part of the past tense. Or he was. She, and her people, were the future.

He saw that now, clearly.

And the American army, slipping from their encampment without his seeing. How long ago had they decided to march on Chillicothe? How long had the judge kept him on, with Tecumseh believing he was cunningly extending his stay, while in reality, the judge was deceiving him? He wouldn't consider Rebecca's part in it.

And now he was walking with his brother, who was also part of the past tense, once, but who was now again part of the present—and potentially the future. And here was a particular bend in the river with an old knotted, hollow tree, as familiar to him as his own arm. It, like all of Chillicothe, exerted a kind of pull, a mental density that grew heavier the nearer he drew to it, to them, to his brother—a sense of inevitability, that he could no more avoid the place than he could avoid shutting his eyes to sleep. But now his people were gone, his home was gone, it was empty land, and it was only he and his brother who had been through some kind of ordeal, a kind of spiritual awakening, but who could be sure? It was up to them, the last living sons of Pucksinwah, the only Shawnee band not to sign the Treaty of Greenville, the only tribe of the great tribes charged by Our Creator to protect them all against the whites. And so Tecumseh had only one question: where could they possibly go from here?

"Our people are only two or three days ahead," Rattle said.

"Little Turtle will stop them, if we do not reach him first."

"Then let's not waste another moment." Rattle clapped him on the back, and pulled him close. "Do not feel sentimental, brother. Say goodbye, and remember, home is nothing but a place you one day outgrow."

West of the Great Miami River, the wind came charging across the prairie like a horse at full gallop. So much flatland made Tecumseh feel lost. With nothing to orient to on the horizon, each direction seemed to offer the same answers, the same bad options, or the complete absence of solutions. He felt exposed to the high, distant sky and already missed the rolling hills of home.

He was in a foul mood: the weather agreed with him. The sky was overcast. The air carried the season's first chill. It was so flat, the wind could knock a man off his feet.

Kekionga, the principle Miami town, sat at the confluence of three rivers. Rattle and Tecumseh approached through forested land from the south. They followed the road but kept off it, concealed in the hardwood and underbrush. Tecumseh weighed the balance of all his questions: his brother's return and what impact that would have on his people, against their need to somehow convince Little Turtle to allow them to settle on Miami land. There was so much he could not predict, it was hard to think of all that was already behind him. Rebecca and Chillicothe, and somewhere the marauding American army.

The Shawnee were camped to the east of Kekionga, with cornfields and the St. Mary's River to their south and woods to the north. The brothers waited on the south bank for nightfall, observing both the Shawnee camp and beyond that, the Miami town.

"It's quiet." Rattle rubbed his hands together.

They lit no fire, wanting to stay concealed. From their vantage point, they could see well enough into the town. There were no cooking pots set boiling and no children playing games outside, as there should have been. Faint wailing sounds rose from the shuttered cabins. Here a horse wandered; here a man's hands shook as he filled his pipe with tobacco.

This, Tecumseh knew, was influenza.

Rattle wrapped his arms around himself, shivering. "I did not know the Miami suffered."

A wind picked up and swirled leaves at their feet, and then the wind died and the leaves too were still. At the edge of the gardens, now dry and empty, a young mother cradled an infant and sang to it. Perhaps by some trick of the water, the way it carried sound, they could her words clearly although she was a hundred yards away. It was a song their mother had sung. She and the child seemed to blend with their surroundings. The brown hides they wore took the color of the earth and the naked trees behind, the color of lost hope.

The Shawnee flight had been hasty and badly organized. The women had wrapped their pottery in blankets, their iron kettles in fishing nets. Men tucked their more precious wampum into the folds of their clothes. The wigwams were meant to be carried and came down easily, or they left them behind. They were waiting on the outskirts of Kekionga for the sickness to pass; they were waiting for permission of the Miami chief, Little Turtle.

Tecumseh slipped through the Shawnee camp, keeping to the shadows, a deer hide pulled over his head so he would not be recognized. He had left Rattle on the south bank, asleep. He had an errand of his own, and he couldn't take his brother with him.

After some time, he found who he was looking for at the edge of camp. Knotted Pine sat before a dying fire, legs crossed, arms resting on his knees. From a distance he appeared to be awake, if lost in his thoughts, but as Tecumseh drew near he saw the old man slept. He hovered several inches off the ground.

"Shaman." Tecumseh touched him on the arm.

The medicine man did not start but slowly opened his eyes. "I was wondering when we'd see you." He lowered himself until he was settled again on the earth, then stretched his legs and leaned forward, reaching as if to coax the fire's last warmth. "How were your weeks with Judge Galloway?"

"I did not sign his treaty."

"Very good." The old man nodded. "You heard the news of your brother then."

"That is why I have come to you."

"We wanted to send word, but there was no time."

"Knotted Pine, my father held you in respect above all other men," Tecumseh said. "So I tell you this honestly: my brother lives."

The shaman coughed, a small disruption in his throat that grew until he was hacking phlegm. Tecumseh put a hand on his back, to steady him. When the fit passed, the medicine man said, "You say he has returned to us from the spirit world?"

"Yes."

"I buried him with my own hands."

"I do not doubt you. And yet, he lives."

He considered this. "You must keep a close eye on him. It may be that Our Creator has some plan that we would do well to follow. Or..."

His voice trailed off, as if he were overwhelmed by the many possibilities, none of them pleasant.

"The *or* you speak of is too terrible to consider," Tecumseh said. "And yet, I know my brother better than any man. I will stay close to him."

Knotted Pine described the ransacking of Chillicothe, the journey to Kekionga, and the uncertainty within the tribe now that the Miami were suffering so great a sickness. Even if Little Turtle agreed to let them settle, there were some who believed they should not stay.

"I will handle the chief," Tecumseh promised. "He will listen to me."

It was time to go—already he had stayed too long. He didn't want to be seen by his people until he made certain of their next move. Even more so for Rattle. The news of his resurrection would frighten some. He wanted to be in control when that reveal came, for it to be on his own terms.

He embraced Knotted Pine, and stood to go.

"What suffering befell you, in your gut?" The shaman gripped his wrist.

"I've said nothing of this," Tecumseh said. "But I took lead shot. I am not suffering."

"Not in the physical sense, perhaps," the man smiled. "But in your mind. Your body moves tenderly, as if expecting to find pain."

He revealed the bandages around his stomach, which he had tried to keep clean and to replace. Knotted Pine touched the wound with his fingertips, muttering as he drew circles and starbursts in the air.

"It is fine work, whoever your healer was," he said. "A

friend with power to heal is one well worth keeping."

The next evening, the brothers crossed the river and met with Little Turtle in the Great Council House of the Miami. The moon was full and bright and lit the seams in the wall. Torches hung in the high corners. Little Turtle and Tecumseh were the same age.

"Brother." The chief embraced them. "Welcome."

Tecumseh rubbed the chief's bald scalp. "Are you waxing? Your head is gleaming—I can see my reflection in it."

Little Turtle had a prominent forehead like the flat of a shell. The globe of his head was shaved to the crown, leaving only a clump of hair at the back, in the warrior style. The overall effect was all skull: a bare and powerful armor. Large, ovular eyes peered out beneath the deep ridge of his brow.

"And you." The chief laughed, gripping his shoulders. "I see your nose hasn't gotten any shorter—you still look like a crow, prancing around, flapping its wings, trying to take flight."

"It is my mating dance," Tecumseh said. "And the female birds flock to me."

"Do they?" Little Turtle looked doubtful. "Then you'll have to teach me. I'm in a bit of a dry patch. More and more squaws marry every day it seems. There are fewer and fewer to choose from."

A dry spell for the chief, he knew, was likely no longer than a week. "You could marry one yourself."

The chief paused for a moment and then laughed. "Let's be serious. What reason have I to marry when I can just import women from the northwest? I've been sampling the Menominee. There is much to recommend them."

Tecumseh introduced his brother, who had so far said nothing.

The chief nodded. "You are welcome in this place."

They sat together. Little Turtle produced a pipe. He pulled several furs around him, and after they smoked a while, said, "I know why you are here."

"The history between the Miami and the Shawnee is long," Tecumseh said. "Together we have caused the white man much sorrow."

The pipe was made of dogwood. A cock's fan hung from the shaft, and beads strung along the tail rattled as the pipe was passed. The bowl was carved from deep, mellow red stone. The bowl was formed as a figurine, but Tecumseh couldn't quite read the details in the dim room. Little Turtle drew and smacked his lips and soon the embers were flickering. The scent of tobacco focused their words. They could somehow hear better through the smoke.

"How many of your people are camped outside my village?" the chief asked.

"A few hundred," Tecumseh said. "We need somewhere to settle. We throw ourselves on your mercy."

The chief passed Tecumseh the pipe. "The Americans

have a new commander now. Not the bumbling St. Clair, but a general named Wayne. His own people call him 'Mad' Wayne. They say he never sleeps. And the men in his command do not sleep. They are not from this world, they say. They are some kind of evil spirits. Death and destruction trail in their wake. They drive the birds and the beasts of the forest before them."

"I have met Wayne's *aide-de-camp*." Tecumseh noticed the figurine on the pipe was a turtle, naturally, but standing on its hind legs with its head extended, so that its open mouth held the tobacco leaves. "They do not fear us."

"And we are right to fear them."

"They will scream and plead for their lives, like all the rest," Tecumseh said. "The truth is, the treaty you signed makes it impossible for us to remain in Chillicothe."

"I am not the only one who signed this treaty. The chiefs are in agreement on this, across tribes. All of us, except for you."

The tobacco held a dark cherry flavor. "We would like to settle here. We are not so many now. We will not overtax the land, and we will not cause you any trouble."

Little Turtle's eyebrows were dark and narrow. When he frowned, his entire face seemed to sink beneath the broad, lustrous dome of his head. "You are my brother, Tecumseh. But we do not want the Shawnee on our land. Trouble follows you. You refuse to sign the treaty. This is why your life is hard. The Miami signed the white man's paper, and so for us, the trouble is past."

Tecumseh gestured with the pipe, although he knew

the chief was impatient to get it back. "Ten years ago we would have ridden together in battle against this American, Wayne. But now you are afraid. Your fear the whites, whom you call devils. You have become your name then: you would prefer to hide beneath your shell."

"These are different times." The chief leaned over and snatched the pipe away. "It is the dawn of a new century. And there have been no good omens for our people."

"It is men like us who write history, brother," Tecumseh said. "We are too young to act so timid."

"You are right that we are young," he said, smiling sadly. "I signed the treaty because I want to grow old."

In silence, they smoked a while longer.

Finally, Rattle said, "There is a sickness in your village."

Little Turtle coughed, exhaling smoke. His eyes began to water, as he waved vaguely at the smoke-trails, trying to clear the air. "It is true what they say about the brother of the great Tecumseh. You are smart and miss very little."

"Your streets are silent as graves."

"They are graves." Little Turtle was no longer smiling. "More than twenty have died, with many more taken ill."

Rattle nodded, hands folded beneath his chin. "Tell your people to gather here. Let them fill this Great Council House. Allow me to address them, and I will drive away this sickness."

Tecumseh felt tightness in his throat and shot his brother a look. He was ignored.

"You know what else they say about you?" The chief of the Miami sneered. "They say you are smart but lazy.

Strong, but a drunk. Like a plant that shrivels in too much shade, your brother Tecumseh casts a long shadow."

"Bring your people to me," Rattle said again.

"What other choice do you have?" Tecumseh said, knowing the same could be said for him. He was following where his brother led.

Little Turtle bowed his head, hands folded. He blinked once, then twice. "I will gather my people here. But know this, Tenskwatawa: the cost of failure will be your life."

Tecumseh waited with his brother. The room was dim, the moon dropping now, the torchlights fading.

This was some essential part of himself, he thought, his addiction to the unfamiliar, to unknown people and places, the way he nurtured a perpetual state of being lost. In a literal sense reaching some fork in the road, never knowing for certain whether to turn right or left, having never been on that road before or encountered these particular people under these specific sets of circumstances—under any circumstance. Needing the sharp edge of the unfamiliar to feel the most like himself, having grown accustomed to unease the way Rattle had once grown accustomed to drink, or the drunken state that alcohol produced, something that was not natural but came to feel natural by prolonged exposure.

Being uncertain of outcomes, or people's reactions, was as close as he came now to feeling right. This was what being lost achieved, then. It revealed different shades of himself, traits or emotions or strengths and yes, sometimes weakness he never knew he had, that he didn't know he contained, until faced with the until-then unknowable.

Rattle's demand had surprised him, but he knew better than to argue. It was foolish to doubt him, especially now, charged as he was with otherworldly confidence. Instead, Tecumseh squatted with his back against the wall, picking absentmindedly at the mortar, while Rattle paced, or what for him passed as pacing: a kind of hurried shuffle-step to the right, then a pause, then a shuffle-step back the way he had come. His lips moved, but Tecumseh couldn't hear what he was saying.

"What are you doing?" he asked him.

"Speaking with our relatives," Rattle said. "There are so many. And all of them have so much to say."

He had to admit that was what it looked like—Rattle speaking with someone Tecumseh couldn't see, then crossing the room to confer with another individual, or maybe two, before returning to placate the first again. They might be relatives, but they seemed to be very needy and opinionated.

Tecumseh cleared his throat. "I don't see anyone."

"They're all here." Rattle waved his hand dismissively. "Father is here somewhere, if the women would quiet down long enough for me to hear him."

He considered. "And Open Door?"

Rattle turned, his expression blank. His skin had a slick sheen. "He is with me always. Even when no one else is with me, our brother is with me."

He resumed his shuffle-step, back and forth across the empty lodge. Soon the space would be filled with the sick and the desperate.

"Is that how you do it then?" Tecumseh wanted to know.

"Do what?"

"All of it. Our relatives—our dead relatives—tell you things? You put them to work for you?"

"Not all the time."

Tecumseh waited, but his brother did not elaborate. He was mumbling, growing more agitated. There was a lot of him using his hands.

He put the question a different way. "Are you planning on healing everyone in this village, tonight?"

Rattle stopped. He looked again at Tecumseh, both scolding and pitying him, as if this were some simple lesson he was failing to grasp.

"I don't think I could do that," Rattle said. "Even if I wanted to."

"I'm just trying to understand how all this works."

"Stop!" He glared from one side of the room to the other. Tecumseh knew he was not the one being addressed. It was as if Rattle were quieting a crowd intent on shouting over one another to be heard. Then he did turn to him and say, "You think the Shawnee talk a lot in this life. Wait until the next."

Tecumseh smiled, and then finally decided to ask the question that most needed an answer, for him. "And Chiksika?"

"No." Rattle folded his hands on his belly. "Our brother is always sulking in the back. He was not ready to cross over. He went before his time."

Tecumseh was surprised when his stomach heaved, forcing him to choke back a sob. "Explain all this to me."

Rattle considered. "Do you remember when you did not know how to swim?"

"No."

"But there was a time when you could not swim," Rattle went on, "and so you stayed far away from the water."

"Presumably, yes."

"And once you knew how to swim, the water became familiar. You learned how to move through it, to read it, to use it for fishing and games and fun."

"Yes."

"My power is like that. Before, I was blind to it. I did not know how to swim. When I died, Our Creator taught me a certain way of seeing, of listening, of moving through the world. Another layer to this world that most cannot see."

"Because they cannot swim."

Rattle nodded. "Exactly."

Those who were too weak were carried inside the Great Council House of the Miami. Others straggled in, short of breath, sweating and shivering. No conversation among them, or not of words—only their shared physical suffering, coughing and restlessly toeing the floor. Amassed, their grief was a low, drawn-out sound that never quite peaked, like a boiling kettle in the moments before the wailing steam. Soon, so many sick and dying filled the room that families passed their children from the front door to the back, relying on strangers to hurry them overhead, to be nearer to Rattle, to his power. Or they tore away a plank in the wall and handed their babies through.

The villagers pressed inside, desperate to be touched by him. Tecumseh kept just off his shoulder, in the event he needed protecting. The air was heavy and stale, a thick cloud of sickly breath.

"My brothers and sisters." Rattle opened his arms wide. "Your suffering is great. But the time of your suffering is almost at an end."

Tecumseh felt his brother's voice in his gut, a voice that had the power to push wind and jounce bones. He saw Rattle open his mouth, but the sound that came out wasn't his, or wasn't one Tecumseh had ever heard. He had to look again to make sure it was his brother talking.

"I have had a vision," Rattle said. "Granted by Our Creator. Three more of you will die. But in five days, those of you who are sick will be well. I have cast the sickness from you. But those three who are yet to die I will not heal, because you practice witchcraft. Our Creator abhors witchcraft, and so you three will die. I will not name you. You must look to your own hearts to see if it is you."

He moved his arms slowly up and down, like the wingstrokes of a large, powerful bird. He began to chant in the ancient language. He moved through the crowd, touching the foreheads of the women; moving the palms of his hands over this little one or that; petting a waifish girl and gripping some of the stronger men by the arms. His hands seemed to convey fire, or a spark: the men jumped a little when he touched them, as if receiving a charge. A woman was blessed and stumbled back, steadied by her husband. Sometimes Tecumseh swore he saw a kind of blue light passing from Rattle's fingers to a bare patch of skin, but it was so quick, almost imperceptible, he could never say whether there was indeed fire or if it was some trick of the light in that dim room, with so many people packed in and fragments of torchlight sometimes flitting between bodies as they swayed.

"I am casting out this sickness," Rattle said. "But three among you have caused this sickness, and to those three I bring death."

Sweat ran down Rattle's face and glistened in pools on his neck. He wheezed through his nose. He was beautiful though. Soon Tecumseh couldn't see the people anymore. There was only his brother, moving through them, the confidence with which he reached for one stranger and then the next, the ease with which he held the crying babies and returned them pacified to their mothers; the way he cupped the face of an old woman in his hands and whispered to her something no one else could hear.

The fearlessness of it, how all the hesitation and doubt was gone from him. It was a righteous pouring out.

Someone tripped and shouted. A woman, no more than twenty, tumbled into him. He caught her, and set her upright, but in doing so the crowd seemed to spring back again and three more people now collapsed against him and Tecumseh, berating them, pulled them off.

"We need space." He set his brother's feet back on the ground. "Give him space, please."

But there were people now on every side, behind them and before them, and some had climbed the support beams to the rafters to get a better view. So much heat, so little air, and the sound, like a disconsolate hive. The need of the villagers collected was something Tecumseh could feel. It was everywhere. He and his brother moved slowly, as in a dream. Still the people pressed in.

"If you have received a blessing, please move toward the door," Tecumseh encouraged them, but one blessing seemed not to be enough. They didn't leave, and they didn't want to make room for their neighbors. He worried about the children, the infants—he thought how desperate their need must be for Rattle to only make one promise and now they all were here, without results. All hope lost then: nothing else to hold onto but his brother's word.

"It's hard for us to breathe, please." Tecumseh shoved a few men back, clearing space.

"Have compassion, brother." Rattle was still at his elbow, moving, touching, whispering. "There's time enough for all of them."

But it was dark in the room, with a fullness that swallowed the shadows and ate up the light. It reminded Tecumseh of diving toward the river bottom, so long ago, when he thought he couldn't be colder until he felt that immediate blackness underwater, that uncertainty of position, of what was up or down. In the Great Council House of the Miami he was no longer sure where the front door stood, or whether the roof was above them or below. It was all darkness, that menacing black bird, taking them again under its wing.

And then he felt a rush of air, the wind nearly knocking him off his feet. He lunged for Rattle and held him: Knotted Pine, the Shawnee medicine man, stood before them, wrapped in bearskin and brandishing a twisted rod. Now the age of untold moons, the man had forced himself inside and parted the crowd. Behind him, distantly, burned the campfires of the Miami.

"Blasphemy," the shaman growled. "You've no right, Tenskwatawa, to give these people hope."

Tecumseh watched his brother's features shrink into his fleshy cheeks. He worked his elbows back and forth, unable to reach across his girth.

"Knotted Pine." Rattle kissed him on both cheeks. "See where your magic has failed you? I am alive and well, and soon these people will also be well."

"You've no right," the shaman said again, spittle flying. "From where do you claim to draw your power to heal?"

Rattle chuckled. He seemed genuinely amused by the question. He made his way to the door. Stepping into the night, he was greeted by his own Shawnee people, gathered to catch a glimpse of their wayward son who had died and who was rumored now to live. They had come into the village from where they were camped, against orders of Little Turtle, not fearing for their own safety, overcome by curiosity.

"Look with your own eyes!" Rattle shouted to them.

Tecumseh too came outside and stood behind him. He guessed there were two hundred Shawnee, maybe more.

"That's why you're here, isn't it?" Rattle asked. "So look, and see. I live."

The crowd backpedaled and then conferred with one another. But Rattle stood taller. He stomped his foot on the ground and the people leaned forward to listen.

"We have moved away from our natural state." He shook his fist. "The state of our innocence. The purity of the way we lived before the white man: that is the blessed condition. That is the state of being most pleasing to Our Creator."

He stopped, apparently too overcome by his emotions to speak. He clasped his hands beneath his chin and took a deep breath. It was not the Shawnee custom to interrupt a man while he was speaking.

He blinked his one good eye. "Once I was a drunk and a scoundrel. I allowed the European way of life to corrupt my natural state. You have too, my brothers and sisters. This is why we suffer. We have adopted the white man's lies and his style of living—it has turned us rotten."

The people showed their restlessness now, whispering and shaking their heads. Tecumseh felt the crowd turning against Rattle. No, he thought—that wasn't quite true. They had always been against him, more or less, his entire life.

But his brother's voice rose above. "There are laws that Our Creator has passed down to me. If we follow them, he will heap blessings upon us. He will make our land bountiful again."

"Let us hear some of your laws." Knotted Pine pounded his staff against the outer wall.

"Rule one." He swallowed. "No more alcohol."

"We know you well enough, Tenskwatawa. You're the biggest drunk of all."

Many laughed. But Rattle's expression did not change. Instead, he lifted his hands. "I have given up all spirituous liquor. I have been dry these past weeks. I will never taste alcohol again."

A woman spat. "A skunk cannot change his stench."

"Two," Rattle said. "It pleases the Great Spirit for a man to have only one wife. Therefore, men shall only take one wife. But if a man has more than one wife, let him keep those wives but take no more."

"Pig!" The woman shook her finger. "Fat pig!"

As boys, when the brothers would visit Knotted Pine, the shaman always seemed to favor Rattle, although Tecumseh could never understand why. On the night before a big hunt, the medicine man would take four tapping sticks, two in each hand, and strike them together.

He would begin to chant, and with the strange, musical sounds came a certain calm that settled over him. The wrinkles around his eyes vanished. He became as one much younger, as if the power he summoned erased the toll of aging. His skin was smooth as a buckeye, his body still but for his lips that chanted in steady meter. Then the song ended, the sticks were quiet, and a cry would go out from the nearby woods—the wolf's howl, a turkey's call—whatever was to be hunted the next day. Knotted Pine had drawn the animal near with his song.

The crowd now was lost, or almost. But Tecumseh saw that same smoothing out now: a defiant calm came over his brother. Rattle relaxed his hands and face. His head drooped and bobbed in a way that seemed to admit defeat. But Tecumseh knew better. It was a gathering of his powers, nothing less.

An almost inaudible moan escaped Rattle's clenched lips. He made fists with his hands and then stretched his fingers wide. Many in the crowd had turned away. But his exultations rose above them as a low, wavering note. He lifted his hands. His body trembled. He began to wail. The crowd turned back to him again and stared at this strange man who'd been a strange boy and who some said had died and come back to life.

He wore a yellow belt. It cinched his shirt below his gut. Chin quivering, the fleshy folds of his neck rippling in waves, he slipped the knot from his waist. The belt was three inches wide, embroidered down its center with a triangular pattern. The knot came loose. He pulled the belt, and the belt unfurled like a whip. He still held one end when the belt began to transform: it was still arcing against the moon-lit sky when the stitches became slithering scales and the full four-foot length of yellow belt became a thick, sulfurous timber rattlesnake.

Rattle held the tail. The serpent curled back on itself and bared its fangs, snapping at the one who held it. Tecumseh wondered what kind of magic this was. It was like nothing he had ever witnessed.

His brother released the snake. The beast dropped heavily to the grass and coiled its body beneath itself. Once collected, the serpent raised to full height. It reared its head back and licked the air with its forked-tongue, its chevron crossbands shivering with venom.

The crowd shouted and all at once pushed away.

"Do you see?" Rattle laughed at them, arms lifted. "We will make a new way of life for our people by reclaiming the ways of the ancients. I am the one who died but has now returned."

No spirituous liquor. Sell nothing to the white man. Trade with the white man only so long as you receive fair value. Eat nothing cooked by whites or from provisions raised by whites. And the white man's dress must be abandoned: the waistcoats and canvas trousers, the wool stockings and black leather shoes. Clothes such as this must be given to the first white man who comes along. Dress in breechcloths and animal skins. And no dogs or cats. They are the white man's devils.

Rattle couldn't keep still. He paced the Great Council House, mumbling to himself and hitching up his pants because the yellow belt he'd worn had slithered off through the underbrush and disappeared. Like a dog that could force its head into a rabbit burrow but not back its way out again, Rattle hadn't quite figured out how to dismount his own powerful magic. Having animated the beast, he hadn't known how to make the snake become a belt again. So he had to keep hitching up his pants.

This was not the boy Tecumseh had grown up with. He could touch his brother and the skin felt the same; his voice sounded as it always had. The heavy breathing through his nose, the bead of sweat on his upper lip, his new eye-patch drooping toward his ear. And yet Rattle was also very far away. The distance seemed intangible or supernatural. Perhaps he'd never really returned from the spirit world, or only a part of him had.

Rattle was beaming. "No one could believe their eyes."

Tecumseh needed to be careful. Rattle was riding a kind of high. The night had gone better than planned. Worlds better. The transformation of the serpent had struck the crowd dumb. There had been no more objections after that.

"You see." He strode toward Tecumseh, wagging his

finger. "I've not been idle while you've been gone. I've been getting stronger. I've been harnessing the power that's been given to me. I feel as if I'm glowing—radiating some kind of energy from my very spirit."

Tecumseh wondered if it were true. Somehow his brother had achieved the one thing Tecumseh wanted for himself: a shot at immortality.

Little Turtle entered then, slamming the door behind him.

"How many are with you?" he shouted. "How many Shawnee?"

"A few hundred." Tecumseh moved to greet him.

But the Miami chief strode through the room, rubbing his hand across his scalp. "My scouts tell me there are now nearly two-thousand in your camp."

"That was not so yesterday."

"Word has spread." It was the chief's chance now to wag his finger. "Word has spread and now I have a Shawnee war camp on the border of my most important town, the place where I live."

It was clear he had no more appetite for conflict. Tecumseh wondered how many more were like him, content to accept their annuities from the whites and hope the peace lasted until Our Creator called them home.

"Your people say you died." Little Turtle accused Rattle. "That they buried you in Chillicothe."

"It is true. But Our Creator sent me home."

"And your prophecy?" The chief stood toe to toe with Rattle, glaring up at him. "Will it come to pass?"

"In five days' time."

"I do not want you here that long." Little Turtle growled and then slammed his hands against the wall. "Go then. East of here is a tributary of the Auglaize. Lush lowland and forest thick with fox and deer. Far from our hunting grounds, and far from our villages. I cannot give you my blessing. I cannot welcome the Shawnee with open arms. But the tributary of the Auglaize is fine, it's fertile soil, and no one will bother you there."

No Shawnee was to take more than one wife. A Shawnee man could no longer take a squaw whenever he desired her. Let that man marry, if he must. And if his wife behaved badly, neglecting the children or chores, refusing to get out of bed in the morning, her husband could strike her into action. But after, when the blows had ended and the point was made, let them hold one another as husband and wife and bear no ill will toward one another.

At the Shawnee camp, many must have embraced Rattle, and wept, and rejoiced that Our Creator had returned him to the living. He who they all had thought was dead. There must have been music, and dancing, and a feast, and fires, and carousing long into the night. There must have been hundreds of stories told in his honor, tales buffed by time and polished by gratitude for what he achieved in Kekionga, for forging a path to a safe, new home. All of this must have happened, but Tecumseh saw only their mother, Methotaske, too frail now to stand, who sat swallowed by her bearskins, reach two whip-thin arms toward Rattle, who fell into her embrace, laughing. Tecumseh had never seen her so glad, sobbing tears of happiness, clutching Rattle to her as if he were an infant again and cooing, "My boy, my boy has come home to me."

It stung Tecumseh—how could it not have? He who was the best of all the Shawnee fighters, who now led a war party like his father and brother had. Who the whites invited to negotiations and entertained because they feared what would happen if they didn't. Where were his tears of joy? His embrace? No, this was simply what she expected of him. And because these were the expectations, he had become as familiar to her as the pot she cooked in—often neglected and taken for granted. So familiar, she hardly even noticed him.

Pray only to the Earth. Beg Our Creator for abundant animals and fish. No longer are medicine men allowed to carry pouches of herbs and powders, or rub magical stones, or study shells and burnt tobacco leaves, or wear mineral tokens around their necks.

Rattle's gamble paid off. Three Miami died, and the rest of Kekionga began to heal.

The Shawnee settled at the confluence of the Tippecanoe and Wabash rivers. An American fort stood nearby, now abandoned. The Shawnee built cabins, reveling in their permanence. They arranged their central square in full if distant view of the fort's breastworks. Tecumseh enjoyed how their settlement defied that American display of strength. He marveled at what it meant for the Shawnee to sow seeds on land once tilled by government field-workers and paraded over by polished, English boots.

It was green land. The water was cold and clear. Gone, though, were the rolling hills of home. This was verdant land but flat, with nothing on the horizon but sky.

Word of Rattle's miracle, and the demonstration of the serpent, spread. Each morning it seemed Tecumseh woke to new clusters of homes. Not only Shawnee and Miami, for many from Kekionga sought them out, but Wyandots too in their black breechcloths, their shaved heads topped with roaches made from porcupine hair. There were two and then three thousand, with more arriving every day.

He could see, without squinting too hard, how Rattle felt the need to claim something in this life. To try and make a name for himself away from the battlefield where, he knew, he himself cast a long shadow. And yet it was difficult to know where the old magic ended and the new sorcery began. Rattle himself trusted nothing and banned not only the medicine bags but modern songs and dances too.

"Keep to the traditions of our ancestors," Rattle told

the crowd that gathered each day to hear him preach. "And in four years there will fall two long days of darkness. During this time of shadows, Our Creator will traverse the world to raise great monsters from the depths, creatures you and I have never seen or even dreamed of. Long gone friends of ours, and family, will also be raised—lovers restored to their dead loves, parents to their dead children. All of these will walk again.

"A hailstorm will follow. This storm will destroy the white men. Those who no longer believe will perish too. But the Shawnee will be warned. We will be given notice ahead of time, and we will flee to the highest mountaintop. And when the storm has passed, we will descend once again into the valley, and our way of life will be restored."

There were men, Tecumseh thought, who dreamed of big things, and there were men who sometimes came close to making those dreams real for themselves through vision or determination. Now, he felt as if his dreams and reality were becoming one. It was a powerful sensation. People he did not know paid him respect in the streets. He ran his war party ragged, training them with war clubs and tomahawks and to shoot from their horse using either hand. For the first time in his life he was comfortable with who he was. He knew he was handsome: he had his choice of women, a different one each night. He knew he had only to smile, to flash his white teeth, to tilt his head so his long, black hair fell ever so slightly to the side, to make the women melt and the men do whatever he asked. Sometimes he imagined not only the women but the men too wanted to sleep with him. This made it easier for him to give commands and carry himself with confidence. And while it wasn't real, it may not have been far from the truth. He was struck sometimes by not just how much people liked him, but by how much people wanted to be liked by him.

His father had joined forces with the British; his brother Chiksika had spent his time conducting river raids and supporting the Chickamauga in Tennessee. Both had lost their lives, and neither had stopped the pale-face swarms. Neither had saved their homes, their hunting grounds, or the places where the spirits of their ancestors lived.

Now Tecumseh was nearly the same age as Chiksika was when he died. And though the momentum seemed to be swinging their way, he worried that all of his life up until now had been little more than talk. That one day the Shawnee would rise to meet their aggressors; that one day they would repel the white forces. As Rebecca had taught him, his ancestors could afford to speak in the future tense. About all that would one day come to pass. No longer though. Tecumseh knew he must root himself in the present, or wither.

Where his father and brother had failed, he would succeed. But the Shawnee alone were not enough to face the whites. They would need the help of other tribes. Consensus was the one thing his father and brother had never been able to build.

"You're up early."

Tecumseh was readying his horse, brushing out her flanks and forking the mud clumps from her hooves. Rattle ambled toward him from the direction of the river. He had never seen his brother awake with the sun still so low in the east.

"Caught a little chill." Rattle pulled his bearskin around him. "Trying to find some sunlight to get warm."

"This is the new you, then," he grinned. "Early to rise?"

"Daylight seems like a terrible thing to waste. We're only given so much of it."

Rattle watched Tecumseh work. At the trading post, where he had purchased the horse, they'd called her a *barb,* fifteen hands high with a toasted nut color and a dark mane. He liked the way her shoulders and neck were sharp and angular, her hindquarters a continuation of the overall linearity of her build.

"Is this one still giving you trouble?" Rattle stroked its croup.

Although she could run indefinitely, hardly ever needing to eat or drink, she was feisty, and sometimes fought the reins, even still. She also seemed to suffer from a case of nerves. That's the only way Tecumseh could describe it. She'd go for days without trouble, and then she'd hear a squirrel rooting through the underbrush and try to bolt. He wondered about her mind. He had no idea how she'd do in a fight.

"She's learning," he hedged.

"The way she carries her tail, so low. Like she's guilty of something."

He leaned against the horse and picked up her back leg, cradling it in his arms. He knocked loose a few stones. "I think she has a heavy conscience. Like the rest of us."

"When will you return?"

"By summer. I will call on the nearby tribes, and then head north. I believe Roundhead will support us, given the proper incentives."

Rattle leaned forward. "Don't worry about us, here. This winter will be lean, as we had little time for planting. But one lean season in exchange for all this, what we are building, is a small price to pay."

"I hate to be leaving now, when so much is going right."

"You don't have to pretend, brother." Rattle swatted him on the back. "We both know you're happier when you're moving. Still, we are counting on your success. Without the support of the other tribes, we cannot achieve all that we wish to achieve."

Tecumseh nodded. "I will think only of home, until then."

"You won't," his brother smiled. "But home will welcome you when you return."

1809

Ohio

HOME WAS SOMETHING THAT CALLED TECUMSEH BACK, but each time upon returning, he seemed to recognize less and less. The geography of home was different now since the Shawnee abandoned their Ohio Country for the Indiana flats, but also some essential quality had changed. He had changed, or they both had. Or perhaps home had never existed apart from an idealized version he held of the place where he was born, where so many had been buried and had helped to form the man he was now. Was home tied to a place, or to an idea? Could he find it now on the banks of the Wabash River, in the thriving new settlement at Tippecanoe?

Sometimes he was convinced he couldn't be from here—these people were not his people. So immersed were they in village life, the day-to-day squabbles, the hard business of survival in a new wilderness, all of which seemed petty, sometimes, and unimportant. Yet he saw a glimmer of himself in the faces of those around him, his neighbors who had lived together their entire lives. So might he have, too. And sometimes he saw himself in the kind gestures that were taken for granted among them, one man holding open a door behind him for a man just coming in: this was something particular to home, to where he was from.

Following a man to the Great Council House door, seeing him enter and knowing he would linger long enough, and pause, with two fingers on the upper corner of the door, so that Tecumseh might reach the threshold and catch it with his foot as it began again its inward swing. Nodding to one another. Thanking him for granting that pause, for acknowledging Tecumseh as what, someone else who also needed to come inside? Saving him the effort of needing to fully open the door? It was more than that—the acknowledgment. It said also, "I am from here, and so are you, and here we pause to hold the door open for one another in this certain way."

That, and the compulsive talking. No one could talk like a Shawnee. They woke and their lips were moving before their feet hit the floor. They talked as if silence were something to fear. They talked to people they knew and to people they didn't. Remarking on the weather; stopping strangers to ask about the harvest or news from the settlements; comparing techniques for fletching arrows and gathering opinions on the advantages of rawhide snares. As if they meant to live by consensus.

Twenty minutes into a conversation with a complete stranger, Tecumseh would realize—it would occur to him suddenly—that although he knew how many children the stranger had, and that the stranger's favorite corn was grown by the Chippewa far to the northwest, that he did not know the stranger's name. Too late to do anything about it then—the stranger was already offering to bring him some of that sweet, lake-fed corn after the late harvest. No reason to interrupt the flow of conversation now just to introduce himself, something that should have been done long before. Knowing everything about a person but their name—that was something particular to home.

Unlike tribes from the East who stalked around wordlessly, glaring. Or tribes from the South where one's name was everything, where one couldn't inquire about something as basic as the crops without reviewing the titles and surnames and family sagas that preceded and precluded your coming into this world—Tecumseh son of Pucksinwah, War Chief of the Kispoko and the Panther Clan of the Shawnee. At home, conversations wandered. The people were hardworking, and at home was a life ready-made for him. He needed only to claim it.

Except that when he was home he also felt as if he were being eaten whole, or suffocated, compressed by the very familiarity he treasured and longed for when he was away.

What drove his need to see the wider world, he didn't know. But he had always contained it, or it had contained him. There was the stress immediately before departure as all the preparations were made; there were the sometimes sorrowful goodbyes to his mother; there was the swearing to himself, as his village receded, that this was the last trip for a while, that he needed a break, that he needed to be around more. And then somewhere many miles on, after he had been traveling a long time, he would turn some bend in a little-used road and find himself on the precipice of a vista he'd never seen. Or he would happen to glance up, and the sun would be slipping from behind a cloud, and he would find it immediately and inexplicably easier to breathe. As if a weight had been lifted. As if a tightening around his shoulders, a persistent and twisted hard coil in his gut, had been released.

He was being recognized in and around the Shawnee villages. Traveling returned some measure of anonymity. And while not being recognized sometimes came as a relief, the truth was, he did not need to be recognized to feel whole. Others he knew required all the familiar components of their lives near them at all times—their blankets, their neighbors, the people who had known them for years. They needed these things in order to feel like the most complete versions of themselves, in order not to fall apart. Whatever it was that made Tecumseh fully himself did not require familiarity, or even recognition. Whatever it was he needed he carried inside of himself or on his back like a snail. And even then: he did not carry home with him wherever he went, but instead he was content anywhere he found himself. Because in some real sense, home for him did not exist, and hadn't for years.

Except that sometimes he swore he heard the river valley calling to him. He wished then that he could fly, or leap higher than the clouds, and hurl himself into the waiting, buckling hills, into the sycamores and hickories, and give his heart, once and for all, back to the place others always referred to as home.

A man was rowing two canoes lashed together with rope. Concealed on the near bank, Tecumseh watched the strange craft come downriver. The pilot was whistling. He wore a tin pot on his head, with the handle turned backwards. His movements were hurried. Rowing madly to one side, then the other, he slid back and forth between canoes as he zigzagged the vessel downstream.

Tecumseh had been traveling. He had lost track of miles, then days. He crossed the Indiana and then the Ohio territories. He dipped into Kentucky, circling home.

This rower now heading toward him: he'd seen it many times before, how the wilderness could overtake some men, suddenly, and cause something inside of them to snap. More than once he'd found a white man running naked through the woods, set on some lonely errand of his own imagining. Sometimes he found only their bodies, later, long after despair had flung them from a cliff or drowned them in a forgotten eddy of the current. This man coming downriver, wearing rags and maneuvering two badly tethered canoes, their contents worth nothing, valuable only to him, was sadly familiar. He wasn't worth the arrowhead it would take to kill him.

But an arrowhead was what he needed, to set him free. Tecumseh could do for him what the man did not have the courage to do himself. Still, Tecumseh watched and waited. He felt some sympathy for the man, for his efforts at navigation. And it did happen sometimes that all a man needed was for someone to speak to him in his own language, to prove the fact of his existence by breaking the silence of the wild, in order to be set straight again.

He followed the canoes for a mile. Finally he watched the vessels land on a rocky beach, amongst burnt-colored reeds. Late winter and the sky was milky white. Wind gusts kicked across the water, carving out shallow moons. Soon the man had a fire going. Tecumseh waited until he settled in, crossing his arms behind his head and leaning back against a log, before he stepped out of the trees.

"Lord have mercy." The traveler leapt up, crossing himself. "I wasn't expecting visitors."

Tecumseh said nothing, but strode past the man and began to root around in the canoes and in the bags he carried. White men always smelled different, and they smelled worse the longer they were in the woods. But this one was particularly ripe, a combination of earthworms and stagnant water. He smelled as if he hadn't bathed in years.

"Chapman." The man followed him, extending his hand. "John Chapman. Son of Captain John Chapman of Leominster, Massachusetts, at your service."

He was a desperate sight. His hunting shirt hung in strips. His pants were cut below the knee and he was barefoot, despite the chill. He'd removed the pot from his head and had it going now over the fire, roasting walnuts and persimmon. He didn't seem afraid at all.

"You're a solider?" Tecumseh put the question to him roughly.

"A soldier? Goodness, no." Chapman folded his hands. "How should I explain? I am on a journey through your country. I visit settlements and help the people there."

Tecumseh held up a hunting sack he'd pulled from the canoes. He reached his hand inside and came away with a fistful of black seeds. "What's this, then?"

"That's what I do." Chapman hurried to the canoe, his blue eyes flickering. "I plant nurseries for the settlements. Those are apple seeds. Here, try one."

Scampering into the far craft, he rummaged through a sack. In a moment he produced two round fruits with dull, greenish skin. He handed one over. When he bit into his, juice sprayed.

"These are Roxbury," he said between bites. "These are my favorite, but don't tell the Rhode Island seeds."

Then he laughed, still chewing, throwing his head back.

Tecumseh had seen fruit like this before. His father had found a crate of apples in a flotilla raid. Rattle and Tecumseh would throw them sometimes and Open Door would fetch, playing dog. But he hadn't seen one since he was a boy. His father had taken an apple and snapped it in half with his hands.

He bit the fruit. His teeth sank in, the back of his tongue flattening out against the sour taste. As his teeth turned the flesh to pulp, a mellow sweetness spread and made the corners of his mouth ache.

"My theory is, settlers need to be planting these seeds and growing up nurseries full of apple trees," Chapman said. "Fruit like this is good for you. And it can be made into all kinds of splendid dishes. Cider, roast apple mash, apple pie...."

Tecumseh didn't trust this white man. He couldn't, not after how he'd been deceived at the Galloway homestead, so many years ago. But there was something about him that he was drawn to. There was serenity, a grace in his long limbs, an alertness in his eyes that implored him to enjoy the offering. And he certainly wasn't crazy—or at least not in the way Tecumseh had expected. Like Boden from his youth, like Rebecca, once, this was a pale skin who might earn his respect.

He bit through the core, and recoiling at the taste of the bitter seeds, tossed the rest of the apple away. But Chapman looked pained. "If you'd like something else, these nuts are almost ready."

"That would be good, yes." Tecumseh sat, rubbing his hands near the flames. "Tell me more of what you've seen on your travels."

Chapman gripped the pan and shook it back and forth. "The biggest news is, Harrison's been made governor of the Indiana Territory."

"Harrison?" He felt a searing heat across his skin.

"William Henry Harrison," he said. "Congressman's kid from Virginia. Fine soldier, too."

"The white men appoint many leaders for themselves. They do not interest me."

"This one should." Chapman turned his attention from the fire and seemed to be tracking something on his own skin, on his chest. "President Adams has granted him powers like nobody else. He doesn't report to anyone but the president, and even then, Harrison runs his own kingdom out here now. What he says, goes. Who lives, who dies. White or Indian. Man or woman even. I saw him execute three dogs myself, just because nobody claimed them."

"He does not hold our lives in his hands," Tecumseh said. "A treaty has been signed. This land is ours."

Chapman found what he was looking for and plucked it from his neck. He held it up for Tecumseh to see: a round, gray tick kicked its legs against the air. Chapman rose and crouched at the edge of the campsite. He placed the tick on a rush leaf and whispered an admonishment.

"Early for those buggers," he said, returning to the fire. "He won't bother us again tonight. What were you saying? Treaties? I've come up through Ohio. I've journeyed just about every tributary and rivulet in the west. All that land you think is yours? Those Western Reserve Lands? They're being promised to soldiers who fought in the War. My own father's been promised ten acres just south of Lake Erie."

"This cannot be so."

"It is so. I just came from there. New sawmills, new roads. Put up a new fort—Fort Industry they're calling it."

Tecumseh's mind was spinning, and he hated that he was surprised. It was only another broken treaty, like all the ones before.

"Anyway." Chapman held out the pan. "These nuts are ready. Try one. They're delicious."

He still sometimes felt the disdain for home that only someone who came from there could truly muster. It made him a little tired, actually, the steady pace of his village, which was never frantic and never slow. Just steady. It was home; it was inside of him; he carried a part of it with him wherever he went; it came through in his accent and his mannerisms and the ways he perceived slights and wrongs, and even to the ways he extended courtesies—it formed his entire world-view in some fundamental way. But sometimes he did wish he were from someplace else, somewhere crowded like the Iroquois towns or cool and remote and shrouded in majesty like the mountains in Tennessee—sometimes the hardwood valleys of home seemed small to him. He felt embarrassed by them. He wanted to dig them up and build them bigger. Wanting grander views, thicker trees, clearer water. He wanted to inspire others to want these things too.

Near the Cuyahoga River, in the Connecticut Western Reserve, Tecumseh met with Roundhead, a Wyandot war chief.

They sat at a long table. The chief propped his elbows on either side of his plate. He had enormous jowls, a nub nose, and a full head of black hair tied off into two shoulder-length locks. His clothes were lined with tassels, his trousers tight and sewn with elk hide.

"It is time for us to set aside our vanities," Tecumseh said. "And our pride. These are new days. We can no longer survive as factions where the Wyandot go one way, the Shawnee another. We have a stronger, more dangerous enemy now."

Roundhead sniffed and wiped his nose. He was also called Bark Carrier because a fire had scarred his hands and arms in his youth. His skin was hard and weathered. "They say your brother has powers because he journeyed to the Spirit World."

Since the miracle at Kekionga, his brother was all anyone wanted to talk about.

"We count our blessings that he was returned to us. Through him we look back to the ways of our ancestors so we might build a better future for our people."

"Looking back so that we might move forward?" Roundhead laughed. "Does a horse look over his shoulder at full gallop? Some might say that kind of thinking would put us in an uncomfortable position. If one should happen to trip, one suddenly finds themselves with their head up their ass."

Tecumseh felt a clenching inside, then flashed his smile. "Think without prejudice on what I have said. The very leaves of the forest drop tears of pity on us as we walk beneath."

The chief sighed, absently straightening the flatware. "What you are trying to do is impossible."

"In our fathers' time—"

"Personal revelations are fine," the chief said. "But the rest of us need more. If Our Creator has revealed to your brother his great plan, let Our Creator reveal the plan to us all."

Tecumseh considered the swelling population of Tippecanoe. Already he led many warriors. But not enough.

"Imagine a child," he said, "who can snap with ease a single hair from a horse's tail, but who cannot break a rope woven of those same hairs."

"Oh, I understand well enough," the chief said. "Your problem is a problem of numbers. You do not have enough warriors to fight the Americans. Well, I have a problem of numbers, too. Here are mine: the Americans are giving us four thousand dollars. And six yearly payments of two thousand dollars. And we keep our rights to hunt and fish here."

"Annuities." Tecumseh swept his plate from the table. It went clattering into the corner. "Our fathers did not live on handouts from the white devils. Once, we were a people who were able to feed ourselves. And what right do they have—does anyone have—to say they will allow us to continue to hunt and fish? This is our land. The Americans steal it from us and then act as if they are doing us a favor by allowing us to use it."

The chief looked away and was quiet for a time. Finally, he said, "You do not say anything to me, Tecumseh, that I have not thought myself. And yet: this is a new world. Our fathers, they did not have to face what we now face, and so, our choices are few and hard."

"Our Creator has a plan—"

"Then let Our Creator show me his plan. Until then, we cannot offer you support."

That night, Tecumseh walked alone. A sliver of moon lay against the sky, half the imprint of a deer's hoof in the black.

When he was out of sight of the Wyandot town, he slipped his tobacco pouch from his pack. He had kept it all these years, since Crazy Jack had given it to him on his Quest long ago, when he'd lost his first horse, Cloudy Girl, and then found her drinking from a desert oasis. He learned later what an oasis was in the stories Rebecca once read to him from a collection, *Arabian Nights Entertainments*. In that book, stars were everywhere: in the sky, on the carpets and walls, in the eyes of lovers. He had never seen stars like the kind the book described in the firmament above all that sand.

He opened the pouch and knocked a few of the leaves into his palm. They were stiff and tasteless. They would burn in an instant. He arranged two stones and found a dry, straight stick. He rubbed the stick against the stones until it sparked and lit the grass. He cupped his hands around the flicker and breathed into it. When the flames swelled, he added more grass and weeds and blew more air and soon the fire was smoking and warm.

Roundhead was not alone in his doubt. All of the chiefs Tecumseh had met with that winter expressed doubt, or even disdain, over what he hoped to achieve. He could see it—why couldn't they?

Crazy Jack had promised that he would appear if Tecumseh burned the tobacco. He had always imagined some dire circumstance, lost and alone and possibly starving, that would drive him to summon his spiritual aide. But in the end, it was nothing so severe. He felt his faith wavering. That was all.

He upended the pouch. Tobacco leaves drifted into the fire. There weren't so many of them now; most of them had been crushed to dust. He let go of the bag, and the flames swallowed it, too. Destroying evidence. This was the old magic, after all. Punishable now by death, according to his brother.

The leaves burned quickly and were soon gone. He waited in the fire's glow, squatting with his arms around his knees. The wind picked up. The fire went out. As quickly as snapping one's fingers. He heard a rustling behind him and turned. His eyes were blurry from having stared too long into the flames.

There was a scent in the air. It reminded him of someone. He breathed in hyacinth and chalk dust. He closed his eyes and was immediately returned to the library in the Galloway home, the open window, the musty smell of books and her hair falling over him, the smell of her on every part of his body. He heard a woman laughing, and for a moment thought his daydream was so vivid that his hearing was somehow affected. But then he opened his eyes and saw Rebecca Galloway curtsying at the edge of the meadow. A perfect moonbeam pouring over her as she lowered herself to the ground and raised back up again, holding the hem of her shift by its corners.

He closed his eyes and shook out the vision. When he opened them again he saw a flash of something white disappear into the trees. Again he heard her laughing.

He bolted after her. He didn't care how she had arrived at this place. All this time he had locked away the complicated emotions of their separation, the purity of their feelings for one another, the impossibility of their ever being together again. And now here she was, darting into the woods as she had so many times in the forest near her home. His legs didn't need to be told to move.

He plunged into the trees, expecting to be met by dense underbrush. Instead he came quickly out the other side, stumbling into a rounded lawn bordered by tall boxwoods. There was a break in the hedge. He ducked through to find himself on another circular lawn bordered by tall stones. He waited, listening. He wiped his forehead but felt no perspiration. This was always his test. Whenever he felt himself in the midst of some powerful magic, he checked for sweat. If he was sweating, it meant his circumstances were real.

He heard her laughing on the other side of the stones. An archway: he scampered through, beneath a marble block. And there she was, standing in the center of the ring. On all sides was water, the ground wet rock, and the water wall rose twenty or thirty feet and then vanished, as if they were standing looking up at where several rivers converged as waterfalls. He couldn't get his mind around it—it matched nothing he had seen before.

She opened her arms. He ran to her, fell into her embrace. He kissed her neck and hair, her face and wrists, the place at the bottom of her throat. She was laughing still, a sound like tinkling crystal.

"I thought you had married," he said, breathless. "I thought I would never see you again."

"Married?" she exhaled.

"To Harrison." His hands roamed freely over her. He had forgotten how fluid she was, how yielding, but his hands still found the places they had charted long ago.

They dropped to their knees, her hands around his neck. His hands were everywhere—on her breasts, her knees, a fistful of her black hair.

And then she was laughing again, and so was he, and she lay down for him and he was over her, burying his face in her nightgown, pawing at the buttons. He put his hands on her back and she lifted herself until he snagged her gown's fabric with his teeth. Thinking this was news, that she had not married Harrison. That now she was here, she had found him, they would forge some way to be together. Even if it meant his giving up the dream of his confederacy—he would move East with her. He would live as the white man. He would live any way she wanted him to. It would be a relief to be done with the chiefs and their squabbling, their fear. Let someone else wrangle them—let Rattle.

Her laughter was a rolling and breakable sound. He put his lips to her stomach, tasting the cloth and feeling her body beneath it. His hands still cupped her from behind and she pushed up into him again. He dropped his mouth to the cottony space between her legs, hearing her laughing—

The laughter changed then, from something careless to a gravely kind of snarl. He tasted leather. He opened his eyes and found he was not holding her at all but instead gripped the rough-cut trousers of a man. He leapt back, spitting out the foul taste, to see not Rebecca but Crazy Jack, leaning on his elbows, his ankles crossed and laughing so hard he wept.

"Couldn't let you get any farther, old boy," the traveler hiccupped. "I was feeling uncomfortable enough as it was, what with all your petting and speaking in such soothing tones."

Tecumseh scrambled to his feet, still gagging on the taste of the man's belt. "You!"

Crazy Jack pouted. "What, you didn't think it was actually her, did you? Come all the way from Old Town just to see you? Here in the Western Reserve?"

He shook his head. "I thought—"

"Thought you were really gonna go through with it." The little man got to his feet and brushed off the seat of his pants. "Might've raped me if I hadn't shifted back just when I did."

"You've no right."

"Don't I? You need to get straight. This is no time to

be playing the love-sick schoolboy. Get her out of your head—permanent. She's good as gone."

"She married Harrison?"

He winced. Shrugged.

Tecumseh couldn't believe the weight of his grief—he hadn't known all that he was holding onto. How much he missed her. The loneliness.

Crazy Jack strutted the length of a log, balancing with both arms out to his side. "So I ask myself, after all this time, why does Tecumseh summon me now? He's had the tobacco leaves since he was a boy. What's so special about tonight?"

He gestured to the right and to the left. Tecumseh saw the water and the stones and all the connected garden rings were gone. Now he and the traveler stood in a little cleared-out place in the woods.

"There's no danger," Crazy Jack said. "Nothing threatening. So I think, maybe Tecumseh just needs a friend. Is that right?"

He shook his head. "Everything I need I carry with me."

"Sure, sure." Crazy Jack folded his arms. "So here's how I'm going to help you. Governor Harrison has settled into his mansion. He has a company of soldiers, nothing more. A hundred of your best men could slaughter them while they slept. So go—pay the governor a visit. Tell him Tippecanoe has grown to five thousand strong."

"Five thousand?" Tecumseh almost laughed. "We are not so many."

But Crazy Jack smiled. "Whatever you say."

There was a clatter of bells, and the little man was gone. In his place, something shone in the moonlight. Tecumseh approached, ashamed of his relief even as he recognized it—so many things he'd been missing and hadn't known.

His pawawka token lay on the log, still threaded with the string he had knotted long ago in Chillicothe. The colors of the quartz were more vibrant than he remembered. He draped it around his neck and held it there until it stopped buzzing and was still.

The American, Chapman, had called it Fort Industry, but that was stretching the truth. Built on a high cliff overlooking the Cuyahoga River, the fort was little more than a blockhouse surrounded by a flimsy picket. A road led up to it through a half-acre of cleared land. Stumps littered the pasture. The second level of the blockhouse hung out over the lower. The roof came to a steep point, so the overall effect was that of an arrowhead planted shaft-first in the ground. The road approached from the south. To the north and east were a rocky cliff and the river.

His pawawka token was giving off short, stinging sparks so he had to wrap it in cloth to protect his skin. Even cloaked, the mineral rock buzzed around his neck, happy to be reunited with its owner.

He felt invincible, his senses honed and sharp. He

felt loose and lean and strong. Most of all, he felt hungry: it was not that Roundhead so valued his annuities, but that he did not believe Tecumseh had enough men, enough skill, to ever win. Well, he would prove him wrong. He would use that doubt, that lack of faith, as motivation. Already he felt it burning inside his belly, propelling him with the spiraling power of a tornado.

He tied his horse a mile downriver. At dusk, he made his way along the bank, the blockhouse rising on the cliff face steadily to his left. A chimney seeped wood smoke into the sunset. From time to time, a rifle muzzle sprang from a second-story portal and then withdrew.

He gathered leaves and trailing vines and underbrush and bundled them with string. Then he lashed four logs together as a makeshift craft. Night fell, the water turned black. He set the bundle on the raft and lit a small fire beneath it, blowing into it and fanning the flames until the bundle was smoking. Soon, flames leapt. Wading into the river up to his waist, he guided the raft into the main current and set it adrift. Then he scrambled up the beach again, to the foot of the rock wall beneath Fort Industry.

"Two if by sea," he mumbled to himself, watching his diversion ease out onto the water.

The Americans expected the cliff face and the river to be a natural barrier to aggressors from the north and east; they no doubt kept careful watch—and had their cannon trained—on the road to the south. He then would do exactly what they least expected.

Soon men were shouting from the blockhouse. His

raft rode the river, lit like a pyre. He imagined the soldiers inside the fort gazing out, startled at first by the flames. If anything, he'd been overzealous: the fire burned bright enough to reveal his place on the shore. He began to climb.

The picket leaned over the water and was splintered in places—hastily erected, indifferently maintained. From the second floor of the blockhouse, men took turns firing for sport at the raft going by, hooting and calling to it. The night was filled with rifle fire and sulfur and the stench of it all burned his nose as he climbed through a cloud of gun smoke, thin like Spanish moss, as if it had leapt from the cliff and now hung suspended.

He reached the top ledge and then was up and over the teetering fence line to press himself against the blockhouse, now fully hidden by the shadow of the overhang. He crept toward the front gate. Here were chicken bones, here a wash tub, here a barrel of dry beans. He peered around the corner and saw two guards at the gate, both armed with flintlock muskets. He kicked over the barrel of beans and sent it scattering. The noise pulled the nearest guard toward him. Tecumseh counted to three and then stepped out from the corner and drove his tomahawk into the guard's face, which split and fell away like pig meat cleaved from the bone. The second guard leveled his rifle, but too late. Tecumseh had already sent his tomahawk sailing end over end where it sank into the man's chest and drove him back several feet, sprawling him against a camp bench.

Tecumseh yanked his weapon from the man's chest and crouched, listening. On the far side of the blockhouse, the gunfire was beginning to fade. Hearing no raised alarm, he knocked three times on the door. Finally it swung open, and a balding, pudgy man stuck out his head.

"Y'oughta come up and see this—"

Tecumseh grabbed the man by both ears and flipped him forward onto his back. He drove his knee into the man's throat.

"How many inside?" Tecumseh hissed.

"Ten," the man gasped.

"All upstairs?"

"We were having us some fun—"

Tecumseh slit his throat and yanked his hair back, opening the wound wide so the blood could flow. He didn't wait for the end, but dashed inside, slamming the door behind him.

To his right, a fire was going in the stone hearth. To his left, a ladder led to the second floor. A pair of white stockings coming down: Tecumseh axed the man behind the knees and he plummeted to the floor. One swing of his tomahawk, and the man's head exploded like a gourd.

A gunshot from above shattered his tomahawk. The blade clattered across the room, leaving him holding the splintered handle. He looked up at the shooter now scrambling down the ladder. He reared back and hurled the handle, flat. The sharp tip of the wood buried itself in the soldier's skull, between the eyes.

The next two men leapt from the hatchway, hoping to take Tecumseh by force. He met the first with a hard kick to the stomach. Ribs gave way and then the man vomited blood and Tecumseh deposited him on the hearth. The second man saw then his disadvantage and sprinted toward the door. Tecumseh unsheathed his knife, crossed behind and drove it through the man's hand, into the doorframe, pinning him there.

Two more gunshots went wide. Tecumseh looked up to see the ladder falling toward him. He caught it as the hatch to the second floor slammed shut. No matter. He righted the ladder and stuck it fast against the hatch, forcing it closed. He could hear feet shuffling on the second floor. Up there were the munitions supply and the heavy cannon. He slid two smoldering logs from the fire and stuck them in the ceiling joists. He brought down a lit lantern from the wall and breathed into it and encouraged the flames to catch. Like the white hunters from his youth who had smoked out pigeons from the trees, he'd do the same with this garrison. They had a choice: face him or burn. He didn't much wonder which they'd choose.

Thinking of Chiksika and his father, he held his breath. Smoke filled the lower room. He knelt beside one slain solider and took his scalp; then the other; then the next; remembering his father's body tied across his brother's horse—how his head had swung from side to side, lifeless.

There was one soldier still alive, the one he'd pinned to the door. He took his scalp as well, savoring the way the soldier screamed as his skin tore away and then his hand was shredded as Tecumseh pushed him backwards into the smoke-filled room.

Outside now, Tecumseh scalped the pudgy man and

then dragged the two dead guards through the gate. He could hear the soldiers on the second floor coughing and shouting for help. Hatches in the roof were thrown open and belched smoke. Hands tore through shingles, trying to claw their way out. The roof began to buckle in places from the heat and from the panicking soldiers, the gun portals not large enough for them to force their bodies through.

When the munitions blew, there was a burst of wood and brick and body parts and timber and all of it went sailing out over the river or scattered across the cut acreage. The sudden light, given depth by the smoke, was beautiful. The cannon did not move but dropped heavily ten feet to the ground, and toppled.

In the shadows of the fire, Tecumseh scalped the two guards and drove pikes through them both and set them upright on either side of the gate. He split them open and unwound their entrails, and draped them around their heads and necks like champion wreaths. He neutered them and shoved their manhoods down their throats.

Let Roundhead look on this. Let Harrison. Let each man consider his options and marvel at the strength of Tecumseh.

1810

Territory of Indiana

IT WAS THE SEASON OF THE HUNT, the season of men.

At Tippecanoe, the hunters had been gone seven days and returned dragging hares and squirrels by their tails. Turkeys were defeathered and strung. Now, the tribe danced to welcome the harvest. They danced for crops and game. They danced to the water drum.

Tecumseh toe-heeled the earth. His feet pressed against the grass and churned up soft mud. It was much too hot for the time of year and his entire body felt one great, constant thirst. The water drum pounded, and he imagined he, too, was full of water, a warm liquid inside of him that rose at the sound of the drum and pleaded to return to the rivers and lakes from which it had been born.

He danced. Toe-heel. Toe-heel. His legs moved in the familiar pattern. An elder before him, a young warrior behind, all of them circling a feast laid out. In the center burned a trembling fire, its flames kicking toward the sky. Tecumseh's feet led his body. His legs began to bend and then to bounce. He twisted a little at the waist. Soon he was thrusting his elbows and chanting. The water drum sang, its wood frame casting sound that could be heard for miles. His ribs shook with it.

This was the Bread Dance, the largest he had ever been part of. Tippecanoe was home now to five thousand souls. Wigwams and longhouses and quonsets dotted two miles of riverbank. There were broad, tasseled cornfields and colorful swaths of pumpkins, squash, and beans. Some homes laid their venison out to dry along their patch-bark roofs.

The water drum hummed. Tecumseh marched. The dancers wore almost nothing: feathers and loin cloths. He slapped his thighs and clapped his hands and smacked his bare chest, the dance an unyielding procession of flesh and the flash of ghostly faces lit for an instant by the fire, of heads bouncing so the slow rhythm of the water drum pushed the dancers left to right but also up and down. Tecumseh straightened and then crouched and then straightened again, limbs flailing, while the elder before him—older than his father would have been—made several jerking motions, suddenly consumed by the power of the moment, by the thrill of the Great Spirit moving through him.

He inhaled deeply: wood ash and the heavy smell of earth stirred up by feet.

The music came faster. Dancing this way, sweat pouring down his arms and along his spine, he bumped his slick elbows against the elbows of those before him and behind, a quick exchange of salt and water. He thought of William Henry Harrison. He conjured the man's face out of the blackness of the night. It hovered there in the center of the circle, wreathed by smoke.

He thought his forces could drive Harrison from the Indiana Territory, but he could not see clearly what came after. He wondered how the U.S. Government would retaliate. Were his forces large enough to repel the Americans in all their military strength?

"Brother, a letter."

Rattle pulled Tecumseh from the dance. Just beyond the firelight stood a man in a U.S. Army uniform, like a specter Tecumseh had conjured up out of his thoughts.

The messenger saluted. "Captain Boyd, at your service."

"From Harrison," his brother said. "Let us retreat to my cabin."

Inside, Rattle lit a candle. The three men sat on blankets. Tecumseh reached for the letter, but Rattle stopped him. "Touch the beans first, brother."

In his hand was a long strand of dried beans, sewn through their centers with string. They were moldy and discolored, the hue of stale sinews. They gave off a rotting odor. He held these up to the light and offered them. "Shake hands with the Prophet."

Tecumseh glared at Rattle, looming in the shadows. He was heavier than he had been even a few short months ago. Sweat stood out on his forehead and nose. He moved differently, as if his arms weren't quite long enough to work around his belly. They were beaver arms, and at this Tecumseh laughed.

"You mock me?" Rattle bared his teeth. "These beads are my flesh. They are made from me. Touching them is shaking hands with my spirit—the spirit of the great

Prophet of the Shawnee. Reject the beads now and you disavow yourself of all Our Creator's blessings."

Tecumseh considered. Finally he reached out and with one finger tapped the strand where his brother let it dangle. The beads shook, swaying once back and then forward.

Rattle snorted to the messenger. "Read the letter."

On Boyd's cheeks was week-old stubble, but the beard on his chin was thick. His lips were chapped and bloody. His hands shook as he broke the governor's seal and slipped the letter from its envelope.

"Just remember," the captain said, "it wasn't me who wrote this letter. I'm just a' readin' it."

Tecumseh and Rattle exchanged a quick smile: the captain feared for his life. The once-white triangles of his shirt collar hung over his jacket like wilted, yellowing petals. There were holes in his trousers and two buttons missing from his jacket. He touched his lapel self-consciously as he read, pulling closed the diamond-shaped gap.

He was not one of Harrison's inner circle, Tecumseh thought. The captain had volunteered, no doubt, so that he might get noticed, receive a better command, earn a raise. And the mission was not without risk, wading into the heart of the last openly hostile tribe in the Northwest, into a den of savages, with a letter that contained uncertain news. No doubt his comrades were making wagers right now on whether or not he would return.

Tecumseh gave it even odds.

Boyd's eyebrows were two drowned caterpillars. A

pale scar ran down his forehead and disappeared behind his hairline. So much depended on the content of the letter, which the captain read at a painfully slow pace, frequently swallowing and clearing his throat, sometimes before each word. The tone of the letter was straightforward and unambiguous. Harrison knew of the great confederacy they had built in Tippecanoe. If they did not disband, he would have no choice but to view their assembly as an act of war.

Boyd finished. He kept the letter in front of his face. The page shook, and the sound of it snapping back and forth was the only sound for quite some time. He held the paper as if he feared that letting it go would mean his life. Finally, Tecumseh reached across and quieted the page. Then he guided the captain's hand to his lap.

"So." Rattle slid toward him, leering with his one terrible eye. "Harrison has declared war?"

"Please—" Boyd stammered.

Tecumseh whistled, sharp and shrill. A girl slipped through the cabin door and stood with her hands folded, waiting. She was a white child, captured as a baby, on a forgotten raid long ago. Something about the turn of her wrist as she straightened her dress reminded him of Rebecca at that same age, who had never shaken the habit of curtsying whenever she entered a room, even after months in the wild.

He pointed to his own chest and then to the captain's. He held his hands six inches apart. The girl nodded and disappeared again.

"Please," Boyd said. "At least make it quick."

The men shifted positions. There wasn't much to say.

"Put a saber through me," the captain pleaded. "Or shoot me in the brain. Please. Just don't make me run no gauntlet."

A hoot-owl bellowed. They heard it pass above the cabin. The beating of its wings shook the shingles.

"And please don't burn me alive." One tear streaked down his cheek. "I'm terrified of fire. I'd die before you even lit the first piece of kindling. Of heart failure."

The girl returned. She entered and knelt before the soldier. Her hair was clipped back with a turkey-bone barrette. The scent of her—lilac and butter—cut the sweaty odors of the room. In one hand she held a needle.

"What is that?" Boyd's eyes were crazy with fear. "Please—make it quick. Just make it quick."

The girl opened her other hand and revealed two brass buttons. They were not an exact match for the ones missing from his uniform, but they would do. Wordlessly, she touched his jacket and worked at the fabric along the lapel. The captain took shallow, fearful breaths as she sewed first one button then the next.

"Return to your Harrison," Tecumseh told him. "Tell him about the power you have witnessed here. Tell him we will pay him a visit during the next full moon. There is much for us to talk about."

The Wabash River receded like old gums. Jagged, limestone teeth jutted at odd angles from the clay. On either bank were maples and shagbark hickories, and overhead one crow called to another.

In the slow current, Tecumseh and his men kept their canoes toward the river's center. Still they sometimes ran up against a sandbar or a downed tree and someone would have to climb out and push off until they found deep enough water again. The canoe bottom grumbled against the sandbar until the current took it.

Four hundred warriors paddled downriver. The heat settled, thick and wet. It was hard to tell the difference between the way it felt to pull their paddles through the water and the way it felt to bring them forward again through the air. Sweat beaded and dripped from Tecumseh's arms and the paddle was slippery in his hands.

The best of the tribes that had assembled at Tippecanoe, their faces painted yellow and red and green, were traveling to Vincennes to meet the governor. Tecumseh wanted to make an impression.

The sky was empty but for the wavering sun, runny as rendered animal fat. Trees pulled back from the water as if yanking hide from the bone. Tecumseh felt raw and exposed. There was no wind, and the trees were reflected in the brown murk of the river. The sky, reflected with the trees, cut a path along the current. Tecumseh paddled and grunted, telling himself to ignore the heat, and followed the deepest current with the sensation of sailing not on the river but through swampy air.

They camped a half-mile from the governor's mansion. A runner arrived at dawn. Already the day shuddered with heat, and crickets screamed.

"I recognize you," Tecumseh said.

He was Sinnantha, whom Tecumseh had fought with in his youth. He now went by Stephen Ruddell, which he said was his Christian name.

"And I you," the messenger said. "It is good to see you."

"How goes the world of the white man?"

"I am prosperous." His paunch and second chin confirmed this. "I have a farm in Kentucky."

"I will stop in and see you, next spring, on my way to Tennessee."

"Sorry, friend." He smiled as if he regretted what he had to say. "I hope that you do not."

Stephen Ruddell was a boy when he was taken by the Shawnee. They had called him Big Fish. He was there the day Tecumseh and Chiksika baited and gutted the first flotilla on the Ohio River; he had been there when Chiksika fell. It was he who had challenged the prisoner Boden in the gauntlet and who Boden had beaten within an inch of his life. Ten years ago or more now, he had taken a small detachment to the north and surrendered to the United States Army. Tecumseh had heard Stephen Ruddell reunited with his white father.

"Governor Harrison will meet you tomorrow," he said. "One hour after sunrise."

"He is not my governor," Tecumseh said, "and I will not address him as if he is."

The messenger blinked. "Governor Harrison requests that you leave the majority of your men here. To avoid hostilities. You may bring a small retinue."

"Brother." He showed the palms of his hands. "Does any red blood still move in you? Or has the white life made you fat and weak?"

"There are plenty of those with red blood who are anxious to make peace," Ruddell said. "Is not the word of Little Turtle and Blue Jacket as good as your own?"

A spider had strung its web between two tree limbs. The woven silk caught the light with its intricacies. A dark form—the spider—perched in the center, glistening just off Ruddell's shoulder.

"Little Turtle only cares about the easy life," Tecumseh said. "He would be content to live in a palace with women to serve him and wash his feet. He is no warrior. As for Blue Jacket—" Tecumseh paused; it pained his heart to talk about the man in such a way. "—he is old, and age dulls the warrior's knife."

"There are those who say a warrior who grows old was no warrior at all."

Tecumseh shrugged. "That is not for me to decide."

A leaf caught on the edge of the web. The spider unfurled one leg, revealing yellow bands along its length, then tucked it beneath himself again, recognizing the quivering strand as something less than prey.

Ruddell adjusted his weight and leaned on his rifle. "Many have said to me—both red and white—that it is not the American settlers who are the problem, but you."

Tecumseh's eyes narrowed. "You know this to be lies."

"I lived with you," Ruddell said. "I was formed under the Shawnee. Still I hear white men call the Shawnee mercenaries, assassins. They say the Shawnee will never sign treaties because yours is a primitive mind—war is all you've ever known. You will never be civilized like the great tribes. You will always be savage and a scourge to better society."

"We do not care what the white man says about us." Tecumseh's eyes flicked from the messenger's face to where he lightly gripped the rifle barrel. "No one with hearts as empty as yours can understand our way of life."

"The Shawnee are scavengers. You settle land that is already owned by other tribes. Many say you must be stamped out."

"And what do you say?"

The messenger straightened his posture and adjusted the powder horn slung around his neck. "I say that I am a Shawnee interpreter in the service of Governor William Henry Harrison."

It was clear then: the boy he'd known, Sinnantha, was gone. "Tell your governor we will meet him tomorrow, one hour after sunrise."

Ruddell nodded crisply, and with a click of his heels, turned to go.

"Sinnantha." He called to him. "How is your Shawnee wife? How are your two children?"

But the man now known as Stephen Ruddell did not turn around again. He continued on until he was enveloped by the trees, and Tecumseh could no longer hear his footsteps.

The sky was just beginning to brighten when they broke camp the next morning. Clouds stretched from the horizon in arcs of pink light. The woods were silent as the Shawnee warriors moved through them, that moment between night songs and the wailing insects of the day.

Despite the heat, they wore blankets over their shoulders. They carried war clubs and tomahawks, and the blankets concealed these. Only Tecumseh's lieutenants would go with him to the house. The others he ordered to wait at the edge of the woods and move closer as the day wore on, until they could hear his voice. If there was trouble, he wanted them ready.

He, along with four men, stepped from the trees in full view of the governor's mansion. Three stories tall, the painted white brick and large, partitioned windows seemed to capture the sun's light and glow with the essence of it. Tecumseh shielded his eyes against the glare. On the west wing of the house stood a two-story veranda, also white, set with tables and tea service. Several uniformed men lounged among the columns and silver place settings. Stairs spilled down three sides of the porch.

He recognized Harrison immediately. He was the one with a nose like a crooked finger.

When the men on the porch saw the warriors emerge

from the woods, there was polite commotion as they straightened their waistcoats and inquired after etiquette. To Tecumseh's right was a stand of walnut trees. He led his men to the grove and waited there. They were still some forty yards from the house.

A shuffle of boots, a tinkling of ceremonial sabers: the honor guard approached, clomping across the manicured lawn. Tecumseh instinctively reached for his tomahawk, spooked by the approach of thirty army regulars in blue jackets and crisp white trousers. But they fell into formation behind a fluttering American flag. Their chests were crossed by white straps. The sun blinked off their belt buckles and sparkled along the lengths of their swords. One stepped forward and put a bugle to his lips.

"We defy their treaty," Tecumseh laughed, "and they throw us a parade."

But the Wyandot leader, Roundhead, who now accompanied Tecumseh, nodded in the direction of the house. "Sinnantha comes with a message."

Roundhead had been a war chief for his people, far to the north. The Wyandot, like the Shawnee, were divided over their allegiance to the Americans. Tecumseh's display at Fort Industry had convinced Roundhead to take his men and join the tribes at Tippecanoe. Tecumseh had been honored by this and quickly made him second-in-command.

Now the former Shawnee brave, Stephen Ruddell, approached. He wore a clean, cream-colored waistcoat and blue stockings. A black hat was cocked on his head.

"You look very pretty." Tecumseh laughed. "I hope

you didn't go to this much trouble on our account."

But Ruddell said, "The Governor is honored by your presence here today. He would like to invite you onto the portico."

Tecumseh glanced at Roundhead and suppressed a smile. *Portico*. Such a fancy word.

Ruddell said, "Seats are arranged where we may counsel."

Tecumseh set his shoulders and gestured to the walnut trees. "We do not wish to hold this council with a roof over our heads. Have Harrison meet us here. In this walnut grove we will hold our council where the Great Spirit can see us."

On the porch, Harrison and his men covered their mouths and spoke to one another, squinting out in the direction of the woods. Finally, the governor seemed to acquiesce. He shrugged his shoulders and raised his palms toward the sky. A dozen men came streaming off the porch then, down the stairs and across the lawn to where Tecumseh and his men waited.

In their wake, black servants scrambled to shuttle chairs from the portico to the yard. When the government men reached the trees they stood around not knowing what to do. Finally, enough chairs were delivered. The men brushed back their riding coats and sat. Tecumseh gestured and his men did the same, curling their legs beneath them in the grass. Spots of sunlight played across their faces. Their rings and silver chains flashed when they shifted.

Harrison looked older than when Tecumseh had last

seen him. This man who called himself governor of Indiana was now very pale—almost translucent. Two blue veins throbbed at his temple. His eyes were set close together, narrow and dark. He wore a wide, black ascot that matched his pitch-colored hair. Swept forward, the hairstyle made him seem taller than he was. He leaned back a little as he gave orders, peering down at those around him from a great height. His body, long and eel-like, was lengthened by his blue, knee-length morning jacket and white riding pants.

Power suited him—he had taken to it.

Roundhead whispered in Tecumseh's ear. "They're armed."

It was true: the government men carried sabers or had coach pistols tucked into their trousers. But he knew also that his warriors terrified these politicians, these sons of affluence and privilege. Bare chests and feathers and war paint were the stuff of their school-boy nightmares.

"Isn't this quaint," Harrison finally said, folding himself into a chair. "A picnic in the walnut grove."

His men laughed. The governor sat with his knees together, hands in his lap.

"It is good to see you again," Harrison said.

"I cannot say the same," Tecumseh replied.

"We've met before, you know." Harrison said this more to his own men than to Tecumseh. "At a fledgling settlement—somewhere in Ohio, wasn't it? I seem to recall a Scottish wench, a real milkmaid. Thighs like fatted calves. Milked me dry, if you want to know the truth about it."

Tecumseh's expression did not change. "You confuse

your metaphors."

Harrison raised one eyebrow, and there was a long pause while the American tried to read him. Then Harrison laughed, louder, then with an outburst that caused his men to laugh too.

"I'd forgotten what a sense of humor you have." The governor snapped his fingers. "She taught you English, our milkmaid. I'd forgotten that until just now. Her father was quite proud. Whatever became of her?"

"I do not know."

Harrison seemed to consider something, then dismiss it. "Well, then."

Tecumseh felt relief flood his heart. All these years—of course she hadn't married this swine. Harrison had no use for someone as strong-willed as Rebecca Galloway. More to the point, she had no use for him. He needed someone meeker, more willing to sacrifice her own life for the good of her husband's career. And she needed a man who didn't dab the sweat from each eyebrow between breaths, as Harrison was doing now.

"How is it treating you?" Tecumseh asked. "All of this?"

"This?"

"You are far from home."

"Far from where I was born," the governor smiled, winningly. "But, of course, as an American, I consider all of this land mine, in the sense that I am proud of it, and feel that it welcomes me with open arms."

It was Tecumseh's turn to laugh. "The entitlement you

people feel—it always surprises me."

"It's easy to feel entitled when you're doing God's work, civilizing the savages and taming the wild."

"Ah, yes," Tecumseh said. "God's work. What is it your Good Book says? 'He that trusteth in his own heart is a fool.'"

Tecumseh saw it, although he thought no one else did—a flash of anger in Harrison's eyes, a spark of disbelief. Nothing else changed. His expression remained as docile and easy as it had been when they sat down.

But the governor leaned forward and gestured for Tecumseh to do the same. "The truth is," he hissed. "I hate it here. But you already know that. I only took this shit-smelling backwater post because they promised I'd report to no one. And once I squash your people like bugs, I can go back East and begin planning my campaign for president. So if you're wondering how all this ends—well, that's how it ends. Let's make this short, shall we?"

He reclined in his chair again and grinned. He looked to his right and to his left and his men seemed at ease.

"Is it true," he said, loudly, as if someone behind him were writing it all down for posterity, "that you refuse to recognize the new boundaries set forth by the Treaty of Fort Wayne?"

Stephen Ruddell, who until then had been silent, seemed to recognize some kind of ceremonial cue and began to translate from English into Shawnee. Tecumseh watched him, waiting for him to finish.

"All done?" he asked once Ruddell was quiet.

The former Shawnee nodded, licking his lips.

Tecumseh glared at William Henry Harrison, and replied in Shawnee. "I am the leader of a great confederacy. I speak for all the tribes when I say we believe the Treaty of Fort Wayne is illegal."

The governor's nose twitched as if he'd caught scent of something unpleasant. "There is the issue of annuities. Your people will no longer receive money from us if you refuse to recognize the new borders."

"We care not for your annuities. We do not want them." He saw the man to the governor's left swat at a mosquito and wince. "We value the land we now occupy. It is enough for us."

Harrison crossed his right leg over his left. He bit his lip. Then he gestured for a servant. A black man, dressed well and wearing white gloves, arrived with a cup of tea. The governor sipped several times before he spoke again.

"The land in dispute," he said, "is owned by the Miami."

Tecumseh shook his head. "There is no Miami. No Shawnee. There is only one nation."

But Harrison raised his finger and cut him short. "That's not how it looks from where I sit. I see the Miami, the Shawnee, the Kickapoo, as separate tribes. Which is what they are, no? You and your bloody histories with one another. These rivalries, by now centuries old, support my position."

There was rustling behind him. His men were anxious. By now, Tecumseh knew, the rest of his warriors had inched their way to within earshot of the walnut grove.

They waited, hidden.

"You say you speak for all Indians," Harrison said. "But I say the Miami have spoken for themselves. Little Turtle has signed the Treaty of Fort Wayne."

"The treaty is invalid and will not be honored," Tecumseh repeated.

But Harrison merely slurped the last of his tea and, finding the cup's bottom, cast it in the grass. "You're a spiritual man. Allow me to couch this in spiritual terms. Your Great Spirit created all the tribes. And all the tribes speak different languages."

Tecumseh wondered how long it would take for him to spring from his seat, slide his tomahawk from his blanket, and bury it at the place where Harrison's neck met his shoulder blade. Half a second? Two? None of these government men would be quick enough to stop him.

"You say you speak for one great Indian nation," Harrison said, "but I call that blasphemy. If your Great Spirit had wanted you to be one tribe, he'd have at least made all you savages able to speak to one another."

"No more." Tecumseh spoke in Shawnee, loud enough to quiet the snickering of the American soldiers. "This man is a liar. He blasphemes Our Creator. He doubts our claim to be one nation. Then let us show this Harrison what it looks like when many become one. Let us run his men through, and drink their blood, so that they become an example to all: we will recognize their treaties no more."

"All of these theatrics," Harrison sighed. "It is only a dozen of us here in this walnut grove."

But then a woman's cry went up from the direction of the house as four hundred native warriors stepped out of the tree line.

"Sir." Ruddell clasped Harrison's arm. "They mean to do us harm."

The governor was out of his chair then, sword drawn, much quicker than Tecumseh would have bet—but not fast enough. Tecumseh flicked his tomahawk from beneath his blanket and met the sabre's steel. Harrison stumbled. Around them, men on both sides groped for weapons.

It would take only minutes, he knew. It would be quick and bloody and then it would be over. One word from him and his men would overrun Vincennes. Murder each and every one of these government men and the women and children, too. It would be nothing worse than the Americans had done to them, a hundred or a thousand times over. He locked eyes with Harrison. This man who called himself governor knew it too—he knew how many men Tecumseh had landed on the banks of the Wabash. He knew they outnumbered his small detachment four to one. And that Harrison knew this made his tough words seem almost comical. Tecumseh could admire the substance of what he said and appreciate the courage it took to say such things in the face of a stark and dangerous disadvantage. To stare death in the face and make unwavering demands: that was the spirit of a true warrior.

Behind him, hands gripped war clubs and tomahawks. He heard the fletching of arrows trembling in their quivers.

Roundhead asked, "Shall I give the signal to strike?"

Up on the porch, a hundred feet away, something caught his eye—a flash of lavender and black hair tumbling down. The woman who had screamed when his warriors emerged was portly, but as she stepped aside he saw a second woman now leaning on the porch rail, gazing out to the walnut grove with sorrow and fear. It was Rebecca—there could be no doubt. He felt a solitary bead of sweat roll from his elbow down the back of his arm and knew that this was no magic. She was here. And the sparkling diamond on her hand meant that she had married Harrison after all.

When Tecumseh was young, he expected to fully realize his most ambitious dreams. He had nothing but years ahead of him. Nothing but time. What held more promise than potential? And potential, he had plenty of it. But as time passed, and he aged, some of these dreams fell away. Chiksika and Open Door would not live to be old men; the Shawnee would not keep their home. But Tecumseh told himself it was all okay, tricking himself into acceptance. Something less would satisfy him then—after all, only a very lucky few achieved everything they wanted to in life.

Rebecca was there on the porch in a coral gown and straw hat. She was his love and his ambition. More than that, she represented a kind of inner peace. The best of man's fulfillment: immortality.

He would not allow her to be slaughtered. Instead, like something approaching but never quite reaching zero, a stick whittled to half, and then half again, he understood then he would halve his dreams not once or twice but a dozen times or more over the course of his life. Until all that was left was a splinter of what he originally set out to do.

He lowered his tomahawk. "There will be no fight today."

He picked up his blanket and draped it over his shoulders. The government men's eyes darted back and forth, communicating something to one another—confusion, also fear. Mostly, relief. They would live another day. Waiting, though, to see what their comrades would do before deciding what they themselves would do. So much hesitation. So much terror now that they were used to big white houses and servants and spending the day indoors. So much to lose—too much for them to want to fight.

"The land you seek to protect was purchased fairly," Harrison growled, hand on his sword. "And we will protect the great Territory of Indiana with the full force of the U.S. Army."

Tecumseh did not look back toward the house. "So be it."

It took only moments for the Shawnee to slip away. They evaporated into the trees like fog that lifts from the field under the breaking sun.

1810

Territory of Indiana

RATTLE STOOD WITH HIS BACK TO TECUMSEH, framed by the doorway. He was gazing out into the yard. Sunbeams came on a low trajectory over the cabins and wigwams to pass beneath his arms, between his fingers, around his ears, causing the dark, rotund shape of him to glimmer with fiery light. Dust lifted and was lit by the glow.

"I forgive you," he said, finally.

Tecumseh harrumphed. "Forgive what, exactly?"

"Your cowardice." Rattle did not turn to face him. "Your weak knees."

He was eating an apple, leaning back on a chair. Now he dropped forward. "There's nothing to forgive."

Rattle turned then, his face contorted, his body twisting with anger. "You should have slaughtered each and every one of them."

Tecumseh had not fully explained his retreat from Vincennes; he'd said nothing about Rebecca. "We would have won the day. But I could not see clearly what came after."

"Then we march now." Rattle strode toward him. "Gather every warrior. Every able man. Return to the governor's mansion and wet the ground with his blood."

"No," Tecumseh said again. "It is not yet time to strike."

Rattle's missing eye itched whenever he was upset. He shoved two fingers beneath his patch and rubbed it out. "And what would you have us do instead? Wait here while Harrison gathers enough of an army to march against us?"

"He will not march now with winter so close."

"You do not know this for certain."

"Whether or not I'm certain, we'll do as I say."

His brother squealed. "This has been my entire life, listening to you. Always doing what I'm told. Because Tecumseh knows best. Well, you're only older by a minute—maybe two."

"This is a war decision. And so it falls to me."

"I am charged by the Great Spirit." He swung at the husked corn cobs strung along the ceiling to dry. The yellow ears dangled and swayed. "I am no longer your kid brother. I am powerful. I speak, and the people listen."

"They listen because they know the tomahawks of my warriors back your words of revolution."

"That's where you're wrong." Rattle shrank a little, gathering himself. "The people follow me because Our Creator speaks through me."

Tecumseh adjusted the matchcoat on his shoulders. "I leave tomorrow, to meet the tribes in the South. When I return, I will have doubled the size of our confederacy. Come spring, we will take back the land that was stolen from us."

Rattle's voice was little more than a whisper, but it stopped Tecumseh at the door. "Why do you move so much, brother?"

He swallowed. "You know I pay respect to other tribes that might help us with our cause."

"Do we not have messengers?" Rattle huddled beneath two bearskins, shivering, although it was warm outside.

"Runners do not carry the same weight as when I go myself."

"And you know that while you are gone, life continues here without you?"

Tecumseh waited, thinking he'd never seen his brother so still. It was as if the air had suddenly changed direction, as if he were gathering all the fluttering currents into himself.

"You can't escape me, brother," Rattle said. "In Tennessee or in Detroit, you are still from here. Your travels do not absolve you of your responsibilities to me. To your family."

"Responsibilities?" Tecumseh took three quick steps and poked him hard in the chest. "I think of nothing but my responsibilities. I am the one our father chose to lead our people. Chiksika raised me. I've had no choice but to become the man they wanted me to be."

"You've done a fine job of it, too." His brother shook his bearskins out from his girth. "But something has been lost. Chiksika raised you as a man of action, but you have become a politician. Traveling with your grovelers. Meeting with chief after chief. Enjoying tea with the governor in a walnut grove. How very pleasant. How very civilized."

"How do you think alliances are formed?"

"Your feet are stuck in the mud, brother," Rattle spat.

"People love to hear you talk. But I see through you. You talk to avoid action: you would talk yourself to death. And why is that, do you think? Is the great Tecumseh afraid? Maybe you've become so important to yourself that you are afraid of losing your life."

"All men fear losing their lives," he said. "I am not so rare."

"And do you value your life more than Chiksika did? More than our father?" Rattle drew himself up and crossed his arms. "I say you've grown timid and are a traitor."

Something splintered in Tecumseh then, as if he heard the sound of wood splitting beneath an axe. It was the sound of ice breaking in the river, the snapping of a neck between his hands. A heartfelt rendering: he threw a punch. But Rattle caught his fist with one hand, absorbing and then pushing back, slowly, against the force of the blow. His brother grinned, and laughed, as Tecumseh couldn't help the look of shock on his face.

"Is that it, then?" Rattle released his hand. "Is Tecumseh a traitor? Come, let us determine your loyalties once and for all."

Outside the Great Council House, a crowd had gathered. Villagers hurried past. Some shot quick and furious looks. Others seemed fearful and made way, veering off as the brothers emerged. Across the yard, a stake was raised with kindling stacked beneath it.

"I've no patience for torture," Tecumseh said.

"Oh." Rattle grabbed his arm. "I think you'll want to see this."

A murmur to their right became shouting and taunts. From the disturbance burst two warriors carrying Knotted Pine between them. The shaman was so old that no one knew his real age. He weighed little more than a beaver pelt: he was thin as a blade of grass. He did not fight. Still, two strong men dragged him to the stake and tied him upright.

"Stop this!" Tecumseh rushed them, but his own people closed in, armed with long knives and war clubs. Their meaning was clear. "You would burn a man our father's father called friend?"

Rattle made a grieved expression. "Sadly, he would not relinquish his medicine bag."

"A bag he's carried since before you or I was born."

When Rattle's men had come to seize it, by rule of the Shawnee code, the shaman had refused. Now the elder was bound to the stake. A brave stepped forward and lit the pyre and small flames jumped back and forth between the medicine man's feet.

"This is madness!" Tecumseh shouted.

"It's witchcraft, brother."

He could not believe Rattle would do this—not to the man who had kept the Eternal Flame longer than either of them had been alive. He who had instructed them, after Open Door died, to look after one another, whose charge still echoed in Tecumseh's ears. Remembering the words of Knotted Pine had stayed his hand more than once and reminded him to take mercy on his wayward brother. It was impossible that Rattle could do this.

The flames shot higher than the shaman's waist. He did not call out. His eyes were open. Only his dry lips moved, offering a prayer at the precipice of death.

Tecumseh sank to his knees. "I don't understand."

"You have a choice, brother." Rattle whispered in his ear. "Prove your loyalty."

"I can still save him—"

"And betray me?" Rattle took him by the shoulders. "The Keeper of the Eternal Flame has no power. Look on him! If he could save himself, do you not think he would? He let Open Door die, not because Our Creator willed it, but because he could not save him. He cannot even save himself. Everything you seek—life everlasting, a new home for our people—is beyond his grasp. Beyond anyone's but mine."

Tecumseh was on his feet again, yanking away from his brother. He circled the pyre, searching for a way through the flames. This was the worst kind of torture: even the lowest animal should not be subjected to such suffering. Treating a man's life as if it were nothing. Not just any life—a Shawnee life. The life of Knotted Pine.

The flames grew too hot and he retreated. He yelled and cursed the wind that fed them. There was a thick, black column of smoke. Knotted Pine vanished in the blaze. There was no way in and anyway, what good would it do now? Tecumseh had been forced to choose to save this man's life or follow his brother and the plan he had laid out for the Shawnee, and Tecumseh had chosen the future of his people.

A warrior approached the fire and emptied the contents of a medicine bag. There was almost nothing—a stone, a few tobacco leaves—and he flung the empty bag onto the crackling wood.

Tecumseh spat near his brother's feet. "This man you have become, I do not recognize him."

Those who were nearby took notice. They turned from the fire to watch the brothers argue, to see which conflagration would be greater. There were Shawnee and Wyandot as before, but now there were Kickapoo and Menominee. Rattle wore new clothes, some kind of knee-length tunic dyed the color of eggplant, with gold embroidery along the hem. His skin seemed to glow.

"I do not wish to fight you," Rattle said. "But we must also have consensus, lest we become divided like the lesser tribes."

Rattle straightened his robe. He wiped sweat from his upper lip. Finally, he gestured for a war club, and a warrior standing nearby gave him his. He held the war club parallel to the ground. Then he placed it at his feet. He backed away, and with his toe drew a four-foot circle around the weapon.

"We are on the verge of building something very great," he said. "But I see that you still do not believe."

"You disgrace our family," Tecumseh said.

Rattle's eyes flashed with anger. "Then pick it up, brother. Pick up the war club. If you can take this club in hand, I will never prophesy again."

Tecumseh wondered what his brother meant—or

what he had planned. Did he mean to knock him over the head when he bent down to retrieve the club? The weapon was sanded smooth, the inside edge was jagged with sharp teeth. It was no challenge to pick up a war club.

He approached the weapon and squatted there, waiting. His brother watched. And the warriors Tecumseh did not know, some of whom still had their knives drawn, watched too.

"Then let this foolishness end," Tecumseh said, and reached for the club.

He wrapped his hand around the grip and lifted. But the war club had some heaviness that would not be moved. The crowd fell silent. Some strong magic anchored the war club to the ground, as if the club had grown twisted roots ten feet deep. Tecumseh pulled with two hands, throwing his weight behind it. He groaned and pushed until sweat ran down his wrists and speckled the dry dirt.

"There will be a sign." Rattle wove through the crowd. "Fire will cut across the sky. Then we will know for certain that the time has come for us to gather all our people here."

Tecumseh shut his eyes. He let in one breath, released it through his nose. He couldn't allow himself to feel defeated by the present. Because the now burned, like being caught in sharp brambles and struggling to claw his way out—he had to ignore the pricks and cuts and skin pinches, keeping the goal always in mind, the moment when he would kick himself loose of the thorns. There was an end in sight here, even if his current actions betrayed an essential part of himself.

There was a bigger goal: the day they drove the Americans back into the great sea. When the Ohio River Valley would again echo with the cries of Shawnee hunting parties. When the forest would return to claim the empty settlements, the way nature eventually claims all things made by men, swallowing them again into wilderness. Then all of this would have been worth it—his people would be free.

He opened his eyes. "I will lead my men to Vincennes at morning light."

"No," Rattle smiled. "I've changed my mind. Go, take yourself to the tribes in the South. Tell them what we are building here. Gather men for our army, so that in the spring we can raise a glass and drink the blood of William Henry Harrison."

1811

South

TECUMSEH RODE HARD FROM TIPPECANOE. His horse seemed to sense his need to put distance between himself and the place he was from. It stretched into a full gallop, Tecumseh leaning over its mane and urging it forward through the countryside.

Travel had always felt like progress, a furthering of his life's work. More than the joy of finding himself someplace new, more than the excitement of strange tribes and customs, a journey carried with it the feeling of success. Behind him, those who preferred to stay home; ahead of him, some new part of himself he had yet to claim, which he would actualize upon arrival. It was not that he thought life was better someplace else. Instead, he traveled so as not to be forgotten. To experience fragments of a varied and complex world, as if re-assembling a broken mirror piece by splintered piece. And to travel to these new places, to be accepted there, even welcomed, made him feel as if he were becoming the fullest version of himself.

Now, there were more practical concerns. The loose confederacy at Tippecanoe fully backed his brother. They would do whatever Rattle asked. So would Tecumseh.

They'd come too far to jeopardize it all because his pride was injured. If there was any hope of defeating Harrison and holding their gains, they needed other tribes to ally with the Shawnee. And wouldn't a good brother be proud of Rattle, of the power he'd found? How he had been recreated fresh? And yet that also was what Tecumseh wanted for himself. The hope that if he kept moving, he would one day leave behind the person he was and transform into someone new.

In Kentucky, the land was rolling hills and thick grass fields flecked with blue. He passed into Tennessee, down through Florida, and west into Alabama. This was weeks along the journey. He met with Cherokee and Chickasaw, Seminole and Creek. He preached the new religion. He lashed out at the Creeks especially. There was a time, he told them, when settlers trembled at their war cries.

"Now your blood is white," he spat. "The spirits of the mighty dead complain. Their tears drop from the weeping skies."

But these southern tribes had received annuities for years. They were convinced they needed them to survive. They told themselves their people were safe even while their land vanished, a little more each day.

"Let the white race perish," Tecumseh said. "They trample on the ashes of your dead. Back when they came: war now, war forever."

In Florida, beneath palm trees, amid salt-stripped shrubs and sand needles, he met with the Choctaw chief Pushmataha, who greeted him in white man's clothes. He rejected Tecumseh's petition and predicted defeat.

The land changed. The beach thinned and disappeared. Trees grew out of the water, straight and tall. Thick clumps of snow-white moss hung from the branches. His horse waded up to its hocks, then its saddle. A shadow fell across him, and he looked up to see a blue heron, legs dangling, wings stretching across the slender spaces in the canopy. Its feathers were the same color as the sky.

Everywhere he looked was water. One channel led to another. The canals were murky brown and sluggish in the heat. He passed through funnel clouds of mosquitos and pulled his blanket around himself, choosing one discomfort over another. Already his skin burned from insect bites.

Daylight faded. His horse slogged through the marsh. There was motion at the surface, something coming up to breathe. Something large by the imprint it left below the water. He felt his horse stumble as if it had been rammed from below. He saw the shadow of something down there, something fleeting that came and was gone.

He trudged on. The night grew increasingly black, the moon hidden by the trees. Without eyes, he felt his other senses sharpen, hearing a skittering on the slough, some water being brushed aside and lapping against the tree roots; smelling a heavy, egg-like odor that he inhaled even when he breathed through his mouth, tasting it behind his teeth.

"Quiet now," he told his horse, rubbing its neck.

The channel emptied out into a broad stretch of slow river. Gaseous and wispy yellow orbs hovered at the surface. Some rose while others sank. They drifted nearer to one another and then parted ways in an aerial dance. From the shadows on the far bank came an unfamiliar call: "Ma, ma. Ma, ma. Ma, ma."

He didn't need to touch the quartzite around his neck to recognize the magic. Still, his pawawka token leapt and strained against its knot. The string that held it cut into his skin. The golden spirits came together in the formation of a diamond. They blinked in rhythm and drew closer.

He swung down from his horse, landing in water up to his armpits. He kicked his way to the closest sliver of land. The lights paused and hovered, still blinking. Watching him. Waiting.

Traders told terrible stories about the swamps. But the stories often contradicted one another. One said the lights warned travelers of danger. Another claimed the orbs were souls of dead children eager to drown the careless traveler. Either way, their sound was deafening. The marsh seemed to shudder with it, like rainwater sloshing in a barrel. Before, he might have mistaken the noise for a chorus of bullfrogs, but it sounded to him now distinctly human.

His horse took a few steps toward the lights, but he

pulled it back and circled once with it, trying to coax it up onto the bank. His horse pivoted then, and Tecumseh stumbled, losing the reins. And then the air was driven from his lungs as he found himself propelled not down into the water but up into the air.

He had heard nothing, then a sound like something rising quickly out of the depths. But too late: whatever it was had him in its clutches and was carrying him off his feet with astonishing speed. His arms were pinned. His legs kicked at the air. He thought it was maybe some kind of bird until he felt himself falling—not dropping so much as being dragged backward. First up, then down.

They hit the water—he and whatever it was that carried him—with so much force he nearly blacked out. There was no time to hold his breath. Water rushed through his mouth and nose and filled his lungs. The creature was incredibly strong. He could feel himself being crushed by its strength even as they dropped through the dark water. And there seemed to be no bottom to this river. Only blackness. Only a hushing sound and maybe a gurgling of the creature breathing in his ear. He closed his eyes. This was it then—this was how it would end. Life would be pushed out of him by something he never saw or heard. It wasn't human, whatever it was.

The last thing he felt before losing consciousness was regret. He wished he could have at least seen this beast, looked his murderer in the eye, and died bravely. But then the river revealed everyone for who they truly were.

And then he was cresting, coming out of the water with the same impossible velocity. He felt himself released. He lashed out with his arms and legs as water exploded from his lungs.

He opened his eyes. Crazy Jack was there, reaching down for him, grabbing his arms and dragging him onto shore. Tecumseh yanked his legs out of the water and scampered for the safety of the trees, taking in great swallows of air. But there was nowhere to go on the fen. He wrapped his arms around the smooth roots of a cypress. Crazy Jack fell back too and together they turned again toward the river.

The orbs floated just off the bank. They moved more quickly now, darting left and right and shooting diagonally into the sky. In their midst was a creature like none Tecumseh had seen. Its face was human, but its legs had green scales. Its hands were claws. It stood eight-feet tall, at least. It hurled its tail against the lights as the orbs attacked and then withdrew. The lights seemed to burn the creature each time they touched it. The beast gave a horrible yell and swatted at them with its talons.

"Letiche!" Crazy Jack shouted, naming the thing.

The monster was half-lizard, half-man. It might have had fangs—it was hard to tell in the darkness, amid the swirl of the yellow spheres. When it had had enough, it screamed one last time, plunged headfirst into the water, and was gone.

The orbs quieted. They approached the two men cowering on the bank. The lamps formed a line and dipped slightly, as if to bow. They blinked once, then shot off into the trees.

Crazy Jack crouched beside him. He withdrew a knife from where he'd plunged it into the ground, up to the hilt. There was blood on the blade.

"Funny thing about those old stories." Crazy Jack laughed. "You never know which ones are true."

"I nearly drowned," Tecumseh whispered.

"Quick thinking, that's all." He wiped the blade on his pants. "C'mon, let's dry you off."

Tecumseh was shaken. More than when he had helped Chiksika take that first flotilla on the river so long ago; more than when Judge Galloway shot him in the gut. It was not that he had never been so close to death—he was ready for death. It was that he had been powerless against that monster, that new magic.

"You saved my life," he told Crazy Jack.

"It wasn't me who rescued you," his friend said for what must have been the tenth time. They had passed into the northernmost stretch of what the whites called French Louisiana. "The orbs drove Letiche away."

"Because we are children of the light."

Crazy Jack winked. "Because if there is anything we believe, it is that the light will one day lead us home."

Tecumseh cracked his reins. He had found his horse a half-mile away, quaking in terror. Crazy Jack had a mount of his own, a tired-looking but hardy mule. They did not camp for the night; they did not make camp for three days. Finally they crossed into the Missouri Territory, in time to witness the burgeoning leaves, the hills curling in the distance. They led their horses along the edge of a cliff, above a narrow river.

"There is new magic," Crazy Jack said. "This Letiche—he is part of the white man's world. He is their creation, their evil."

He wore a style of clothes Tecumseh had never seen. The pants ballooned from his hips. They matched the shirt he wore, with their gold and brown stripes. There were no sleeves, so his bare arms hung out. On his head was a high-crowned velvet hat.

"It's how they're all dressing in New Orleans," the traveler said. "Well, the Portuguese anyway, whom I tend to feel warmest toward, given a chance to choose."

Crazy Jack went on to describe the magic he'd seen in that port city, and the collection of unsavory characters making a killing there, many literally. "If a city can be wild, it's that one. Even if they decide one day who it belongs to, don't expect it to behave. Whatever sorcery lives down there has no regard for claims of ownership, believe you me."

But Tecumseh was thinking about the old magic of his own people and all that had been driven from the Ohio Country. The Eternal Flame that had burned for generations was another kind of light, another kind of safe-harbor. What had happened to it? Had it been banished by his brother, along with the medicine bags and the ancient songs that called the animals to the fire? Extinguished like Knotted Pine? Tecumseh felt shame that he didn't know the answer—he hadn't been home long enough to ask.

"It was simpler in the days of our fathers," he said.

"Every generation says that," Crazy Jack grinned. "It's just not true."

But Tecumseh felt complicit in the new magic, as though he stood accused of something. It was wrapped up in his sense that the old ways were gone and somehow he was to blame—or that he alone stood against whatever new power had begun to establish itself on the frontier. The choices he faced, the extent to which it seemed Our Grandmother had abandoned them: indeed no Shawnee had faced quite these same impossible odds.

"You're exhausted," Crazy Jack said.

It was true—he had never felt so tired. He swatted a gnat from his brow and his hair felt brittle, like stale hay. How long since he'd bathed? He had no idea.

"And you're all alone." The traveler sighed. "Which is why I thought I'd pay a visit."

He touched the quartzite around his neck. It dangled below his throat, lifeless as any stone, its colors dull. Once, Crazy Jack was notorious in the Ohio Country. That was whom Tecumseh had befriended on his Quest. Who knew how old he really was? He hadn't aged a day.

"We've known one another many years," Tecumseh said.

"Thirty moons." He cleared one nostril, then the other. "Would you have guessed, so long ago, when I led you—a lost, little lamb—to find your horse, that now I'd be the only one you could still call friend?"

"I have a thousand warriors."

"Perhaps." Crazy Jack spat into the ravine, leaning out over the rock to watch it fall. "But your brothers? Where are they? The old medicine man, or the girl—"

"Don't say her name." He silenced him. "Do me that one favor, at least."

But he wondered at the traveler's words—at what lay behind them. All his life he had told himself that he was achieving, or at the very least carrying on his family's great work. Repelling the Americans. Reclaiming Shawnee land. But there was another way to frame his life story: perhaps, all this time, he had only been perfecting the art of losing.

Because it was true what Jack said—he had no one left. He had betrayed, or been betrayed by, everyone he ever loved in one way or another. But those betrayals had seemed such minor things when they occurred, and he could excuse them then because they were a sacrifice to the greater Cause, that of his life's work.

"You've betrayed no one." Jack clapped him on the arm, having read his thoughts—they were no doubt etched deep into his expression. "You've devoted your life to bettering the lives of your people. There's no shame in that."

He shut his eyes, opened them. "Have you always been able to read minds?"

Jack laughed. "It's the first trick anyone learns who

has even the faintest interest in magic. Didn't your brother teach you anything?"

The Osage were known as "the people of the middle water" and built their villages on the banks of a long river. Tecumseh had never seen such a settlement: their main road ran east-west, and on either side lived the two divisions of the tribe—an Osage was either part of the Sky People or part of the Earth People. Homes were symmetrically arranged outward. Families lived together in one wigwam, some running nearly a hundred feet long. Tall saplings were bent and woven with other trees and mats to form the uprights. It was the closest thing he'd seen to architecture on par with the white cities in the north.

Crazy Jack had bid him farewell, something about needing to get back to New Orleans because he'd promised someone he wouldn't be gone long. He didn't say, but Tecumseh suspected this someone was female, and possibly into a kind of black magic—not of this land, but from across the ocean. Crazy Jack said he was learning a thing or two, and not only about voodoo, if you caught his drift, wink wink, which Tecumseh did.

As evening came on, Tecumseh entered the Osage village. It was a far cry from the scattered chaos at Tippecanoe, where many families were still sleeping out in the open, and even those that had built shelters gave little thought to where they built them. They certainly had no road as straight as the one that divided this village between north and south, between the people of the earth and those who flew.

He arrived feeling grateful to have survived his encounter with Letiche. He arrived tired and hungry. And he arrived to find a scene that would not have been out of place in his own Shawnee village: in the center of town, a man was being tortured.

The white man was tied by his hands to a stake, with enough slack in the rope for him to stumble his way around the pole. But he had little energy left for that. Whether he walked right or left, a squaw was there to burn him with the heated end of a stick. Others held muskets, loaded with powder. They pressed the barrels against the man's flesh and pulled the triggers, leaving tidy, black-charred circles on his skin. His body was white as a meal worm. His face was painted black. He wore military trousers—all that remained of his uniform. Men danced around him, lashing out to club him with the blunt end of their tomahawks.

Tecumseh swung down from his horse and grabbed the arm of a boy who happened to be standing there, gaping.

"Who is he?" he demanded.

"An American scout," the boy said. "A gift from the Creeks."

A squaw had loaded hot coals on a board. She approached the prisoner and flung the burning embers: he pitched forward, howling, but found himself snapped back again by the tether. He collapsed, whimpering, as he shook off the red-hot coal dust.

Tecumseh remembered the strength of the prisoner Boden from his youth, the way the man had braved the gauntlet twice and nearly escaped.

He pushed through the ring of onlookers. "Enough."

The Osage were a race of giants. Their men stood well over six-feet tall—some more than seven feet. With shocks of red-dyed hair at the backs of their heads and painted war bands spiraling down their arms, they were an intimidating group. For sheer savagery, their treatment of enemies rivaled the Shawnee. Still, they backed away at Tecumseh's words.

"Most of you know who I am." He let the crowd take him in. "For those who do not, I am Tecumseh of the Shawnee, the Great Panther Crossing the Sky, brother of the Prophet. This, what you are doing here, does not please the Great Spirit."

He looked each man and woman in the eye. Some wanted very badly to continue the torture. Others weren't sure what to make of this foreigner, breaking up their gathering and now making demands.

"Is this prisoner to be executed?" he asked them.

A warrior replied, "He is to die tonight."

"Taking prisoners is costly." He put his foot against the white man's back and pushed with little force: he collapsed, unable to support himself. "They must be fed, guarded, cared for. If this man is to die, let him die. But be swift about it."

There was dissent. A squaw said, "The whites treat our prisoners no better."

"We have more to do with our time than torture little boys," he said, because in truth the prisoner was seventeen or eighteen, still baby-faced and soft. "If a man is to be executed, let it be so. If not, return him to his home. It is not our concern: let us look to more important matters."

He stepped away. Two men helped the prisoner to his feet and tied him upright against the stake. Others worked swiftly to assemble the kindling and soon the fire was lit and the prisoner was consumed by flames.

"Brothers." Tecumseh swung back into his saddle, needing the advantage of height to address them. "We all belong to one family. We are all children of the Great Spirit. I know you have just ended a conflict with the Choctaw. Lay that enmity to rest."

This was something he hadn't tried. No longer would he make requests, or implore these tribes to join him. He would speak only the truth, and speak it harshly. He was finished asking questions. If Chiksika had taught him anything, it was that most men wanted to be told what to do as badly as he wanted to tell them to do it—maybe more.

His horse bucked and he steadied the reins. "The blood of our many fathers and brothers has run like water on the ground to satisfy the avarice of white men. We shared with them whatever the Great Spirit had given his red children. But the whites are like poisonous serpents: when chilled, they are feeble and harmless. But invigorate them with warmth, and they sting their benefactors to death."

His horse pranced side to side, snorting. Some of the

warriors nodded to one another. His words were gaining traction.

Behind him, flames spit and kicked. "You have heard of the great deeds of my brother, who many call the Prophet. You know me by reputation, and that my words are as sure as my tomahawk. The Shawnee and Wyandot are brave and numerous, but the white army is still too strong. I ask you now to join us. Who are the Americans that we should fear them? They cannot run fast. They are good marks to shoot at. They are only men—and our fathers have killed many of them."

Cheers rose, and war whoops. The braves stomped their feet and beat their fists against their chests. He thought that yes, finally he had found an ally.

"Tecumseh."

Someone spoke his name—he barely heard it above the din of the crowd. But there was authority in the voice. He turned and saw Roundhead, the Wyandot chief, standing at the Great Council House. He must have ridden weeks from Tippecanoe.

Tecumseh maneuvered his steed to greet him. "Brother, what news?"

Roundhead did not offer a smile. "I have been waiting for you."

"Then let us council. I am relieved to see a friendly face."

He wore two white feathers at his crown. The neckline of his shirt was embroidered with white and black beads. He nodded toward the assemblage, where many still waved their weapons in the air, shouting. "It is best if we talk somewhere private."

It was not good news. It could not be. Tecumseh knew Roundhead had not come this far to deliver good news. And so, as he followed his lieutenant inside the lodge, he prepared himself for whatever he might say.

Both Osage leaders were there, and the Wyandot sat with them and began passing a tobacco pipe. Tecumseh did not sit but paced small circles, shaking out his legs. His thighs were chapped and bloody from the long ride.

"Speak, brother," he said finally. "Your words can do no more damage to me than my imagination already has."

"It is not good news." The chief opened and closed his massive hands, making fists, considering his words. "Tippecanoe has fallen."

Tecumseh blinked as if the room had become suddenly very bright. "Fallen?"

"Your brother." He looked at him squarely. "I am sorry to tell you this."

"Speak then." Tecumseh squatted, accepting the pipe. "Start from the beginning."

Roundhead began slowly, then his words took on more force. He described how shortly after Tecumseh had gone, Rattle built a larger medicine lodge. Here he spent most of his days and nights with two or three boys to help him with his magical arts.

"We saw him very little," Roundhead said. "And when we did, he was often alone, mimicking the movements of a bear, growling and grunting, or calling out like some great bird. The spirits were very much affecting him. And yet we never doubted the Great Spirit spoke through him."

Despite what Tecumseh had predicted, William Henry Harrison had marched from Vincennes with a thousand men. He sailed down the Wabash and camped a half-mile from Tippecanoe. When Shawnee delegates went to meet him, he assured them he only wanted peace, and agreed to a council the following day.

Roundhead shrugged. "Remember that many in Tippecanoe had gone home in your absence to care for their fall harvests. We had but five hundred men when Harrison arrived."

Rattle told his warriors not to fear: the Great Spirit had delivered a message, that the bullets of the white men would not harm them but would pass through them.

That night was very dark. There was no moon, and the winds were hard. Many gathered outside the medicine lodge, taking comfort in one another, fearing the large army camped so close. Strange noises and flashes of light came from within the lodge, but no one dared enter.

Finally the Prophet emerged. He had painted a white circle around his empty eye socket. He wore a turban and dozens of silver bracelets and clasps. He wore one heavy earring in the shape of a star and another in the shape of a crescent moon. Around his neck hung his bear-tooth necklace and the moldy beans he always carried.

"He seemed to fall into a trance," Roundhead said. Even now he seemed to have trouble believing all that he had seen. "He chanted and trembled, and raised his arms. He said we would not wait for the morning's council. We were to attack Harrison's army that night, while the white man's eyes were clouded with dark."

They would attack before dawn, while the Americans slept. But Harrison had roused his men early. The Shawnee lost the element of surprise.

"Their guard collapsed beneath our first wave," Roundhead said. "But it was soon clear that all was not as it should be. Despite what the Prophet had foreseen, our men were dying."

During the fight, Rattle had stayed well behind the lines, chanting and pounding on a water drum.

"I ran to him and told him all was not as he had promised," the chief said. "We were dying in great numbers. But the Prophet said it would be some time before the prophecy took effect."

The night was terrifying because of the total blackness. They could not see the enemy or know whom they were fighting. By dawn, the Prophet had abandoned his drum and retreated past Tippecanoe with the women and children. They had fled to a camp ten miles north.

"We slaughtered four of theirs for every one of ours," Roundhead said. "But there were too many. The next morning, Harrison's men burned Tippecanoe—they burned everything. Five thousand bushels of corn and beans. Our supply for the winter."

Tecumseh waited to feel something—anything—other than what he felt, which was a void expanding from his chest to the edges of his limbs. He lost, somewhere, the sense of his body having borders. It was all emptiness. And he was falling from a great height. He put his hands on the ground to steady himself.

"Where is my brother now?" he asked.

"We caught him," Roundhead said. "Some wanted to kill him. But we agreed to hold him until you returned. His fate is in your hands."

Tecumseh stood. He knew his friend was waiting for him to say something, to make some proclamation. But he turned away. He stumbled to the door, where he steadied himself against the bent saplings. He breathed in, thinking he could smell the dank ground where the roots had been pulled from—the wood smelled like rich earth, pungent life. Thinking how far the trees were from home. How far he himself was, and his goal still further away yet. Caught somewhere in the middle then, with nowhere to hide. And Roundhead's eyes on him. He was waiting for some decision, or outburst, something to reassure him this was not the end.

He closed his eyes. He heard voices outside, villagers passing along the main road. Men and women. Strange that there should be so many, so late in the day.

He felt as if he were the animal skin stretched taut across the uprights of the council house. But inside—nothing to guard, or care for. An empty room. An empty bowl. The way a drop of water spilled onto dirt quickly disappears. All at once the hundreds upon hundreds of miles he'd traveled seemed to take hold. He felt exhaustion, like a sticky vine, snare his ankles and legs. For the first time in his life, sleep was the only thing he really wanted.

More voices outside now. A lot of people were gathered in the street, where men were shouting.

He pushed open the door and stepped out. Evening had come, then night. The street was filled with Osage warriors, all looking at the sky.

He turned. Up among the thousand luminaries, the stars like jewels on black cloth, one cut a bright trajectory across the felt. It seemed to cast aside everything in its path. A comet, blazing.

All the miles traveled—every leave he had taken, each new sight—crashed down on him at once. His heart was sucked up by a devil wind, his spirit corkscrewing through the air. Why tonight, of all nights, was there a comet? When he'd only just learned that all was lost, that Tippecanoe had fallen, that his last brother had betrayed him?

"This is a sign," he said, although he did not know that anyone was listening. "Our Creator reminds us to have strong hearts."

The crowd pressed in. They shouted his words back to him. Two hundred heartbeats, two hundred souls. They were waiting for his direction.

"This is only the first sign." He lifted his arms. "I will return to Tippecanoe. When I reach that place, I will stamp my foot on the ground. My foot will cause a great rumbling in the earth. And when it does, you will know the second sign has come, and what I have spoken is true. You will know why Our Creator has sent me. You will join me as part of a new nation."

Tecumseh felt unreasonably, almost insanely good. There was a little mist, and the birds were chattering, and on the horizon the sun was shining through the clouds. Despite the setback at Tippecanoe, the Osage had sworn their support. Together with the Wyandot chief, he rode hard for home.

"I thought you left the prophecies to your brother," Roundhead said.

"All will be as I predicted," he said.

His lieutenant growled. "The trouble with prophecies is that if you are wrong, you will lose their loyalty forever."

"Not true." He winked. "The beauty of predictions is that the world only remembers the ones you get right."

"So you hope."

"Reputations have been built on less."

It was not in Tecumseh to accept defeat. He would not. He would fight Harrison with three men, or two, or alone. He would fight with every breath Our Grandmother allotted him. Seeing his birthright cross the sky had clarified certain things. It was as if what he'd suspected all along, his deepest, unspoken dreams, were coming true. When he'd made his prediction about the earthquake, he knew that what he said would come to pass with the same certainty he knew the sun would rise each morning. How had Rattle once described it? Maybe he was finally learning to swim.

"And what about your brother?" Roundhead asked. "What are your plans for him?"

His heart clenched, and the light withdrew from his eyes. "I will paint my brother's face black. I will tie him to the back of a horse. I will drag him from town to town so that each man and woman who he has betrayed can cut off a piece of his fat, useless body—a finger, a nose—and in doing so scatter his worthless flesh across the river valley."

They traveled north along the Mississippi River. They saw no one. There were few signs that anyone had passed this way in quite some time. It was still wild land and no one bothered them.

They rested near the mouth of the Ohio. They tied their horses, and the horses drank. On the far bank, trees stood jagged against the sky. Tecumseh crouched and drew water into his skin. He looked at the current, shut his eyes, and looked again. He thought his vision must be playing tricks on him. To his right was due north, but the water here seemed to be flowing from his left—from the south.

"Odd," he said, mostly to himself. He kept watching. A log, floating near the center of the river, dipped and twisted and passed left to right. Without question, the river was flowing north. He called for Roundhead.

"There's something strange with the current," he said.

"It could be an illusion, created by the confluence of the rivers."

Some animal, a fox or raccoon, had drowned. They spotted it at the farthest southern turn. They watched it bob past and disappear around the bend.

"It's no illusion," Tecumseh said.

"Some magic then?"

"Wait." He put the palm of his hand to the ground. "Do you feel that?"

As a child, learning to hunt meant learning to recognize vibrations. By putting his ear to the mud, he knew how many horses were coming, or how many men. Carriages had their own timbre, as did feet—one or a hundred soldiers running created their own singular reverberations. Thunder had a rolling wave that resounded long after the sound had gone. But what he felt now was different.

He stood and wiped his hands. Beneath his feet he felt a short and unsteady hammering. The ground was trembling, not as something struck, but more deeply: the earth was shaking somewhere in its belly. All at once there was no sure footing.

Across the river, the sharp silhouette of the tree line heaved and pitched. Trees snapped and moments later the sound reached him: the shrieking splinter of wood.

He staggered, caught himself, reached for his companion. "The horses."

They ran. The earth swayed. The horses stamped and

whinnied. He reached his own mount and snatched the reins. He turned again toward the river in time to see a column of water, a quarter-mile through its center, shoot sixty feet into the air. Behind the column came a wave that swelled and crested and seemed to him like a giant's hand in the moment before slapping down.

He swung himself into the saddle. He cracked the reins. His horse bolted, crashing through underbrush. They would put distance between themselves and the coming flood. But he could hear the rumbling now, the deep baritone of the earth. His horse stumbled and caught its balance and dodged a falling pine and kept on. Roundhead caught up with him in another mile and together they rode and did not look back.

1811

Kentucky

THEY FOUND AN ALTERED TERRAIN: trees uprooted, great mounds of earth churned and folded. Along the river, as far as they could see, was now barren land.

They passed piles of lumber and tin that once had been cabin homes—smashed by the flood. Fires burned in distant fields and livestock wandered free.

Despite the appearance of the comet, despite the earthquake coming just as Tecumseh predicted, there was no way to look favorably on the loss they had incurred at Tippecanoe. There was, he thought, no coming back from that—the future too was altered now, and would be different than it might have been had Rattle not foolishly attacked, or had Tippecanoe not fallen. Again Tecumseh was forced to lower his expectations, to halve his dreams. To harbor a more modest hope for the Shawnee: perhaps not to reclaim their land but to defend what little they had left.

He would not admit this, of course. He would continue to exude the confidence of one who was favored. Of one who had earned and kept the graces of Our Grandmother. Of one who led a people with a long and storied and certain future. And yet his personal plumb stone had been cast. He'd bet on black; it had come up white.

There were scattered refugees, families displaced by the quake, wandering in the wilderness. They carried what they could, leading cattle and packhorses, mules and wagons. They paid no attention to two braves on horseback. The country had changed. There was nothing for them to fear.

Even when the land was sacred Shawnee hunting ground, Tecumseh's people did not consider the land theirs, any more than they might claim ownership of the rivers and sky. It had seemed such an absurd idea when the white man came asking to purchase this or that parcel. What value could be placed on something that was abundantly free? But then those same white men sold those parcels for many times what they paid and suddenly the lands were filled with homesteaders. The animals flushed out, the Shawnee no longer welcome in woods that had been hunted by their ancestors. Only then was it clear: there was no reconciling their race with the way the white man lived. When ownership, the idea of staking one's claim, was the god you prayed to, there was no room for anyone else. The white men consumed, and then consumed still more, but this consumption did not fill them. It was like eating sweets that tasted pleasant on the tongue but left you hungry. Greed drove a bigger and bigger need, bore a deeper and deeper hole. It was not something that would ever be filled.

What had Rebecca said once? That consumption didn't strike her as very "Christian." The man they prayed to, Jesus, never owned a thing. How ironic that so much since had been claimed in his name.

Tecumseh and Roundhead made their way along the river. They had not seen anyone in quite some time. Soon they would need to either ford the water or swim: the bridge was gone. Great Horned Snake or no, Tecumseh tried not to get wet when he could avoid it. The river had given and taken an equal amount from him over the course of his life. He had no desire to test it.

They were resting in the thick woods, eating supper, when they heard the sound of a woman's voice from somewhere up the road. Tecumseh noted the melody and then, without thinking too much about it, found himself humming along. A song called "Logan's Water," which had been one of Rebecca's favorites. On his belly, he crawled to the edge of the undergrowth and squinted down the road. A voice sang:

At e'en, when hope amaist is gane,
I daunder dowie an' forlane,
Or sit beneath the trystin'-tree,
Where first he spak' o' love to me.

A horse-drawn wagon was coming toward them. Two American soldiers, on horseback, trailed at twenty paces. The wagon driver wore a military uniform, topped with a tricorn hat. Rebecca Galloway rode beside him, bracing herself with one hand against the unsteady road. In her other hand she held a book. She held the pages close to her nose, all the while maintaining the haunting, down-turned melody. The wagon was filled with dry goods and furniture. And books.

Roundhead settled in beside him, and Tecumseh asked, "Do you see anyone else?"

"No." Then, "Is that the governor's wife?"

He shrugged his pack and handed it over. "Take my horse, return to Tippecanoe. I will meet you there in a few days' time."

"Didn't you two have a bit of a turn, a long time ago?"

Tecumseh glared at him. "Please, I am asking you this one favor."

The Wyandot war chief peered again at the road. "Are you sure you don't want my help?"

"This one is mine, brother."

Roundhead seemed disappointed, and shrugged. "Well, have fun."

Tecumseh sprinted through the woods, heading uphill even as he made his way east along the road, keeping it in sight, wanting to get ahead of the wagon. He stepped high, clearing roots and underbrush. His legs worked like wheels, lifting but also pushing himself forward. He remembered his training sessions with Chiksika long ago, when his older brother marked the trees with targets. Now, Tecumseh moved more quickly through the forest than most men ran at full speed on flat ground. Soon he was a hundred yards ahead of the wagon, then two hundred. The terrain presented itself; his body moved without his command. His feet chose each step, every leap, and varied his stride to compensate for the uneven ground. Pounding steadily uphill, he found he wasn't thinking at all.

Which was good, because most of his thinking was consumed by what to do once he stopped running. Rebecca Galloway: what did he want from her? What could she possibly give him now? He had made his choices, and so had she. He did not blame her. But also he felt no guilt over what he himself had chosen—the future of his people over their love for one another. There was nothing left to talk about. In the years since, he had mostly succeeded in closing his heart against the memory of her, although he still sometimes dreamt of her even though other, more recent memories had long since vanished. Yet something was sending him blasting through the woods, with so much speed he felt his heart slamming against his chest, like a bullfrog trapped in a crate. Something drove his legs faster, three hundred yards now out in front. He wanted one more chance with her alone, to look into her eyes and see for himself. Her words, the things she said, would not matter at all. Her eyes would give him all the answers he needed.

He dropped behind an outcropping on the hill. The ground rose steeply from the creek and the road that ran along it. Tecumseh knelt behind the rock pile, swatting away funnel clouds of gnats. He was thirty yards above with a clear view to the west. He saw the wagon materialize as a smudge of color against the trees, then heard its creaking axles, the horses breathing heavily, a rifle butt knocking against the saddle horn, someone scratching his knee, the pages of a book being turned: a whisk punctuated by a snap. Whisk—snap. Whisk—snap. Rebecca smartly dispensing with the printed words whenever she turned the page.

And then they were close enough for Tecumseh to see the dark brown patches on the flanks of the smallest horse, how one of the mounted men leaned out and spat tobacco juice, how Rebecca sat impossibly erect—she looked impossibly clean, really. Her skin shone beneath her black hair, still long and thick and pulled tight to her scalp. Whenever she turned a page, sunlight caught the ring on her left hand, the cut gem that Tecumseh felt symbolized the death of everything he had ever wanted for himself, or had been foolish enough to allow himself to ever consider.

He nocked an arrow, pulled the bowstring, and took measure down its length. It would be a difficult shot, through the branches, down a steep slope. Difficult for most, anyway.

His first arrow found its mark in the center of a mounted soldier's chest. There was no sound. The arrow flew, hit, and then the rider slumped and fell from his horse. The other cavalryman didn't notice—and then he noticed too late. He was swinging his rifle level when Tecumseh's second arrow ripped into his throat. He spat great quantities of blood across his horse and down the back of the wagon. It was the spray that made Rebecca look up from her book: she saw the two riders down and then the driver beside her leapt up as if he'd been stung, clutching the arrow shaft in his side. Tecumseh's third shot hadn't been perfect, but his fourth caught the man in the forearm when he raised his hand just as Tecumseh fired.

"Now you're really making a mess of it," he muttered to himself, stringing his fifth arrow.

The driver stood in his seat, flailing. Tecumseh fired and drove the shaft into the man's belly. He toppled forward, laying briefly across the reins, then pitched to the ground. There was only Rebecca then, her face expressionless, her book resting in her lap, hands folded across the cover. As calm as if she were sitting in church.

Tecumseh came down out of the trees. He waltzed into the center of the path and let her recognize him. He approached the wagon, not saying anything, but making his way toward the harnessed horses which had paused in the road.

She looked to either side, then behind her. "It's only you, then?"

What a thing to say, he thought. Of all the ways to greet him. Of all the words at her disposal.

The wagon driver was still alive, crawling for the creek. Tecumseh crouched and slit his throat and then peeled the silver scalp from his head. When the hair pulled clear, he tossed the clump into the wagon where it landed at Rebecca's feet.

She shifted her shoes away from it. "We had a cat once. Brought us dead things in the night. Mouse hearts. Bird beaks. Is that what this is?"

He checked the two riders. They were dead, and he scalped them as well, flinging each piece of flesh into the wagon. Their horses were wandering just up the road, so he stripped their saddles and slapped their rumps and set them running off the opposite direction. The saddles he piled in the back of the wagon.

"Are you taking me prisoner?" she asked.

He still hadn't said anything. He collected the rifles and ammunition from the dead men. He considered taking their clothes but decided against it—it just wasn't worth the money he might sell them for. Then he pulled himself into the wagon, bumping Rebecca a little so she had to make room for him on the bench.

"What are you reading?" he asked, taking the reins in hand.

"*Confessions*." He heard her gather courage. "Of St. Augustine."

He rubbed his chin. "Have you something to confess?"

"Only as much as the next. After all, we're accountable for our suffering."

Some blood had spattered on her cheek, so he licked his fingertip and wiped away the marks from her skin. She did not flinch. She might have even bowed her head slightly, leaning into his touch.

"I admit the wife of the governor of Indiana would be a fine prisoner," he said. "But I wonder if you'd be any use.

How long has it been since you worked the fields, or made your own lye?"

"I might return a nice ransom."

"Perhaps. Although one might ask himself how much the governor of Indiana values his bride to let her travel with only three escorts."

"This is no longer Indian country."

He turned from her and cracked the reins. "It will always be Indian country."

The horses heaved the wagon forward. She wanted to know where he was taking her. He considered his reply, how weighted his answer would be. How the word meant something so much different to her than it did to him.

"Home," he said.

The road was passable. The horses did not struggle with their load. Before long, Rebecca slipped her arm through his and they rode like that, not saying anything.

"I used to fanaticize about this," she said. "A proper ride."

"With me?"

"With a gentleman."

"A proper ride," he said. "And yet the things you and I have used a wagon for haven't been proper at all."

There were moments from yesterday, or last month, or last year, which felt further away than the last time he'd sat beside Rebecca Galloway. How often in the ensuing years had their time together come rushing forward to greet him when he least expected it, erupting from the long, dark storm cloud of memory to interrupt moments of intimacy with women he cared far less for. Or the way her voice sometimes woke him in the middle of the night, although he never found her there. It should have felt odd, or at least remarkable, for them to be sitting beside one another then, in a wagon, in Kentucky, having found her among so much wild and barely guarded. But it did not feel odd or even noteworthy. It felt like it had always been; it felt like yesterday and tomorrow. Things were finally as they should be. A pocket of air where he could finally, if briefly, breathe.

"All of these years, you never wrote," she said. "There was no word from you at all."

So he'd written no letters, sent her nothing, had not been within fifty miles of her until seeing her at Vincennes. Wasn't it like her to pin the blame on his ego, his disregard?

"I'm not the one who married," he said.

He'd meant it to hurt, but when her eyes flashed and became hard, angry glass, he thought maybe he'd struck too fast, too true.

"I hate you." She turned from him, yanking her arm from his. "I wish you were dead. I wish my father had killed you."

This wasn't what he intended, not at all. This wasn't how he wanted the conversation to go. But he couldn't clear his mind. He closed his eyes and saw her with Harrison and this imagining made his entire body burn from inside. His hands ached, and he opened and closed them. But the only thing that would bring relief, he knew, would be to pound them against something—to cause something to break.

"I did not write you," he said, "because despite your best efforts in teaching me, I still do not write well."

She wouldn't look at him, but wiped the back of her hand across her face. "I don't care how well you write."

"More than that, even if I were more eloquent than Shakespeare, I would not have written you. Think on it: would you have had us correspond at length? Exchange pleasantries, inquire after one another's loves and losses? Afraid of realizing we had moved on, or terrified we hadn't?"

"Love has no end," she said, finally looking at him. "And yet, there are practicalities."

"Better to let what we had continue to exist, where it lives, now and forever, in the past. Unblemished."

"Unexplored."

He shook his head, wanting to reach for her hand but afraid to. "Better not to cheapen what we shared with these current, lesser versions of ourselves. To soil it with the compromises we've made, the civilities we've grown accustomed to. To allow one thing in this world to remain perfect and untouched. The purity of what we had. It was raw; it was real."

"Our silence gives it too much power," she said. "We have not spoken since that time in my father's house. Whenever I think of you—"

"Your feelings are as strong as they were then."

Their silence since that time in her father's house was an admission. Unspoken, perhaps unrecognized, even by them. That there might be other loves—spouses or children. But the love they shared would be buried like a pirate buries his loot: perfectly preserved, undiscovered for centuries. Priceless.

"The dreams," he said. "They come so often."

She allowed a smile. "No one else interrupts my sleep as frequently or as powerfully. I find I am able to recreate you perfectly in my dreams, even after all these years."

It was the saddest conversation he had ever had. The most truthful, too. He had never felt so impotent. There was nothing to be done. No solution, even if they wanted one. Nothing to do but continue on. In another place, maybe. Some other life.

"We're cursed," she sighed, threading her arm through his again.

He thought yes, that was precisely so. He was cursed, they were cursed, and the Shawnee were at best no longer favored—which amounted to pretty much the same thing.

So he and Rebecca would keep buried that which they had shared. He might glimpse it from time to time, the way he might catch sight of a deer darting through the trees, there and gone so quickly he wasn't sure he'd seen it. Stumbling upon soft, mossy lights in the woods might bring to mind the girl she'd been, her fearlessness and ready laughter; the smell of an open book would always stir his groin in a way no other scent could, all those trysts in her father's library. And in his most desperate and lonely hours, he would think of her and feel trapped between his desire and his need to let her go. Which, he knew, he would never quite allow himself to do.

"Do you love him?" he asked.

"It's calm." She held his gaze, so that he would understand. "With him there is order, structure. It's less volatile."

"He's made a good life for you."

"So why come to me now?"

He set his jaw. He wanted to be the one who asked questions. "I simply recognized you among the refugees."

She laughed, tossing her hair. "Don't think that I believe that, even for a moment."

They turned a bend, and the horses pressed on. They could hear the rushing water and something scrambling through the dried leaves—a squirrel, or birds looking for seeds.

"When I saw you at Vincennes," he said, "my heart flew from my body. I became disconnected from myself. All the parts of me seemed far away. The experience was mystical. That you could marry him—"

"I won't be judged for my decisions."

"And I have only your best interest in mind. That is why I never wrote, or came to you again: because it would be easier for you if I didn't."

"What a thing to say. What arrogance."

"No." He shook his head. "I hoped you would seal me somewhere deep inside, and hate me—that would make it bearable."

"But I nearly died thinking you no longer loved me," she said. "Wondering how you could walk away from all we built and shared. Wondering what it had meant, once you left."

He was finished looking for meaning though. He was pretty sure there wasn't any. "I wanted to see you now to know if the woman I loved still lives."

"And why does it matter to you if she does?"

"Because I am still the man who loved you. And I want to know if I am the only one of us who feels as if his life ended the day I fled your father's library with a bullet in my belly."

She smiled and rested her head on his shoulder. "No. There are two of us."

They camped for the night. She slept in the wagon. He made his bed on the ground. She was married now and insisted they respect that. He was willing, although as he lay there, wrapped in his blanket on the hard dirt, he felt his desire for her like a rope pulled taut between them. He slept poorly.

In the morning, they covered the last few miles to the edge of the woods where her family's property began. He would go no further.

"What will you do?" she asked. "The governor has broken your confederacy."

"But not defeated," he said, noting her use of *governor* and not *husband*. Not even calling him by name. "The Osage will support us. The Wyandots."

"It is not nearly enough."

"No. Which is why I will pledge my warriors to the

British." Ashamed, he could not look at her because he didn't want to see her expression, which he knew would show only disappointment. "I will demand to be a general in their ranks; I will command my own men."

"The great Tecumseh," she teased, "stooping to join their little war."

"It's not their war," he said. "It is Tecumseh's War. That is how it will be remembered."

He had taken the second horse to ride back to Tippecanoe. The first would pull the wagon the remaining miles. More than likely, her family's field hands would find her within the hour.

As he was preparing his saddle, she came to him. She stopped short of an embrace. She put her hand on his chest.

"We should probably pretend we never saw one another," she said.

His thoughts were jumbled. Blood pounded in his ears. He felt connected to the earth by the thinnest thread. His heart was so full—he wanted to scream, or explode, to somehow change all this.

"I still love you," he said.

Her hand paused on his chest, her eyes downcast, as if she were listening, perhaps, to the vibrations of his heart against her palm.

"I am with child," she said.

And then she was stepping back with her words still hanging in the air. She was climbing into the wagon when Tecumseh fully understood. But his feet were stuck in the mud. He had no words—they were trapped at the base of his throat. He fell into a coughing fit and retched, and tried to push it all out of his stomach, the spirit of her which had always and would forever inhabit him completely.

She did not look back at him, not even once. He knew because he stood watching her wagon recede like the wavering of a candle flame in the moment before it dies, having melted the wax beneath it and come to the end of its thin, black wick, and finding no future there.

1811

Territory of Indiana

IT WAS HOME NOW, and bore many resemblances to the place where he had grown up. Which is why, perhaps, returning to Tippecanoe made Tecumseh think of his father.

He thought about him often, of course—every day. Mostly he wondered what Pucksinwah would think about something someone had said, or he'd come across. What his opinion might be, whether he'd be for or against. Knowing his father always thought about things in the long term, aligned his perspective with whatever side he considered just, and above all saw things as a Shawnee. Conjecture, of course: Tecumseh had been so young when he had died. He hadn't known him the way Chiksika had. All he remembered were scenes, out of context. He wasn't around much. Tecumseh supposed that in this way, they were the same.

He was jealous of Rattle. If his brother could speak with their ancestors like he claimed, then he'd been able to forge a relationship with their father, had been able to know him as a man, as an equal, in a way Tecumseh never would.

Tecumseh remembered that morning at the river, where the brothers dove for their pawawka tokens. If he closed his eyes, he could hear the deer-call whistle his father had carved from a plump stick. And finally, the crate of apples he brought home once after a raid. The way he'd eaten the apple through its core, stem and all.

It was the apples that were on Tecumseh's mind as he arrived at Tippecanoe. Cooking fires were being lit; children were called in from the fields. The village was, as Roundhead had warned, overrun. Gutted, a blackened skeleton. He exhaled against the cold and saw his breath. There was smoke too from the cooking fires as he strode past, and beneath the piles of wreckage and waste were still-hot embers that had been smoldering for weeks.

Against this backdrop he noticed the apple trees.

It was a small grove of half a dozen trees, the branches bare. Only if he looked close enough did he notice the hard, reddish buds. Knobby things containing life, preparing for winter. The trees were a few years old, but he'd never noticed them before.

"Next year." Roundhead found him, having noticed his approach. "Next spring this orchard may finally produce fruit good enough to eat."

"Not before now?" Tecumseh ran his fingers over the smooth, shiny bark.

"Soon." The Wyandot cleared his throat.

The man he'd met, John Chapman of Massachusetts, who preferred the Roxbury to the Rhode Island seeds: he was making progress. He had obviously been through, some time ago, and convinced whoever needed convincing to plant these trees. There was logic in his ideas. Apples were hearty, versatile. Although non-native—foreign, like the Shawnee. And yet they thrived here. Chapman's dream had been to see the river valley flushed with orchards.

"My brother?" Tecumseh asked.

Roundhead nodded. "I'll take you to him."

The new medicine lodge Rattle had built was now a burned-out shell. The rear wall was charred, the roof gone. The front was as it had been. Although he could have walked around the lodge and entered from any side he chose—in fact, might have spoken to Rattle directly, standing in the yard, and seen his face—Tecumseh felt the formality of knocking on the front door was important somehow. So he and Roundhead knocked and then waited, breathing through their mouths against the acrid smell.

Only seeing it with his own eyes did it become clear: whether or not Tippecanoe ever had the chance of feeling like home, it never would now. No one had bothered to rebuild. Cabin foundations and half-circles where wigwams once stood were burned into the earth. This was all that remained. They'd been so close, and it had been taken from them. Starting again would be worse than starting from nothing. When you started from nothing, you had hope. Having nearly succeeded and fallen so far, hope was something he would not let himself feel again.

A young man opened the door. Tecumseh focused on only what was before him as he was led inside. Roundhead followed. There were candles; a few managed to stay lit against the air. Tobacco smoke curled, rising from the floor. In one corner, where half of a wall remained, a boy of about twelve brushed his palms against a skin-drum. There was a fire going. The aide added two lengths of kindling, snapping them in his hands. When the fire had picked up he went to Rattle and whispered in his ear. After a long while Rattle rose to greet his guests.

He opened his arms in welcome. "Brothers."

Tecumseh's mind flooded with murderous thoughts. He didn't know how his brother could smile like that.

"After everything," he said, "still you sit here and put on airs."

Rattle held a finger to his lips. "Let us speak quietly, brother. Talon is sleeping."

"Who's Talon?" Roundhead whispered.

Tecumseh didn't know.

The aide cleared his throat. He nodded toward where the boy sat beating the drum. Tecumseh's eyes adjusted and he saw finally a shape beside the boy, a human-like form. The figure was concealed beneath a blanket and did not move. The aide went to it and propped it higher where it had slumped against the wall. It had the shape of a body wrapped in canvas.

"Man cannot look upon Talon's face," Rattle said. "This world is hard, and so the Prophet does his best to keep Talon comfortable."

"Who is that man?" Tecumseh asked.

"Calling Talon a man does Talon an injustice."

"It is someone dead you are keeping for your magic."

There was something else about the apples: he remembered a walk through the woods, accompanying his father. How Pucksinwah always kept a little bit ahead. How Tecumseh hurried to keep up. How in the early morning, the leaves beneath their feet were stiff with the cold. The air smelled like ice.

Tecumseh crossed his arms, planted his feet. "You disobeyed my orders."

There was an odor in the room. Something spoiled or unwashed, the heavy smell of decay. He thought it must be emanating from the far corner, from the figure beneath the blanket.

"And who are you to give orders to the Prophet?" Rattle already seemed bored by the conversation. "The Prophet follows only the Great Spirit."

"Everything we tried to build," he said, "you have treated as carelessly as a drunk treats his whore."

His brother offered a wan smile. "What an apt metaphor. What is the Prophet to you but a drunk and a whore? Even after all this time."

The boy in the corner stopped playing the drum. The aide stoked the fire, listening. Tecumseh breathed in through his mouth. It was all past. The sorrow, the disappointment. He had made his decision. Let Rattle have this last moment.

"What a burden the Prophet must be on you." Rattle moved his hands as if parting invisible brambles. "He must constantly disappoint. Of course, all men cannot be like the great Tecumseh. The Prophet is sorry he can't stomp his foot and cause the ground to tremble or the flood waters to rise."

He cracked his neck from side to side. He went to the corner and bent to adjust the figure hidden beneath the blanket. He cooed to it as a mother settles a child.

"What you don't realize," he said, standing, "is that the Prophet never needed you."

On that morning walk with his father, after they were a long way from home, once there were woods all around and a path that only Pucksinwah could see, through the trees, his father said he had a surprise. Something he'd taken on a raid. From the sack he carried, he produced a round, green fruit. He called it an *apple* and said that it was very rare. It had traveled a great distance from white orchards in Iroquois country to the east.

"But you need the Prophet." Rattle moved through the rank, smoky room. "The Prophet plays an important role in the story you tell yourself about your life. The Prophet is someone to try to save. Have you saved the Prophet, brother? Will you succeed with him where you failed with Open Door, with Chiksika? Or will you fail the way our father failed?"

There was no one else in the world who could say these things to him—no one but his brother. No one else filled him with this incendiary blend of anger and shame. And hopelessness. He tasted bile on the back of his tongue, sour guilt and disbelief. And rage. Enough to kill his brother. Roundhead wouldn't stop him, and no one in Tippecanoe would care. There were some who believed death was the only just punishment. Rattle's fate was his alone to decide.

"I should have you executed," he told his brother. "I have every right."

"Yes." Rattle fell to his knees and threw his arms around Tecumseh. The stink followed him, or perhaps came from him. "It is what the Prophet wants most—to be set free." He was weeping now. "To no longer be dogged by incompetence or dreams he can't live up to."

He clutched at Tecumseh's clothes; he pawed his chest, face upturned. Tears flooded his cheeks. "Death will be a mercy for the Prophet—release him from his fleshy, waddling prison of a body."

Tecumseh considered that word, *death*. There were many ways to die. One might die by his own hand, sacrificing oneself to the darkness, as Rattle had once. Or one might die in glory, like his father and Chiksika, in battle for a cause. Death was to be honored, and it came for each man in turn. But there would be no honor in killing his brother now. In fact, death would always deserve better.

"In the morning, my men will escort you to Upper Canada," Tecumseh said. "There you will live out the rest of your days with the old men and those who are no longer fit for fighting."

He jerked his legs from Rattle's grasp. His brother collapsed, the sad mass of him shaking, his head buried in his arms. Tecumseh turned to go. He'd almost made the door when his brother spoke his name.

"Tecumseh," Rattle begged. "Kill me."

It was hard, being brothers. No one knew you so closely. No one could get under your skin in quite the same way. They were you and yet not you. Intimately familiar but impossible to understand. Raised the same but formed into something set apart. To see your sibling was to see someone who was as like to you as your own hand, yet a total stranger.

"Put guards around the lodge," Tecumseh told Roundhead. "Make sure my brother gets food and water. Let no one enter, and do not let him leave. The aide and the boy, of course, are free to go. In fact, make them."

That morning, long ago, he and his father had walked, and Pucksinwah had found a straight path through the trees. But Tecumseh remembered nothing of what they spoke about. Maybe they walked in silence, each man to his thoughts. Or one man, and the boy who would succeed him. His son, the Great Panther Crossing the Sky. Maybe the forest honored the quiet between them. Even now it felt as if they should have talked about something important. But in the end he recalled only the walk, and the woods, and the privileged feeling of being alone with his father. It happened so rarely.

As they walked, his father put both hands on the apple and twisted. The fruit came apart cleanly, as two perfect half-moons. His father handed him one, and Tecumseh held the crescent to his lips, thrilled by the gift, his face tickled by a spray of juice as he bit into it and, one by one, spit out the hard, black seeds.

CREDITS

"Barbara Allen," Traditional
"Highland Widow's Lament," Traditional
"Logan's Water," Traditional

ABOUT THE COVER ARTIST

Doug Hall's paintings reflect his admiration and respect for the culture of early Eastern Woodland Native Americans. Most influential in his development has been mentor Bob Tommey, a master of color who resides in Carthage, Missouri. Hall grew up painting in Neosho, Missouri, and now lives in McDonald County surrounded by the Huckleberry State Forest. He is an avid black powder shooter and horseback rider. Past recognition includes the George Phippen Memorial Fine Art Award, Prescott, Arizona, 2002; First place in oils, Sedona, Arizona, 2003; Artists' Choice and the H.E. Williams Award, Midwest Gathering of the Artists, 2004; and Best of Show, Stillwater, Oklahoma, 2005. See more of his work at https://www.somersetfineart.com/s-1446-hall-doug.aspx.

ACKNOWLEDGMENTS

This book owes particular gratitude to James H. Howard's *Shawnee!* (Ohio University Press), which was both the inspiration and the guiding light for this novel, as well as Allan W. Eckert's fictionalized but exhaustively researched account of Tecumseh's life, *A Sorrow in Our Heart: The Life of Tecumseh* (Bantam Books).

Allan A. MacFarlan's *Exploring the Outdoors with Indian Secrets* (Stackpole Books) and *Recreating the American Longhunter: 1740-1790* (Graphics/Fine Arts Press) helped flesh out environmental details and would be excellent reading for anyone interested in learning more about this period of American history. As would two riveting collections of captivity narratives: *Captured by the Indians: 15 Firsthand Accounts, 1750-1870* (Dover) and *Women's Indian Captivity Narratives* (Penguin).

Thank you to the Greene County Historical Society, stewards of the Galloway House in Xenia, Ohio, and the staff who kept the doors open late to give me and my wife personal tours.

Thank you to Linda Hobson and the NC Writers' Network, Heather Dewar (my indispensable reader), Patricia A. Lynch, Alana Dunn, R.E. McDermott, Nancy Peacock, and Doug Hall and Somerset Fine Art.

To my parents, Lyle and Ro, my sister, Cara, and my nephews, Isaac and Luca, who continue to make the place where I grew up somewhere I'm always excited to come back to.

To my daughter, Eloise, and to my wife Amelia—my first reader and always the classier half of our *duprass*.

CPSIA information can be obtained
at www.ICGtesting.com
Printed in the USA
LVOW12s1553200317
527826LV00005B/1159/P